OUT FOR JUSTICE

Published by Mundania Press
Also by Vicki M. Taylor

Not Without Anna
Trust in the Wind

OUT FOR JUSTICE

VICKI M. TAYLOR

Edited by Sarah-Jane Lehoux
Cover Art © 2012 by Skyla Dawn Cameron

Published by:
Mundania Press LLC
6457 Glenway Ave., #109
Cincinnati, OH 45211

First edition November, 2012 ISBN 13-978-1-60659-361-5

Second Edition, April, 2025 ISBN 978-0-9838586-8-3

Production by Mundania Press LLC
Printed in the United States of America

10   9   8   7   6   5   4   3   2   1

DEDICATION

For my children, Amber, Michelle, and Kyle.
You are my greatest accomplishments.

PROLOGUE

The boy knew he shouldn't wander too far away from the campsite, but it was too tempting. Not a baby anymore but a big boy of four years old, he fought the urge, but in the end curiosity won out. He followed the large white bird as it ambled and picked its way up the beach. The sleek curved line of its long white neck silhouetted in the sky.

The voices of his mother and sisters grew fainter in the wind as it whipped along the shore. Small waves crashed into the sandy beach strewn with broken shells and seaweed.

He left his shoes next to the pile of shells he'd collected for his mom. He tried hard to remember to pick them up on his way back because he knew his mom would be upset if he lost them. Never had he seen such a big bird on the ground before; he would follow for a little while longer.

Careful where he placed his little bare feet, the boy skipped along to keep up with the bird. Ignoring him, it appeared more intent on finding bugs to eat and unconcerned with the antics of one small boy.

The sun was setting and the shadows were long. Bird and shadow mingled together.

The boy had no trouble keeping up, until a quick movement in the small brush near the trees caught his eye. Another animal. Smaller. Quick footed. The boy knew the name of this animal. Squirrel. The bird forgotten like an abandoned, used toy, the boy ventured closer to the chattering brown squirrel.

The light from the setting sun didn't reach far into the trees. The boy's sun kissed skin shivered in the cooler shade, a small breeze making its way through the tall branches, whistling noises among the tops of the trees. With only his short bib overalls and no shirt, he wasn't dressed for a trek through the woods. Branches from the low-lying brush and kudzu vines grabbed at his skin and scratched his arms and back.

A small voice in his head told him he'd better turn back and return to the campsite. At the same time, he heard louder voices just beyond a large rock covered with green vines. The voices sounded interesting. The squirrel forgotten, he moved a little closer. There, he could see who was talking.

He stepped on a stick that broke beneath his foot. The sharp end punctured his tender skin and he cried out in pain.

The voices stopped.

Suddenly realizing he had gone too far, the boy turned only to find himself tangled and confused in the kudzu vines and low branches. He shivered again. This time not from the coolness of the woods.

Long forgotten, the big white bird ambled its way down the beach, toward tastier prospects and away from the humans.

Chapter One

Karen Sykes pushed some stray hairs behind her left ear. Her short brown hair lay damp against her neck, stuck to her skin in the thickening humid heat that was Tampa, Florida. Heat waves rose from the hot basketball court where she'd been taking challenges for the last forty minutes. Standing with her feet spread apart, she put her hands on her hips and asked, "Are we gonna go through this again?" She tucked her yellow t-shirt back into the top of her jeans.

A rare cool breeze stirred the treetops overhead. For a second, she closed her eyes and imagined a tall glass of ice-cold lemonade. Then she opened her eyes and made a face at the man she'd been calling partner for only short time. His gray hair stood on end in a short brush cut. He'd run his hands through it so many times during their basketball game, it now stood out at various angles. He was in reasonable shape for a man in his fifties, but too many days sitting behind a desk had given him a small paunch he swore on a daily basis wasn't there yesterday.

With his shirtsleeves rolled up and his shirttail untucked, he looked a bit frazzled. They'd been playing hard and Karen knew he was about to call the game even if he wasn't losing.

"Come on, old man, throw in the towel, she's got you beat," a voice called from the small crowd of onlookers and recent losers of Karen's earlier challenges.

It had been a slow morning at the Warehouse, the loosely affectionate term the detectives gave to the large county building that housed their offices along with the rest of the Hillsborough County Sheriff department, and they didn't want to waste any of the good weather that temporarily graced them.

Throughout her thirty-odd years, she'd led a competitive life.

Girls against boys. Karen against everyone else. Karen dribbled the ball, looked up at the basket, then back down to the ball. She set her feet and bent her knees. She held her breath, ready to push off with her arms.

"Sykes, Anderson. Get in here."

Karen hissed a sigh. "Damn, I had it too." She wiped at the sweat rolling down the side of her temple. She didn't like leaving anything half finished. Even if it was a friendly game of basketball.

Sam walked over and patted her on the shoulder as they headed into the office. "Good game."

"You too, Sam."

Lieutenant Santiago waited for them in the main room. "I need you to check out a new case. Over in the Hamilton Davis Park Campground."

Back inside, the air-conditioned air felt cold and refreshing. "Sure, no problem, Lieutenant." Karen accepted the folder the lieutenant held out. She grabbed her dark blue blazer from the back of a chair and shrugged into it.

"Hey, wait a minute," the lieutenant said.

"Yeah?" Sam hesitated then turned around while Karen stood expectantly.

"It's a kid."

Eyes widened, Karen's throat tightened. She swallowed hard to work past the lump that suddenly developed. This was it. She'd waited more than two years for this moment. Her first homicide case. Already, their lightheartedness on the basketball court faded into a distant memory. Real life had a way of crowding in and changing moods.

"Shit," Sam swore. "All right. Thanks for the heads up, Lieutenant."

Karen could feel Lieutenant Santiago's eyes watching her as she headed out the door. He probably thought Sam competent enough to handle the case. But what did he think about her? She was tough. She had to be, growing up with parents that barely recognized her existence. It wasn't their fault. The blame lay with her and what happened a long time ago. She lived with the guilt for more than twenty-five years. The guilt kept her company and almost felt like a familiar, comfortable sweater on a chilly night.

Following Sam out of the Warehouse to the parking lot, Karen knew he would help her along with her first homicide case. She couldn't have a better teacher than Sam. She'd been told that plenty of times from the other detectives. She trusted his judgment. If he figured she was ready then damn it, she'd show everyone how ready she could be.

Karen rubbed her sweaty palms on her jeans before letting her fingers splay across her thigh near her knee. She shifted in her seat on the passenger side of the car. She had a thousand questions to ask and didn't know where to start. She knew the case was serious. Any case that involved a child was, and that whatever she did between now and when the case closed could affect the lives of the victim's family members and the killer himself. It was up to her and Sam to get it right. Something Sam would be good at, while he kept Karen from screwing up. She didn't know whether to sit quietly and let Sam think while he drove or to let loose with a barrage of questions.

One of the stipulations Sam had when she was assigned to him was that he drove. From what Karen could figure out, he hated to be a passenger. Sam needed to be in control. That was cool with her. Glad to let him take the wheel, it gave her more time to think about the case and where they were going. She wanted to review all the procedures in her head and make sure she left nothing out.

Heading west on 580, Sam drove toward Oldsmar. Karen figured the campground must be close to the Pinellas/Hillsborough county border and right on Tampa Bay. She couldn't remember ever seeing a sign for the place but remembered a lot of undeveloped land out that way. The area wasn't as built up as most, but getting close. Looking out the window, watching the palmettos race by, she hoped that the big housing developments continued to bypass this area. More nature and less development.

Having never been to the campground she didn't know what to expect. She imagined thick brush, oak trees, sandy beaches, and lots of palm trees. She turned to her partner. "Ever been to this campground?"

"Once or twice, when the kids were young." Sam didn't take his eyes off the road. "It's an older place, attracts mostly families."

Karen stole a quick glance at her homicide partner. Sam never would tell her his exact age, preferring to tell people he was older than dirt. She knew he had a wife. He kept a picture of her in his office. The only personal thing on his desk. Karen wondered if he had grandchildren. She hoped he did. She pictured him rolling on the floor with a few little ones tumbling around, climbing all over him.

Pushing her hair back behind one ear reminded Karen that she needed to get a haircut soon. She'd been pushing the lengthy pieces behind her ear long enough. Shifting in her seat, she tried to keep her voice casual. "How many kids have you done?"

Sam didn't ask her to explain. "More than I'd like to remember. Not enough to throw a number at it." He rubbed at his face with one hand in a weary sort of way. "Not all of these missing kid cases end up with a happy ending. Every Amber Alert that comes across our desk needs to be solved as quickly as possible. Every minute we're not working the case gives crazy sickos like this one a chance to snatch a kid and do God knows what to them before they end up killing them."

Sam glanced over at Karen. His eyes widened. She realized her face must have given away the strained feeling his words caused. With a little effort, she got herself back under control in time to hear Sam continue.

"Don't worry about a thing. Just stick close to me. If you need to barf, remember to do it away from the scene, okay?"

"Yeah, okay." Karen shifted in her seat. "Yeah, I'll be fine." She gave her head a little shake. "There's a first for everything, right?" The bravado in her voice did little to help alleviate her jitters.

Sam sighed. "These kinds of firsts we could do without." Karen made a fist with her left hand and used her nails to scratch at the inside of her palm. She wasn't nervous. More anticipatory. She didn't want to be the girl who couldn't hack it in Homicide. She didn't want to let anyone down.

She wasn't exactly sure what to expect and didn't know how to ask without looking like a total idiot. What the hell, it was Sam after all. If she couldn't ask her partner and teacher, whom could she ask? "So, what can I expect?"

"A crowd. We won't be the first on scene." Karen let out an inward sigh of relief.

"The Crime Scene Techs will be there." He paused. "Stay out of their way." Sam cast a quick glance at her, his eyes serious. "And don't touch anything." His voice lowered. "We want to nail the son of a bitch who did this, so nothing gets compromised. Got it?"

Throwing a salute with her right hand, Karen said, "Yes, sir!" When she saw Sam's face frown, her smirk disappeared. "Don't worry, Sam, I'll be fine. I'm just getting out some nervous energy right now. This is my first, you know, and I want to—"

"I know, Sykes." Sam sighed. "I know."

Signaling to turn left, Sam waited for the traffic to clear. Cars along the busy road that usually sped by at sixty plus miles per hour now slowed to a crawl to get a good look at the police cars parked along the side of the road.

Karen glanced at the entrance to the campground. The heavy pine sign to the right of the entrance had the name of the campground burned into the wood. The owners must have been from up north; she thought it had a northern folksy kind of air about it. The kind of places her parents used to take her before they moved to Florida and her world turned upside down.

Police cars flanked both sides of the entrance and uniformed officers directed traffic away from the road that led into the campground. Not so long ago, she would have been one of the uniformed; directing traffic, keeping the curious and media hounds out, doing the grunt work for the detectives. Now, here she was, on her way to her first homicide. *Please don't let me screw anything up*, she pleaded silently.

Sam slowly maneuvered the car forward until the officer stopped them. They showed their badges and ID. The officer told them to follow the road to the left, deep into the campground, take the third right and follow the flashing lights.

Large straight pine trees and a thick canopy of oak trees created a dark ceiling that kept out most of the sun's intense glare. Karen rolled down her window and took a deep breath. The humid air smelled earthy, almost musty. She took another breath and caught a crisper scent, tinged with the faint odor of drying seaweed. The bay. It was so close she could nearly make out the faint sound of waves lapping at the shore. At another time, this might have been a pleasant new experience. Instead, Karen knew only tragedy awaited her.

Sam pulled his sedan into a space between a county sheriff's patrol car and a black SUV. "Looks like Connelly and Parker are already here. That's their truck."

"Who?" Karen looked around. She saw emblems from state, county, and city police cars. It looked like everyone showed up.

"Crime Scene Techs."

"Oh, gotcha." Karen pushed open her car door, stretched, then closed the door behind her. The area was abuzz with activity. Cops in various uniforms and civilian clothes gathered into groups of three or four and stood around talking in low voices. Karen heard crying and looked in that direction. Without being told, she knew this was the family of the child. She nudged Sam. "Guess we start with the family?"

Karen watched the faces in the subdued group. Grief emanated from those gathered to console the family with anguish on their faces, reflecting in those around them. Two women supported a crying woman who collapsed in their arms. They hugged and soothed her. Was she the mother?

The air practically suffocated Karen with misery. Already the heat index climbed past the eighties and into the nineties. The once cool breeze of the morning all but disappeared in the thick woods, leaving a stifling humidity that built upon her skin like a second layer. Underneath her lightweight blazer, her t-shirt stuck to the space between her shoulder blades. Moisture gathered at her forehead and between her breasts. Memories of another summer day, dense with suffering and anguish gathered at the back of her mind, attempting to break through and force her to confront them. Karen closed her eyes, forced her mind to clear, then looked up at the sky. She couldn't see them, but she knew clouds were forming on the horizon.

Hurricane Season in Florida. The day's summer shower hadn't arrived yet. Everyone at the scene would work against time to finish before the afternoon rains brought a slight reprieve to the intense heat and washed away any evidence.

Karen liked summer, even if it meant destructive hurricanes lined up in the Atlantic to take their shot at Florida. She wouldn't forget the summer several hit, and knew she wouldn't forget today either.

Sam pulled her to the side and motioned her toward two people walking their way from a trail that led into the oak trees. He waved and they headed in their direction.

"Connelly. Parker. Good to see you two on the case," Sam said.

"Thanks, man. Not my favorite kind of case, though." The powerfully built, younger man pushed a pen into his front shirt pocket and slid a notebook in after it.

Blonde hair and good looks aside, Karen noted an air of confidence radiating from him. His attitude meant business. Probably uptight. He didn't even have the good manners to sweat like the rest of them.

"Hi, I'm Susan Parker." The dark, tall woman stripped off a purple latex glove and stretched out a hand to Karen. Looking up, Karen met kind dark brown eyes. The woman was muscular, her skin dark like Godiva's best chocolate, the surface slightly slick with sweat. She had a strong grip. Her dark, curly hair, cut short to the scalp, had a leaf caught in it. Making a motion with her hand, Karen pointed it out to her and received a murmured 'thanks' from Susan.

"Oh, right. Introductions." Sam pointed. "Mike Connelly. Susan Parker. Meet my new partner, Karen Sykes." They shook hands and exchanged cards.

"Hey," Mike said barely glancing at her. Then he took a slower, more appraising look.

Karen bristled at his obvious review. "Hey, yourself," she threw back at him. Where did he think he was? A local bar during happy hour? She gave his handsome good looks and deep blue eyes a brief glance, then focused back to what Sam was asking Susan.

"What do we have?"

Susan flipped back a few pages in her notepad. "Male, age four, appears to be asphyxiated by strangulation. Scratches on the skin appear to be from local vegetation; no other visible signs of stress."

Without looking at her, Sam motioned for Karen to take out her notepad and start writing. Karen waved the pad that was already in her hand, in front of his face. He gave her the thumbs up sign and went back to asking questions.

"Where were the parents?"

Susan checked her notes. "According to the officers first on the scene, the father claims he was fishing, the mother says she was at the campsite. The parents reported the boy missing late last night, somewhere around midnight. Search and Rescue covered the area, then ZCI brought in Jake and they started again. Jake found the body this morning approximately three miles from the parent's campsite, just on the other side of that trail, mostly hidden by leaves and brush."

Karen sent a questioning look to her partner. He explained about Jake. "Jake is a Bloodhound from the Zephyrhills Correctional Institution's tracking unit. They offer a free community service when searching for missing kids. He's got a great success rate."

"The way the body was hidden, we might not have found it so quickly and could have lost valuable evidence," Mike said with a look to Karen that said volumes. Karen felt small and insignificant under his stare. Did he think her incompetent because she didn't know about the search dog, Jake?

Sam clapped his hands together. "Well, let's get over there and take a look at the scene."

"We haven't removed anything yet, wanted to wait for you to check it out first," Susan said.

Karen walked with the others down the trail through big oaks and tall pine trees. Dried pine needles and small, brown, oval oak leaves from last season crunched beneath their feet.

The air was cooler here; the sun not as intense, but the humidity was the same—stifling. She tried to quell the butterflies in her stomach. This was her job. This was what she trained the last two years for. She knew she could do it. She just needed to convince her stomach. Willing the queasiness to settle down, she lengthened her stride to keep up with the others.

Bright yellow and black tape wrapped around several trees surrounding the crime scene. Mike lifted a section and they all ducked under it. He gave Karen a long searching look before she took her turn. If he was wondering whether she could do her job, she would show him.

For some reason, Karen felt that Mike disliked her and she didn't know why. Maybe because she was a woman or she was new, but she got the overall impression that he didn't approve of her. He judged her abilities before she could prove herself. That irked her. Besides, she was a likable person. Damn it.

Susan drew on a fresh pair of gloves then pointed out to Karen how she was putting the boy's hands in paper bags and securing them. "We want to preserve as much evidence as possible. If the kid put up any kind of fight, he could have skin, fibers, or hair under his nails."

Karen smiled politely, not sure if she should explain to Susan that she knew this from her classes. Looking at the boy's body lying on the ground, she fought against another image floating up from the recesses of her memory. *This isn't the same thing*, she told herself. *Get a grip*. Although able to quiet her mind, she couldn't ignore the tug at her heart. Such a little boy. So young.

Susan moved on to the second hand. "We'll scrape the fingers at the medical examiner's office, then take any evidence we find back to the lab with us."

Karen looked down as she moved to the side and saw a small section of rope laid out around what appeared to be a footprint. Making sure to step away from the rope, she looked around for a safe place to stand out of the way.

"Hey," Mike called out. "Watch where you're stepping. We have a good footprint there and we don't want to lose it."

Fire burned in Karen's cheeks. She clenched her teeth and choked back a curt reply. She wouldn't embarrass Sam and say anything.

She wasn't going to step on the footprint. She wasn't that stupid; she paid attention. If Mike asked, she even knew how to make a plaster mold of the print to protect it. Although Karen doubted he'd be asking her to do anything involved with this case. Apparently, she wasn't good enough.

Looking back over her shoulder, she studied Mike Connelly. What was it about her that rubbed him the wrong way? Or was he always this charming? Why did she even care? She shouldn't. A small voice inside vowed to prove she could handle the job despite the tiny spark of curiosity that piqued her interest about Mike Connelly.

Having taken all the notes she could think of and not sure what else to do at the moment, Karen watched Parker and Connelly help the medical examiner. They laid out a white sheet and gently lifted the boy's body onto it. The bit of sun that did make it through the trees glinted off the shiny metal snap of his overalls.

"Wait," Karen said thinking aloud. "Those snaps on his overalls. Has anyone checked them for prints?" Just as quickly as she spoke, she wondered if she should have voiced her thought, but it was too late to take it back now.

"It's a long shot, Sykes," said Connelly.

"Well, I was thinking that if the killer picked him up at any time to carry him, then he might have left a print. I mean, this place is what? Three miles from the boy's camp, right? Do you think he walked the whole way?" Karen pointed out. "It's worth a shot, isn't it?"

Susan must have thought so too because she hurried to get out her fingerprinting kit and kneeled down next to the boy's body, making sure not to touch any other part.

"She's right," Susan said after dusting the snap. "I found a print." "Yes," Karen whispered to herself.

"We'll see what kind of a match we get," said Connelly looking at Karen as if he just swallowed something bitter. "It's more than likely the mother's print from dressing him."

"Have you printed the parents yet?" Sam asked moving closer to Karen. "Nice catch, Sykes," he whispered for her ears only.

"Thanks, Sam." Karen's face flushed with pride. She'd saved valuable evidence. Even the high and mighty Mike Connelly couldn't deprive her of that fact.

"We're printing the parents after we finish up here." Susan stood up to stretch while backing away from the body. "By the way, Karen, nice save on the snaps." She packed up her crime scene case. "I'm sure we would have caught it and printed it back in the lab, but by then, it could have been smudged. Out here we got a clean print." She looked over at her partner. "Mike might be right, it could be one of the parent's print. But we have to cover all our bases. We could get lucky on this one. We'll compare it to the parents' prints, then we'll run it through our local database and then with the FBI's AFIS if we have to. We'll let you know if we come up with anything."

Karen lowered her voice and closed the gap between Susan and her. "So, what's up with Mike? Is he always this pleasant?"

"That's Mike. Straightforward and ready to doubt at the drop of a hat. I wouldn't put much stock in his growls, he doesn't usually make a good first impression," whispered Susan. "He doesn't like anyone telling him how to do his job."

"Or even making suggestions. What about you?"

"Me? I just go with the flow, girlfriend. Just go with the flow." Susan smiled. "Mike and I have a good working relationship. I respect him and he respects me. But, it wasn't always like that. We had our moments."

"He sure isn't shy about his feelings."

"Sure he is. He definitely doesn't like mixing business with pleasure."

"What do you mean?"

"Honey. Mike has just come across a new puzzle. You."

"Me?"

"Yup. You, darlin', are going to cause Mr. Connelly a few sleepless nights. I can guarantee it."

"You're kidding, right?"

Mike, interested in her? He didn't even like her. Besides, he wasn't her type. Too sure of himself. But, something deep inside stirred.

"Nope. Not a bit. If I know anything, I know my partner. He's intrigued." Susan laughed quickly then motioned to where Mike folded a white sheet carefully over the body.

"See how he keeps everything turned in, toward the body? That's so any evidence on the body that falls off will catch in the sheet."

Karen smiled at Susan. "Yeah, they taught us that in class too."

"Sorry, it's the teacher in me."

They watched Mike zip the little body into a black bag and help the medical examiner lift it and carry it across the leaf covered ground to place it onto the gurney for the bumpy ride over the trail to the waiting van.

"Where does the body go from here?"

"Mike goes with the body to the medical examiner's office. I'll finish up here."

"Got it." Karen was glad the boy's body wouldn't be alone.

"Hey," Susan called after Karen as she and Sam headed toward the first group of witnesses and the parents of the murdered little boy.

"Yeah?"

"Want to get together sometime for a cup of coffee or something?"

"That'd be great." Karen smiled. It would be nice to have a new friend in the business. "I have your card. I'll call you." Susan might even be able to shed some more light on the complicated Mike Connelly. Curiosity simmered. He wasn't the only one intrigued about their encounter.

Chapter Two

Karen and Sam had pulled the grieving parents aside to a remote picnic table to hold their inquiry. "If we could just get back to the question at hand, please." Karen tried to turn the discussion back into a calm interview session, instead of resembling the chaotic stage of the Jerry Springer show.

The young man with long hair hovered over his slouched wife. Her hair hung in her dirty face and she picked at her nails. They'd been arguing for ten minutes and had yet to agree on anything pertaining to the disappearance of their son. Karen tried to get them to focus, but the husband spoke up again.

"I told you I was going fishin' and that was that."

"Well, you also promised Logan you'd take him with you, didn't ya?" The wife mumbled, barely speaking above a whisper, but loud enough for Karen to hear. Karen took the opportunity to ask her a question.

"Ma'am, please. Where were you exactly when you discovered your son missing?" A pen, poised over her notebook, Karen softly pursed her lips, then forcefully let out the breath she'd been holding. She waited for the young woman who sat with rounded shoulders at the metal picnic table to answer her question. These arguments were obviously not the first for this couple, nor would they be the last.

"Like I told that other policeman, I was getting supper ready for the kids. I called to Amber and Ashley to find their little brother and bring him to the table. We were having Logan's favorite, hot dogs." Her voice caught as she gasped once again for air and held her grimy fist to her mouth. The nails chewed down to the quick; blood seeped from the edge around one torn thumbnail.

"Mrs. Hunt, how long did your daughters search for your son?"

"I don't know. Maybe ten minutes or so. They looked in all his favorite spots to play. On the beach, behind the truck, inside the tent." She swiped an eye with the back of her hand in an attempt to stave off the falling tears. It merely smeared the dirt.

"If you couldn't have been watching him, you should have had the girls watching him." Mr. Hunt once again interrupted the interview. "Someone should have been watching him, dammit." He stopped his pacing to look accusingly at his wife. His eyes flashed with anger, his dirty face streaked with dried tears.

Karen looked at Sam who nodded slightly. "Mr. Hunt, could you please tell me where you were, exactly, when you found out your son was missing?"

"I don't know how many times I gotta tell this to you people, but I was fishing. Right off the south point. In about three or four feet of water. Damn near up to my chest." He pushed dirty hands through even dirtier hair. Bits of dried leaves still clung to some of the long strands. "I had a good lead on and was just ready to set the hook when I heard them girls screaming their fool heads off at me to come in. Nothin' makes a fish swim away faster than a bunch of screaming."

"Mr. Hunt, how long did you and your wife look for your son before you notified the police?" Karen noticed Mr. Hunt's hands shook when he brushed back his long hair. Was he nervous because of the questioning? He could be upset about his son, but she sensed it went deeper than that.

"I don't know. It seemed like hours. We looked all around, even got some of the neighbor campers to help look. After finding his shoes on the beach, we all looked 'til way past sundown. We crawled through bushes and briars, even under other people's trailers." He held out his hands. "Man, just look at the dirt on my hands. You can't say we weren't looking for my son."

"No one is accusing you of not looking for you son, sir." Karen kept her voice level.

"Ya'll better not. We looked for hours you know. Hours." Mr. Hunt patted his shirt pocket as if looking for something. He checked his pants pockets as well and still came up empty.

"Mr. Hunt, whose decision was it to call the police?"

"Well, some of the folks kept saying 'call the police,' 'call the police,' but Kelly and me, we said we'd keep looking on our own and we'd wait. Little Logan couldn't have gotten far and we felt for sure we'd find him lost in someone else's camp." Mr. Hunt looked at his wife for a long moment.

Karen made some notes on her pad, then looked up at the man who again began pacing back and forth behind his wife. "Mr. Hunt, can you explain why you waited nearly eight hours before you called the police?"

"We didn't want no trouble." He nodded at his wife. "Kelly and me, we figured if Logan was just playing, then we'd get the police involved for nothin', so we waited until we were real sure. We checked with all the campers first. Looked everywhere we could, then we called."

Karen knew he was hiding something. She took a deep breath and asked, "Mr. Hunt, have you ever been arrested?"

The man stopped pacing and stared at Karen as if he'd just seen her for the first time. "What's that got to do with anything?" His eyes narrowed and his shoulders tensed. He was coiled to spring.

"Honey, I'm sure they don't mean nothin' by it." Kelly Hunt tugged at her husband's arm and turned a pleading look toward Karen. "It's just routine questions, right?"

Checking her notes, Karen flipped back a few pages to where she recorded the information she received from dispatch after running Mark Hunt through their system and then asked, "Weren't you arrested a year ago on a domestic disturbance?"

"They just run me into the station. It wasn't like Kelly pressed charges or anything." He looked around quickly then said, "It was those damn cops that pressed the charges. Ain't none of their business what goes on between a man and his woman."

"We just had a misunderstanding, me and Mark. Sometimes we argue." Kelly tucked a wayward strand of hair behind one ear, saw her dirty hand then tried to hide it in her lap. "Sometimes we get loud when we argue. Seems like someone's always calling the police or something." A hesitant smile found its way to her chapped and chewed lips. "Mark, he don't mean nothin' by it when he makes me see where I'd done wrong. It's mostly me that messes up. And Mark, he promised to quit. He ain't done nothin' in months. Honest. Not since that last time." Her eyes widened as she stared at Karen.

Karen carefully watched the young woman's face. She was protecting the man who stood next to her, his hand gripping her shoulder. "Mrs. Hunt, if you'd like we can continue our questions over there, separate from your husband." Karen paused then reiterated, "If you'd like."

"You ain't taking her away from me. She's staying right here!" Mr. Hunt tightened his grip on his wife's shoulder.

"Please, no. I'd much rather stay right here, if you don't mind."

"Very well." Karen cleared her throat, wishing she'd remembered to grab a bottle of water from the cooler in the back of their car. "Mr. Hunt, do you hit your children?"

"What? What kind of questions are these? Just what are you trying to say?" Mark shrugged away his wife's attempt at soothing him and pushed back away from her. He turned as if he were going to walk away from the picnic table.

"Mr. Hunt, please sit down. We're not finished." Sam took a few steps closer and looked the angry man in the eye. The men stood toe to toe for a few long seconds before Mark Hunt must have realized that Sam wasn't going to back down.

"Mark, please sit. Don't give them no cause to take you in. We don't need that on top of this too. I don't think I can handle much more of this." Kelly buried her face into her hands. Her slumped shoulders shook. "Where's my girls? I want to see my girls."

Sam answered. "They're being looked after while we ask you a few more questions. Don't worry. They're in good hands."

Looking up with tears streaking dirty paths down her cheeks, Kelly pleaded with Karen. "Please, we never hurt no one, 'specially our kids. Please, find the man who did this to my little boy."

Karen looked deep into Kelly Hunt's eyes. She was younger than Karen, but she looked older. Tired. Faded. Karen felt a familiar rush of sympathy for this young mother. She wanted to tell her everything was going to be all right, but she couldn't. For Kelly Hunt, nothing was ever going to be all right in her world ever again.

Karen turned to Kelly's husband. She sighed. If this man didn't like the direction of their questions so far, he sure as hell wasn't going to like being fingerprinted. She made a motion to Sam who understood she was finished with her questions. He turned and whistled. Susan's head swung up. Signaling that she got the message, she started toward their table.

"Mr. and Mrs. Hunt, we're going to finish up here in a few minutes. We have one more procedure for you." Sam cleared his throat.

His voice deepened. "We'll have to take your fingerprints."

"What for?" Now, it was Kelly's turn to act suspicious of their motives.

Karen answered. "Ma'am, we may find fingerprints on the body. If we do, we'll need to differentiate between your fingerprints and someone else's. This will help us to get that much closer to finding the person who did this."

Mark Hunt shifted restlessly in his seat. He stood, turned then sat again. "Fingerprints? What kind of shit is this, taking our fingerprints."

"Mark, hush. It'll be all right." Kelly Hunt looked up with trusting eyes. "Right, detective?"

"We don't anticipate any trouble." Karen rested one hand over Kelly's shaking one. "All we need to do is compare your fingerprints to any we find on the body. It'll just help us do our job, ma'am."

"I don't know why you need my fingerprints, anyway," Mark Hunt argued. "It's not like I haven't touched my boy. We're always messing around. You know? I mean, how long do fingerprints last anyway?"

Susan stood quietly to one side of the table and listened intently to the conversation. Hearing the question about fingerprints, she stepped in to answer. "The best time to lift fingerprints from the skin is within the first twelve hours. After that the image deteriorates."

"Oh. Deteriorates? Does that mean go away?" Mark Hunt looked visibly relieved. "Well, anyway, I don't see why—"

"Yeah, we know," Sam spoke up. "Look, you're either gonna sit here and piss and moan about getting your fingerprints taken, or you can shut up and deal with it." Sam pushed one hand through his short cropped graying hair. "We've got a job to do. Find out who murdered your little boy. And you're gonna help us do our job. Now sit down."

Karen looked at Sam, her mouth opened slightly, jaw dropped. She looked at Susan and saw a bemused expression on Susan's face.

Karen figured Susan had seen this kind of outburst from Sam before.

Motioning to Susan, Sam said, "Now let's take those fingerprints and move on."

Mark and Kelly Hunt both sat quietly at the metal picnic table and watched as Susan opened her case and arranged white cards with printed squares, an inkpad, and other items along the table in front of her.

Chapter Three

Using her toe, Karen nudged the hot water handle to the on position then leaned back and let the warm steamy water swirl about her body.

It had been a long day.

Shifting slightly, she let her head loll to one side of the inflatable plastic pillow shaped like a shell. Warm water rushed in to replace the cooler water along her back. Bubbles floated lazily along the top of the bath. The light scent of coconut drifted and settled around her in the humid air. As if her arm weighed a ton, Karen slowly lifted it to scoop a handful of bubbles and rub them along her right arm, from wrist to elbow. The ache in her arm subsided a bit while she massaged it. She never felt writer's cramp like this, not even in the academy when she took hundreds of pages of notes during lectures. Today, not wanting to miss a single thing while they worked the scene and interviewed the witnesses, she wrote until she couldn't write anymore. She took so many notes that by the end of the day she filled up two of her notebooks and Sam's.

With a twist of her foot, she turned the water off. Sam had told her she did a great job. She hoped so. She didn't want to let her partner down and for some strange reason she wanted to show that condescending Mike Connelly she could do her job just as well as anyone else.

As if he would really be interested in her. Susan didn't know what she was talking about. Or did she? She was Mike's partner. She probably knew him better than most people. Even though he acted tough, she sensed a softer side beneath the surface. She didn't know how, but instinct told her he wasn't always so grumpy.

Karen smiled. She knew she got lucky with the snap on the overalls. She could still hear Sam telling her it was a nice catch. Her head swelled just a little. So this was what it felt like to be a real detective. She was going to keep her fingers crossed that the fingerprint on the metal clasp led them to a suspect.

Karen closed her eyes and remembered the look on the parents' faces. They seemed sincere enough in their grief. It was always hard to tell though, until the case was solved. Sam told her not to be so trusting, to remember the sensationalized stories of parents grieving on television news shows for a child that they themselves killed. They had to be prepared for the worst until the evidence showed otherwise. Karen had her doubts about the boy's father. He was a class A jerk and should be hauled away on domestic abuse charges immediately. But she wasn't as sure about the mother. She reminded herself that the mother could be just as guilty as the father. Parents could be a child's greatest protector or their worst enemy.

There was something in the mother's eyes that still haunted Karen. The anguish and pain struck deep into her soul. If this mother was lying she was doing a damn good job of hiding it from the authorities.

What did those eyes remind her of? Then it hit her. Her own mother's eyes.

Her mother's grieving, sad eyes.

And another murder. So long ago. But never completely forgotten.

Karen caught her breath as if it had been knocked out of her. Through all the pressure of working her first homicide, she didn't let the memories of her sister's death distract her but, now, sitting here in her bath, relaxing, she was overwhelmed with memories.

Her little sister Sarah was only a couple years older than the boy they found today. Karen wondered if there would ever be a time when she would be able to think about her little sister without that "fist to the gut" sensation. It took her a lot of years to pull through the despair and anguish surrounding her sister's death. A lot of years to recover in a family that never forgot how special her sister was, and how important it was to never forget what a joy Sarah was to the family. Karen's eyes welled with tears as she felt the chilling horror this mother must feel knowing that someone killed her little boy and took away her most precious reason for living.

In her own instinctive way, Karen knew that the mother at least

had nothing to do with the murder. She couldn't. But if she didn't, who did? The father? Possible. He was less than convincing with his alibi and it looked as if the parents didn't get along that well. Not only did they argue about who was supposed to be watching the boy, they argued about who was more upset.

It didn't make sense. Karen wondered why one child and not the others. She knew of cases where parents abused one child but not another. Unfortunately, Tampa had seen too much of it in the past couple of years. Maybe this child wasn't his? Extramarital affairs have produced unwanted children before, why not in this case?

Karen pulled herself back a bit and reined in the flow of her thoughts. She didn't even have the results of the fingerprint yet, or the Crime Scene Tech's report. Susan promised to call her as soon as it was available. Before she spent too much energy chasing down imaginary leads, she'd better concentrate on what she knew.

She ticked off the items on her fingers. She had a strangled boy found outdoors in a concealed part of a popular campground that had approximately one hundred people in the area; about half of them overnight campers. She had a fingerprint. She had a footprint. She had parents who claim to have had nothing to do with their son's death and about twenty witnesses who so far saw nothing.

Karen laughed at herself. She didn't have much.

Later, wrapped in a light robe and a cup of tea in hand, Karen sat on a patio chair on the balcony of her townhouse. The afternoon rain had cooled the temperatures and for once, the mosquitoes weren't targeting her like miniature kamikaze planes.

It was moments like this when she wondered if she'd ever find someone to share her life with on a more intimate level. Sure, she had friends, and even a few short-term relationships. But nothing lasting. Nothing that tugged at her heart and made her want to open her soul to another person.

She sat her cup down on a small table next to her chair and rested her chin on the tips of her fingers. Be serious, she told herself. When would she ever find the time to have a lasting relationship? She lived and breathed her job now. What made her think that there would be room in her life for another person?

Statistics showed that she'd more than likely end up with someone in the same field of work, only because she had a better chance of meeting someone during her working hours. Karen thought about that and figured it might be true. She sure as hell wasn't going to troll for someone in a bar. She had her share of one-night stands when she was younger and that just wasn't part of her life anymore. Not since she turned thirty a couple of years ago. She hoped she'd grown more since then and at least matured enough to get to know someone a little bit longer before jumping into bed with them. Her job was dangerous enough; she didn't need to live her life dangerously as well.

Chapter Four

"Sykes here." Karen absently picked up her telephone on its second ring while trying to concentrate on the file in front of her.

"Susan Parker. You ready for this?"

"Whatcha got?" Karen sat up straighter in her chair and covered her other ear with her hand. Even though the office wasn't crowded, she wanted to make sure she heard every word.

"We got a hit in our local database, girlfriend. We got a hit."

"Can you fax me the report?"

"Already on its way."

"Awesome. So it wasn't one of the parents." Karen leaned back in her chair and brushed her hand across her forehead, pushing away a few stray hairs. Damn, she needed that haircut! She looked around for Sam to give him the news.

"Well, as of yet it wasn't one of the parents. But, according to this fingerprint, someone else touched that boy. And that someone else has a name. Whether he's connected with the parents is something we'll find out when you go talk to this sucker."

Karen grabbed a pen from her desk and pulled a notepad closer. "Don't keep me in suspense, give."

"Raymond Alan Thomas."

"Raymond Alan Thomas." Karen repeated the name, letting it roll off her tongue. She had a name to go with a fingerprint. Life was sweet.

"Don't let me down now. His last known address is on the fax. He should be an easy pick up."

"Okay. I gotta ask because I'm dying to know. What did Mike think when you told him that the print wasn't one of the parents?" Karen twisted the phone cord around one finger.

"Him? Why do you want to know what he thought? Oh, yeah, I get it, girlfriend. You like this guy right?"

"Well, I—"

"You don't have to say anything. I got the picture. I told you that he looked interested, now that I know you're interested too I can work with this. Mike? He gave a typical Mike response. He said you got lucky."

"Lucky? Why that egotistical...thick-headed...," Karen sputtered, running out of words to describe the man who had definitely gotten under her skin.

Susan laughed. "Don't worry. I won't say anything, unless you want me to?"

"No, Susan. Please don't. I was just wondering for professional reasons, of course."

"Uh huh."

"Thanks for letting me know about the print. I'll go pick up that fax now and get right on it."

"You do that. Let me know how it goes. Don't forget about us getting together for coffee some night after work."

"Sure thing. Thanks. Bye."

Karen hung up the telephone and twirled in her seat looking for Sam. She slammed her hand on her desk and let out a whoop of joy. Several officers turned in her direction and gave her questioning looks. Karen asked, "Anyone know where Sam is?"

With shrugs and fingers pointing in different directions, the guys gave what they considered an answer. Karen blew a raspberry at them and headed for the fax machine. The least she could do was get started on finding this guy. She'd catch up with Sam as soon as she could.

CHAPTER FIVE

Sitting in her supervisor's office, Susan hung up the phone after talking to Karen and sat back in the chair. Rocking gently with one toe, she thought about Karen and Mike. It could happen. Stranger things have been known to take place. Would Mike go for it? Susan shook her head. Not if he stuck to his rule of not dating anyone who worked in the police business. Basically anyone he'd come into contact in his job was off limits.

As long as she'd been his partner, Susan knew Mike stood by that rule. He had good reason to and she understood that. But she also knew Mike and what she saw in his eyes yesterday when he met Karen was more than casual interest. Susan caught him really looking at Karen and that must have unnerved him. If Susan knew Mike, and she thought she did, he was probably trying to keep as far away from Karen as possible right now so that he could sort out what happened to him.

But Susan had other plans and it didn't include keeping those two apart. Not if she could help it. She had good instincts and she knew that Mike and Karen needed each other. All she needed was a chance to sit and talk to Karen and verify a few things, and she'd know for sure.

Laughing softly to herself, she pushed up and out of the chair then headed down the hall back to her lab to continue separating the vegetation and sand particles from the boy's short overalls.

CHAPTER SIX

The house and yard had an air of neglect. Chipped and broken ceramic pots on the two steps up to the door held long ago memories of an occasion forgotten and dried bits of a plant that once was. The flat lawn, littered with children's faded and broken toys, appeared tired and worn as if it had been beaten down for good and would never be green and lush again. Thirsty, aggressive weeds held the majority of the yard's small patches of weakened grass at bay.

Karen followed Sam up the sidewalk and to the front of the house. A dull, faded plastic Christmas wreath hung on the door, long past the holiday season. Sam reached out and knocked rapidly and sharply. Karen stood to one side, Sam on the other. They waited. Alert for any noise, however slight, that might come from the other side of the door.

The door opened a crack and a woman's worn-out face appeared and a tired voice asked, "Can I help you?"

Sam answered. "Ma'am, we're here to ask Raymond Alan Thomas a few questions. Is he at home?"

"There ain't no Raymond Alan Thomas here."

"Can you tell me the whereabouts of Mr. Thomas?"

The door opened the rest of the way. The woman inside clutched at the front of her faded button down blouse in a disconcerted sort of way. A small child clung to one of her legs. Another was pushing a truck along the hard floor in the living room behind her. She lifted weary eyes and made eye contact with Karen. Karen gave the woman a small smile while keeping herself vigilant for any other activity inside the house.

"I don't know no one by that name." The child clinging to her let go with one hand to casually pick her nose. Without looking, the

woman slapped her hand away. The child laughed.

"Ma'am, can you tell us how long you've lived here?" Karen spoke for the first time.

"I don't know. I guess maybe eight, nine months. Maybe less." Dull, listless eyes stared back at Karen and Sam.

"Did you know the previous owner?"

"Ain't no previous owner. We're renting. The owner, his name is Mr. Menendez."

Karen took out her notebook and pen. "Would you happen to know how we could contact Mr. Menendez? Would you have his phone number?"

The woman sighed and let out a deep breath. "Sure, I guess. He ain't in any trouble is he? We just can't move again."

"We need to talk to Mr. Menendez, ma'am." Sam said. Agitated, the woman sighed and looked at her children, first the one clinging to her leg, and then the other sitting in the living room. She seemed to weigh her answer before speaking. "Well, hang on. Let me go get his number for you. I have it taped to the fridge." She left the door open as she hobbled her way down a short hall into the kitchen. On the way, she untangled herself from the child that clung to her leg and sat her on the floor of the hall. Sniffling, the little girl looked from the door to her mother before letting out a loud whine of displeasure.

Sam and Karen watched silently, exchanging one knowing look. Karen nodded. She waited, pen in hand.

"Here it is. You can copy it off this." She handed Karen a slip of paper. Turning to the whining child, she said, "Shut up, now. Quit that yelling." Turning to Sam, she said, "Kids, ya know?"

Sam nodded back to her then looked over Karen's shoulder to see what was written on the slip of paper. While Karen wrote, Sam said, "We'll need your name also, ma'am. Just for our records."

"Yeah, no problem. It's Sherry. Sherry Edwards. With a 'y'." "And a telephone number where we can reach you?" "Oh, we ain't got no phone. We just use the neighbor's if'fin we need to call somebody."

"Thank you, ma'am. We appreciate your cooperation."

Sam and Karen said their goodbyes and walked back to their car. Once inside, Karen flipped the notebook shut and wiped the sweat from her forehead. This didn't end here. She wouldn't let it.

Clenching her teeth, she silently vowed that this murder wouldn't go unsolved. She would bring justice to the parents of that little boy. More than her parents ever received.

Sam started the car and backed out of the small driveway. Karen pulled out her cell phone and dialed Mr. Menendez's number.

CHAPTER SEVEN

"So, then what happened?"

"Basically, we hit another dead end." Karen sipped her latte then leaned back in her chair. "The landlord didn't have a forwarding address and was as eager to find him as we were. Apparently he owes some back rent."

Susan waved her hand as if she swatted at an imaginary fly, dismissing the landlord's needs. "That sucks."

"Yeah, tell me about it." Karen sighed. "Now we go looking for anyone he's ever hung out with. Any buddies he might still have around Tampa. Maybe someone's seen him lately and will tell us they've seen him."

"Right, someone's gotta be giving him up. Good luck."

"Thanks, we're going to need it." Setting her cup down, Karen leaned her cheek on her hand. "I know this case isn't easy, but we've gotta catch a break."

"Your first one, huh?"

"Yeah, how'd you know?" Karen looked up at her new friend.

"Sam getting a new partner was a big hint. Not seeing you around the other homicide cases was another."

"Yeah, this is my first homicide case. I want so bad to get it solved too." Karen lowered her voice. She hesitated, looked into Susan's eyes and figured she could trust her. "It's kind of personal." "Oh, girl. You can't be getting personally involved in a case. Don't you know that?"

Karen kept her voice low, her tone quietly soft. "I was eight years old when my little sister was killed. I watched how it ate up my parents. Year after year went by and the murderer was never found. My poor parents never saw justice done. They never had the satisfaction of watching the killer stand trial for Sarah's murder. To this day, it haunts them. I can't let these parents go through the same thing. Not if I can help it."

"Wow. Honey, I didn't know." Susan reached out a hand and gently patted Karen's arm. "Are you sure you should be working on this case?"

Karen looked down at the dark brown hand covering her own lighter one. Susan's concern was genuine. She could feel it. Having a friend who understood meant a lot.

"Absolutely." Karen shook her head as if to clear her mind. She sat up straighter in her chair. "I was meant to work on this case. I'm gonna find this guy, damn it." She slammed her hand down on the table, then guiltily looked around Starbucks. Relieved, Karen saw everyone seemed oblivious to her outburst and went about their business. They were totally unaware that only a few feet from them was a conversation of murder and killers. The noise of other conversations buzzed around them.

"Well, good luck. We'll do our best to preserve all the evidence and help you nail this guy when you find him."

"Thanks."

"No problem. Hey, not to change the subject or anything, but I've been sitting here now for nearly an hour and you haven't asked about Mike."

"Huh? Him? What do I want to ask about him for?" Karen fixated on her coffee cup, not meeting Susan's eyes.

"Uh huh. Just as I thought. Want me to drop a hint to him that you're available?"

"God, no! That sounds too desperate, doesn't it?" Musing about her mournful contemplation about ever finding someone to share her life with from the other night, Karen double backed. Did she want to be alone forever? Some bitter, man hating, old detective with a collection of cats and a taste for frozen dinners? Throwing caution to the wind, she added, "Oh, why the hell not. It's not like I'm doing any better on my own." Feeling brazen and spontaneous, Karen decided that there must be more to Mike than she's seen so far, and if getting to know him better meant being set up, well, then why not. Maybe she was even right about him having a softer side. She made an instant decision that she would be more active about balancing out the personal side of her life.

36 • Vicki M. taylOr

"Honey, we all need a little help sometimes. Don't worry, my hints are real subtle like. Before I'm done, he'll think the whole thing was his idea." Susan grinned and winked at Karen.

Karen eyed her new friend with suspicion. "What 'whole thing'?"

"Now you just hush, and let Auntie Susan do her job." Susan rolled her eyes upward to the ceiling. "And, boy, do I have my work cut out for me. Did I ever tell you that Mike doesn't date anyone in the business?"

"No, can't say that you have."

"Well, it's true. And it's my job. And yours, honey, to make him change his mind."

Karen looked doubtful. "Uh, what if he doesn't want his mind changed?"

"Well, that's for us to fix. He just doesn't know what's good for him right now. You and I are going to take care of that."

"We are?"

"Yep. I saw the way that man looked at you and he's interested. We just have to help him along with being interested. Make him so interested that he'll forget all about his silly dating rule."

"Do you really think so?" A little nervous laugh escaped Karen's lips. "Maybe this isn't such a great idea. I mean—"

"Of course it is."

"It's been hard, Susan. I haven't been really that successful in the 'relationship'," Karen made little quote marks in the air with her fingers, "area and I'm not sure this is going to work out." Worried, she folded her paper napkin over and over until it began to look like an accordion.

Susan sat up straight in her chair and took one of Karen's hands. "Listen. I hope I didn't give you the wrong impression earlier about Mike. He's not a 'fling' kinda guy. He's dedicated, thoughtful, and considerate. He isn't reckless or mean spirited." She patted Karen's hand and let go. "He's a good man, Karen."

"I've been down the 'fling' road in my twenties, and now that I'm in my thirties I think I want something more. Something that means more. I want to belong…to a set. Become a pair. Find my other half. Do you know what I'm trying to say?"

"Yeah, I do, and I think you are at a good time in your life to be looking for something more. Something to complete your life. Mike is too, he just doesn't know it yet."

"Right, you keep saying that." Karen smiled. "Are you doing him any favors by ambushing him like this? I mean the guy just might not want to have his life arranged for him, even if it is by a friend."

"I've known Mike for a long time. And I stood by him through some painful moments. He's like a little brother to me. You caught his interest and I can't stand idly by while he's too stubborn to act upon it. I'll give him the little push he needs and then step back. Fate will take care of the rest."

"You're like a fairy godmother." Karen laughed, her voice carrying in the small coffee shop.

"You think so? Is my tiara on crooked?" Susan looked around the table. "Now what did I do with my magic wand?"

The two women laughed together, their combined cheerful voices causing more than one customer to glance in their direction and smile.

CHAPTER EIGHT

"Damn it, woman, how many times do I have to tell you to keep those kids quiet when I come home?" Mark threw the remote control for the television across the room, nearly hitting Kelly's head. It bounced off her shoulder and landed on the worn carpet floor near her feet.

With an inward sigh, Kelly picked up the remote control and carried it back to her husband. She handed it over without saying a word. That was one lesson she'd learned a long time ago. Don't ever make a comment about him throwing something. Not unless you wanted it thrown at you again, with better aim. She walked away from the living room and its loud noise from the television to go into her daughters' bedroom. The girls had hurried to their room as soon as they heard their father's truck pull up into the driveway. It was better that way.

Walking slowly down the short hallway, she passed the closed door to her son Logan's room. She gently placed a hand on the door and swallowed hard. It hurt. It hurt real bad. Swiping at her eyes, she sniffed loudly. It didn't help to cry anymore. If Mark caught her crying again, he'd yell at her to stop her sniveling and dry up. He'd had enough of her crying, he said. She couldn't understand why he was trying to push Logan's memory away. It wasn't like the rest of them could forget as easily or hide their emotions as well.

She missed her baby. She missed holding his soft, chubby body, the smell of sunshine and baby shampoo in his hair, and the way his bright blue eyes lit up when she'd wake him in the morning. She missed kissing him goodnight and tucking him into his little bed. Most of all, she ached and hurt as if a piece of her had been torn out and left a gaping wound that would never heal.

Taking a deep breath, Kelly wiped a hand under each eye and pulled herself together. She pushed open the door to her daughters' room and said, "Girls, hush now. Your daddy's home and he needs his quiet while he's watching TV."

Two blonde heads looked up in unison. Two pairs of blue eyes stared back at Kelly with slight apprehension on their faces.

"We're sorry, Mama," eight-year-old Ashley said as she smoothed the hair down on her little doll's head. She laid her doll on the floor in front of her and covered it with a small scrap of old cloth she used as a blanket.

"Mama?"

"Yes, Amber?" Kelly knelt down next to her daughters and busied herself with folding doll clothes and putting them in one pile.

"I miss Logan," Amber said in a low voice as she cast a quick glance at her bedroom door.

Looking at the sad, innocent face of her six-year-old daughter, Kelly nearly burst into tears. Of course her girls missed their brother. What family wouldn't? But what child needed to watch what she said in case her daddy could hear and possibly punish her for talking about things he'd forbidden them to talk about? Kelly cringed inside, a small spark of stubbornness slowly fading away, knowing that she had to protect her children, knowing that she'd already failed miserably and knowing that she would probably fail again.

Kelly sat on the floor between her daughters and pulled her knees up under her chin. She put an arm around each girl and held them tight. Tears ran unchecked down her cheeks, but she made no noise. She'd spent many long nights of her life learning how to cry without making a sound so that Mark wouldn't hear her and slap her for bothering him. Tonight, she cried for her son for having to go to heaven so young. She cried for her daughters for having a mother with no courage to help teach them to be strong. She didn't cry for herself; she had no tears for self-pity. She knew the kind of life she'd lead by marrying Mark Hunt and she went into it willingly. Despite what others may think, she loved her husband. Loved him enough to forgive him yet again for his lapses of physical roughness.

After a few moments, she wiped her face with the back of her hand, kissed her girls, then left their room after making them promise to keep the noise down. She walked slowly back toward the living room and the man who was going to be upset over what she had to say.

"Mark?" Kelly waited to interrupt him until a commercial came on the television.

"What?" Mark responded with a loud burp and a demand for a fresh beer.

"We need to talk about something." She kept her voice even as she opened the refrigerator.

"What?" Mark's voice rose along with his temper.

Kelly knew she was heading into dangerous territory. She waited to answer until she was back in the living room. She handed her husband a cold beer then swallowed hard before she said, "Logan's funeral." She rushed on before Mark could stop her. "I got a call from the Medical Examiner's office today. The autopsy is finished and they're ready to release his body. They needed the name of the funeral home we'd be using."

"You know we can't afford no damn funeral."

"I know that. But can't we afford to at least have his body cremated? We could borrow the money from my—"

"Don't say it." Mark rose from his chair and stomped into the kitchen. He opened and slammed cupboards as if looking for something, but not able to find it.

"I'm sure they'd be happy to do it. Mama already said if there was anything they could do to help, just to let them know."

"I ain't borrowing no money from your daddy." Mark slammed shut another cupboard door. It bounced back open from the force. "Damn it, don't we have any chips or anything to eat around here?"

Kelly hurried into the kitchen and opened a lower cupboard door. She pulled out a new bag of potato chips and pushed them into her husband's hands.

"What are you handing me these for? Put 'em in a damn bowl first."

"I'm sorry." Kelly caught the bag of chips as Mark threw it at her. She found a large bowl and hurriedly dumped the bag into it then handed it to Mark.

"That's better. Damn. You'd think by now you'd learn, what are you stupid or something?" He wandered back to his chair in the living room.

Kelly knew her husband wasn't looking for her to respond so she kept her comments to herself. Instead she continued on about her son's burial arrangements. "One of the neighbors said that a fund had been started at the local bank for Logan and that we might get enough money to take care of the arrangements."

"What fund?" Mark stopped shoving chips into his mouth and looked up with interest. His eyes got the greedy gleam to them she'd seen before when her parents first offered them money to get started. The gleam had gone out quickly when Mark found out that Kelly's daddy expected some type of payment in return, either in cash or physical labor. Mark hadn't planned on returning either.

Kelly picked up a dry dishtowel and started wiping the dishes sitting in the strainer that she'd washed earlier in the evening after supper. "Mrs. Cooper said that someone started an account at the bank on the corner in Logan's name. Said people have been donating to it after they put something about it in the newspaper."

"What the hell are they putting stuff like that in the newspaper for?"

"I dunno. She said it was in the article about Logan's killing." Kelly gripped the counter until the knuckles on her hands turned white. She wouldn't start crying again. She wouldn't.

Setting the bowl of chips onto the scratched coffee table, Mark clapped his hands and rubbed them together quickly. "Well, this changes everything, don't it?"

"What do you mean?"

"Well, if'fin we get enough donations, we might be able to come out of this ahead, don't you think?"

Watching her husband cautiously, Kelly said, "No, I don't think I understand. Mrs. Cooper said that the money was to go to any arrangements that needed to be made for Logan. I don't think she meant—"

"I don't care what you think, woman." Mark exploded. "They can't tell me what to do with my own son's money. My only son who's been ripped from my life by some damn, good for nothin' murderer." Mark stood and paced the small living room between the still blaring television and the couch. He turned rapidly and shoved a fist into his right hand. "You still got the number of that reporter who came by?"

"Ummm, I don't know." Kelly searched her mind for where she may have placed it.

"What?" Mark yelled. "Do you got it or not, woman?"

"Yes, I think so." Kelly turned away from the sink and started searching on the counter next to the telephone.

"Damn it, if you done gone and lost it there'll be hell to pay," Mark threatened.

Searching frantically, Kelly pushed papers around on the counter until the familiar business card appeared. "I found it. I found it."

"Damn right, you found it." Mark strode into the kitchen and shoved Kelly aside from in front of the telephone. "Give it here," he said as he picked up the receiver.

Chapter Nine

Karen watched intently out the car window as Sam drove as slowly as possible down busy Nebraska Avenue. Raymond Alan

Thomas was not going to be an easy man to find. If they were lucky, they'd find someone who knew him and could point them in the right direction. Finding someone who was willing to squeal on his buddy wouldn't be too difficult if they knew the right person to squeeze.

Women with weary, bored expressions on their faces walked the street, attempting to make eye contact with the drivers who sped by. Karen knew that many of them looked older than their actual years. Life on the street did that to them. Life on the street and drugs. It was always about the drugs. The hard life of prostitution took a toll on the body and never gave back change. Having spent a number of years with the narcotics squad, Karen knew that most of these women walking the streets were just working for their next fix. Their next smoke. Their next high. They only existed for that next druginduced thrill and then they concentrated on the next one after that. It was never enough. Nothing else mattered in between.

When she went undercover, Karen walked those streets along side of them. Busting the johns wasn't her idea of a good time, but it was necessary. Arresting the girls didn't work because they were right back on the street the next day. They went after the source. The guys who paid for the services. Getting them right where it hurt. Their pockets and their privacy. Walking the streets was hot, dirty, hard work, especially during the humid days of summer. Especially when the line of johns seemed never ending. Karen tried not to let the job get to her, but it was frustrating at times to know that for every john they arrested, two more took his place. For as long as men and women have existed, paying for sex was a part of life. It wasn't just on the streets. Karen saw the other cases too, when she was a patrol officer, where women received bruises and broken arms. The best cases were when those women realized that price was too high to pay and got out.

There was always a price to pay. Karen was going to make sure she was there to collect the payment due on little Logan Hunt's murder.

Clearing her head, Karen went back to watching the action on the other side of her car window. More women walked the street. Choking on the exhaust from the buses and trucks, sweat stains on their clothes, pooling between sagging breasts and in the middle of their backs. These women guarded their stretch of Nebraska Avenue fiercely. Karen's chest tightened. She wished desperately to save each one of them and help turn their life around.

Clearing her throat, looking up the next block, Karen pointed ahead. They found what they were looking for. A small neighborhood grocery store, little more than a hole in the wall, with grimy, boarded windows and faded lettering. A small group of men huddled around the entrance. Sam turned right onto the first side street and parked the car near the corner. A blast of oven-like heat and humidity hit them as they got out of the air-conditioned comfort.

Approaching the group of men, Sam spoke first. "Gentlemen, we'd like to ask you a couple of questions."

"Hey, man. Whatcha want?" One man from the group broke away and moved toward them. He gave off a quality of superiority to the other men that held them back from talking. "We ain't talking to no cops."

Tough guy image, Karen thought.

"Suit yourself. We can have a nice conversation here, or we can all go down to the station and talk there." Sam spread out his hands to include everyone. "It's your choice."

The other men murmured among themselves in Spanish. Karen understood enough to know that they were not thrilled about going down to the station and wanted the first guy to shut up. Dissention in the ranks. A perfect opportunity to use them against each other.

"Hey, you." Karen pointed to one of the men. His eyes shifted away from her then back. He tucked a hand into his pants pocket then pulled out a pack of cigarettes. With hands that weren't quite steady, he lit one, and then put the pack back into his pocket. His

pants slid low on his hips. The ragged cuffs dragged along the ground. His shirt hung on his thin frame, untucked, dirty, and worn. "What's your name?"

"Juan," he mumbled.

"Juan?"

"*Sí.* Yes."

"Juan, we're looking for one of your buddies. Raymond. Have you seen him around lately?"

"No."

"No, you haven't seen him?"

"No, I haven't seen him."

"Are you sure?"

"What do you mean, 'are you sure?' He said he hasn't seen him." Karen turned back to the tough guy.

"Was I talking to you? I don't think so. You just stand back and be quiet."

The other men laughed. Karen had a feeling tough guy didn't like to be laughed at and especially didn't like being told what to do by a woman.

"Now, Juan. When was the last time you saw Raymond?"

Juan looked hesitantly around at his friends. Some shook their heads. Juan turned back to Karen. "I don't know. A week. Two."

"Where'd you see him last?"

"Here." Juan pointed to the storefront. "He was bragging about his new girlfriend again." The other men muttered broken comments in Spanish.

"Girlfriend, huh? Karen asked as she exchanged a look with Sam. "A crazy bitch with little ta-tas?" Some of the men's heads lifted quickly when Karen repeated their comments back to them in English. She knew they were going to be more guarded about their comments from then on. "Did this girlfriend have a name?"

"We just called her 'crazy bitch'."

"Do you know where I can find Raymond and his crazy bitch?"

A chorus of "I dunno" answered her back. Karen sighed. She needed to change her tactics. She was getting nowhere with this group. "All right, Sam. Call dispatch to send a few patrol cars and have them come and pick these guys up."

"Hey, we're not doin' nothin'—" "What for?"

"I'm outa here."

"Hold on there." Sam grabbed the man's arm to keep him from leaving. "We're looking for a little cooperation. If we don't get it, we'll take you down to the station and charge you with loitering and then maybe obstruction or aiding and abetting a known felon. Now, does anyone want to change their answer?"

"Don't be such a hardass man."

"Yeah, man. It's too hot to be comin' down so hard. Be cool."

"Look," Karen said, wiping the sweat from her brow. "Do you know where I can find Raymond?"

The men looked at each other as if to weigh their options. An unspoken agreement spread between them. "Yeah, man. He lives about ten blocks from here, down that way." Tough guy pointed down the same road they had parked their car. "Blue house."

"There are little dwarf statues in the yard."

"Nah, man. They're not dwarfs, they're elves."

"Gnomes, asshole. How many times does that crazy bitch have to tell you?"

"All right, we get it. There are little statues in the yard." Karen pulled out her notebook and made a few notes. "Thanks."

While Sam drove, Karen keyed the address information into the computer and waited to find out if there were any prior calls. Sam parked across from the blue house. One domestic disturbance showed up on the screen as they sat across the street. Sure enough, the front yard had little gnome statues. Chipped and faded looking, they matched the unkempt exterior of the house. The weeds grew tall where grass should be growing making the house look even smaller. Waving in the breeze, torn screens hung from dirty windows, some of the frames banging against the house.

"Do you think this guy could be our killer?" Karen asked.

"We'll know soon enough. Stay alert. Who knows what kind of crap he'll pull once he finds out who we are and why we're here."

"Just let me run the tag on the car in the driveway." Karen leaned over the computer to press the button to send the car's license plate information.

Sam leaned back against the headrest and shifted his body slightly. The rasp and crinkling of the mock leather seats echoed loudly in the car.

"Here we go. Car's registered to Thomas. Tag's expired. Noth-

ing else."

"All right, then. Let's go see who's home."

CHAPTER TEN

Susan tossed her shoes inside the locker and slammed the door shut. The rattle echoed across the tiles in the empty locker room.

"Parker, you in there?"

"Yeah, Mike. Sure am. Just finishing up."

"Move your ass. We got work to do."

"Hush your mouth, boy. You kiss your momma with that mouth?" Susan pulled on a light windbreaker and zipped it half way as she walked out of the locker room.

"No, I kiss my momma with my other mouth. Sheesh." Mike slid into step along side his partner. She was tall and walked nearly shoulder to shoulder with him. "What kind of crap are you giving me today?"

"Whatever works."

"I am not one of your kids, Susan," Mike said as he held the door for her to walk outside. The sun shone on her skin and reflected the color of coffee. Rich and dark. She was a beautiful woman with the eyes of a warrior queen. He knew life was hard on her, with no husband to help her take care of her three children, but she didn't complain. She didn't complain after her husband was shot on patrol after interrupting a burglary, and she didn't complain when her youngest needed to attend a special needs school, and she didn't complain now. "Good thing too. Or else there'd be hell to pay," she told him.

"Uh huh." Mike checked his pockets to make sure he had everything he needed. "Looks like we got another dead body to deal with. Somewhere on the Courtney Campbell Causeway."

"Great. It's raining dead bodies this week." They walked across the parking lot toward their vehicle.

"Seems that way." Mike thought for a minute. "Wasn't it like this last year about this time? Didn't we have that floater in the Hillsborough River and then that shooting over at Radio Shack? Then that domestic violence call where some guy shot his ex wife and kids? Let's keep our fingers crossed history isn't repeating itself."

"I hear that."

They did a quick check of their vehicle to make sure they had all the supplies they needed then climbed into their black SUV. Susan let Mike drive. Mike knew he did a better job and she was smart enough to admit it. He handled the traffic better and found ways through back ups that she would be too timid to try.

Once they turned off Lois Avenue and were heading toward State Route 60, Susan took over the conversation.

"How've you been lately, Mike?"

"Not bad. You?"

"About the same. The kids are always up to something, but I got them well in hand. The oldest, he joined the band this year. Drum Corp if you can believe it. That's all I need around the house is someone beating a drum. But, he likes it and I don't want to spoil his dream."

"Jamal? Good for him."

"Yeah. That's what I thought too." Susan shifted slightly in her seat. "So, Mike. Are you seeing anyone lately?"

"Nah. Not lately." Mike cast a quick glance in Susan's direction, taking his eyes off the road for a mere second. "Why?"

"Just wondering. Thought maybe if you weren't seeing anyone right now you might be interested in taking out Karen Sykes." "Who?" Mike asked a little too quickly. Damn.

"You know who I'm talking about. Karen Sykes. Sam's new partner. We were on a case with them the other day. I'm sure you remember." Susan nudged an elbow toward him in a sign of camaraderie.

"What made you think of her? Why would you even think I'd be interested?"

"Oh come on, Mike. I saw the way you looked at her. You were interested. You just didn't want to be interested."

Rounding the curve near Tampa International Airport, Mike said, "Well, what if I was. It wouldn't work out. Besides, I don't date women in the force."

"It's a silly old rule."

"It's a smart rule."

"Well, I for one think it stinks. Get rid of it. Who better to understand your schedule and be sympathetic about your job than a fellow officer?"

"I tried that once. Remember?" Mike slapped the steering wheel. "It didn't work." Boy, how it didn't work.

"Oh, pooh. Melissa? Good night, that woman was a mess. It didn't have anything to do with you two working together. You're lucky to be rid of her."

"She needed me and I wasn't there for her."

Susan waved her hand as if waving away a fly. "Boy, she messed with your head something awful, didn't she? It didn't matter how much you did for that girl, it was never enough and it never would be. She wasn't your type plain and simple. It had nothing to do with who worked where."

"But, still—"

"Listen. You need to get over that and move on. I think a date with Karen would be the perfect way to show how much you've moved on."

"You're relentless, you know that?" Mike laughed a short laugh. "I'm a mother."

Heading west, Mike turned the vehicle onto the Courtney Campbell Causeway. Driving past Rocky Point, Mike said, "Okay, the report that came in said the body was found on the north side, before the boat launch. You see anything yet?"

"Not yet, but we're just getting on the causeway now."

"Keep your eyes peeled. Traffic along here is ripping by at sixty or seventy miles an hour. It's gonna make it difficult to find a safe place to stop."

"I see lights now up ahead."

"So do I. Watch for a place to turn in and follow the side street. I'll probably have to—" Mike hit the brakes. "Wait, there's one now. Watch our back. I'm gonna make this turn."

Braking quickly and deftly turning the car onto the access road, Mike slowed down. They bounced along the unevenly paved road until they reached a point where so many police cars and rescue trucks were parked they could no longer pass.

rs

Seagulls flew overhead, crying loudly. Fluffy cotton ball clouds dotted the deep blue sky. Susan quickly glanced at the sun. It was going to be another hot day. Hot and humid. Far off to the east, she could see a buildup of clouds. Maybe if they were lucky it'd rain this evening. She crossed her fingers that the rain would hold off until they finished working.

She looked to her right out over the rocks clinging to the shoreline. The Courtney Campbell Causeway divided a portion of Tampa Bay. It was actually divided in thirds by the Howard Frankland and Gandy bridges as well. The causeway bridge was the furthest north.

Hurrying to meet with the officer in charge, Mike and Susan carried their cases of equipment necessary to work the scene.

"Connelly, Parker, glad it's you two." The officer in charge wiped a large hand across his face, wiped it on the side of his trousers, and then held it out for them to shake.

"Hey, Shafer. What do you got here?" Mike asked.

"Jogger saw something suspicious in the brush, called it in as a 911. Patrol arrived to check it out and found the body, fully clothed. Looks like its laying right where it fell."

"Shot?"

"Not so far as we can tell. No blood stain."

"We'll check it out closer and let you know. Is the scene secure?" Susan interrupted the all male chatter.

"Yes, ma'am. Patrol secured it then cordoned off a generous portion of the scene just for you folks. No one's been in there since."

"Well, let us get in and get to work."

Susan opened her case and grabbed the camera. First thing she needed to do was to take photos of everything, from the body to the rest of the area surrounding it. While she was recording the scene with the camera Mike would sketch and measure to record it on paper. It was a good thing that the county let them use digital cameras now. She never did like having to change out the film and carry around all those film canisters.

Thirty minutes later, Susan stopped for a moment to wipe away the sweat so she could see through the viewfinder. Blinking, she checked the image again. The hairs on the back of her neck tingled with uneasy familiarity. She called out, "Yo, Mike. Come and take a look at this."

Winding up the tape measure, watching where he placed his feet, Mike made his way carefully to Susan who was standing just slightly away from the body. "What'd you find?"

"Something very interesting."

"Yeah?"

"Take a look at this." She pointed to the ground. "Look familiar?"

"You've gotta be kidding."

"Yeah, right. As if this one wasn't strange enough."

"Want me to handle it?"

"Nah, I was just finishing up with the shots anyway. I'll go get the casting stuff out of the back of the truck."

"What do you think the odds are that we'd find the same kind of footprint at two separate scenes in less than a week?"

Susan shook her head in disbelief as she made her way back to the SUV. They'd been lucky with this footprint. If it had been winter, the ground would be too hard and dry. With the rains they'd been having every day, it kept the ground moist enough to hold a print.

On her way back to the cordoned off scene, Susan saw Mike talking to Officer Shafer. She figured he was telling him about the print and their case the other day. Ducking slightly, she walked under the police tape. She placed the casting materials on the ground near her and checked the print. She wouldn't need much, just enough to cover the print; it wasn't deep into the ground like last time.

Letting her mind wander a bit while she mixed up the water and plaster, Susan thought that this would be the perfect opportunity for Mike to speak to Karen. He could be the one to tell her about the similar footprint. Susan smiled to herself. Anything for love.

Having finished recording the scene and waiting for the cast to dry, Mike and Susan turned their attention to the body. Moving carefully so as not to disturb the drying mold, they used gloved hands to search for obvious signs of trauma. Finding none, they examined the head.

"He could have fallen and hit his head on one of those rocks," Susan pointed out.

"Yeah, except there's no swelling."

"So, he's walking along and just drops dead?"

"Stranger things have happened."

"Maybe." Susan pondered the situation. "Did you check for ID?" "Yeah, didn't find anything. So far, he's Mr. John Doe."

Susan turned to the body. "Well, Mr. Doe, what's your story? And how much of it are you going to tell us?"

"I doubt he's gonna do much talking until we get him on a table. Maybe a tox report will give us some answers."

"Let me go grab a sheet and a bag. Why don't you let Shafer know what we found out so far."

"Don't you mean what we didn't find out?"

"You trying to get smart with me?"

"No, ma'am." Mike grinned as he ducked under the police tape surrounding the scene. "Just stating a fact."

"Hey, Mike," Susan called him back. "Since you're in such a good mood. How about I arrange a date for you?"

"Who?"

"What do you mean who? Karen Sykes."

"What? Didn't we just have this conversation?" Mike frowned. "No way."

"Come on. Just do it for me? I know you two would get along great if you just gave yourself a chance."

"I don't know."

"Give yourself a chance."

"She probably wouldn't want to go anyway." Mike slapped the gloves he's been wearing against his thigh. "I haven't had much luck lately." He choked back a laugh. "What am I telling you all this for, anyway?"

"I know. I know. That's why I think you should just listen to your Auntie Susan and let me handle all the details."

"I gotta be stupid."

"No, you're not. You're finally doing something smart." "We'll see."

"Just leave it up to me. I'll make all the arrangements. I'll let you know when and where, you just be there."

"Connelly? What'd you two come up with?" Shafer called out.

"Seriously, Mike. I'll take care of it."

"Connelly?"

Mike turned as if to head toward the officer in charge, but stopped in mid step and turned back. "Fine," he muttered and stalked off toward the biggest group gathered around Officer Shafer's car. Susan watched him fall into conversation with them probably explaining the lack of injury to the body.

After retrieving the sheet and black body bag, Susan checked it carefully to make sure it didn't contain any stray evidence from a previous occupant.

Susan called out to Mike, "Hey, Mike. I'm gonna need your help here."

"Sure thing. I'm on my way." Mike turned from the group and headed back to the scene.

Unfolding the sheet with Mike's help, they placed it next to the body. After lifting the body onto the sheet, they folded it over carefully then lifted the body, sheet and all into the bag.

"I'll ride along with the body and collect the clothes and fingerprints," Susan said after she packed up her equipment.

"You sure?"

"Yeah. I don't mind. You took the last one."

"Okay, then. Meet you back at the lab?"

"See you there."

Susan climbed into the transport vehicle and pulled out her cell phone. While she waited for the technician to drive to the medical examiner's facility, she placed a call to Karen.

"Yo, girlfriend."

"Hi, Susan, what's up? I'm sitting in front of a suspect's house. Can you make it quick?"

"Do you have any plans for tonight?"

"Tonight? No, not really. I did have a date with a frozen dinner and my television but I can always cancel. What do you want to do?"

"Not me. Mike." Susan smiled as the medical technician climbed behind the steering wheel and started the van. In seconds they were heading back east on the Courtney Campbell Causeway back toward Tampa and the office.

"What?"

"Yep. I convinced Mike to give you a chance. So don't blow this."

"Blow this? I haven't even said I'll go."

"You'll go. You know you will. You can't say no. I already told him you would."

"Oh, God, Susan. He must think I'm the most desperate female in all of Tampa."

"Not quite."

Karen chuckled. "Very funny."

"Now see, that's what I'm talking about. Get yourself in a good mood. This is gonna be fun, for both of you." Susan smiled. She knew her two friends were going to hit it off.

Sounding resigned but excited, Karen asked. "Okay, so where am I meeting Mike?"

"I was thinking Miguel's Mexican Café, over on Kennedy? It's a nice place and friendly. You do like Mexican food, right?"

"Yeah, I do. I take it Mike does too?"

"It's his favorite."

"Of course it is." Karen sighed. "Fine. Tell him I'll meet him there at seven thirty. Gotta go. Bad guys to catch."

Susan hung up her cell phone and let out a whoop. She startled the driver then laughed. She hadn't felt so good in years. She thought she might just go into the matchmaking business and give up all this death nonsense.

CHAPTER ELEVEN

After hanging up with Susan, Karen radioed dispatch their exact location before stepping out of the car. The hot afternoon dragged on. It looked as if it were going to rain today, but not until much later. The fluffy clouds were too high and scattered. If she had a better view of the east she might be able to see if there were any storms forming. What was certain was the thumping of Karen's heart as they drew nearer to the house. The killer was here. She could feel it in her bones. Forgotten was the conversation she just had with her friend Susan and her date with Mike tonight. All her instincts were trained on this moment.

Sam climbed the wobbly, rickety steps to the door. He knocked twice. Karen kept guard from below where she had a view of the front yard and the car. If Thomas attempted an escape this way, he wouldn't get past her.

Karen looked at Sam. He shrugged and knocked again.

"Someone's coming," Sam said, indicating that he heard noises on the other side of the door.

"I've got your back."

The door swung open wide. "Can I help you?" a small, woman with a tentative voice and short, blonde, curly hair asked. She was dressed in a Disney character t-shirt and a pair of torn jean shorts. Her feet were bare.

"Ma'am, I'm Detective Anderson and this is Detective Sykes." Sam motioned to Karen. "We're from the Hillsborough County Sheriff's Office and we're looking for a Mr. Raymond Alan Thomas. Ma'am, is there anyone by that name living here?"

"Ray? Yeah. Ray lives here." The blonde looked to her left.

Alerted, Sam immediately drew his gun all the way from his holster. Karen put her hand under her blazer and felt for her gun. "Ma'am, is Mr. Thomas in the house right now?"

"Ray? No. Not right now. He stepped out for a few minutes." She ran her hand through her short, blonde curls. They bounced then settled back against her head. "Said he'd be back later," she sighed. "He always comes back later." She gaped at the gun in Sam's hand.

"Is Ray in some kind of trouble?"

"We're not sure yet. We need to talk to him," Sam answered the woman then looked to her left. He shook his head letting Karen know he didn't see anything. He motioned to her to start taking notes.

Karen took her hand off her gun and pulled out her notebook. Sam kept his drawn. He eased forward a bit on the small front step and leaned into the house looking to his left and right. Karen asked the woman, "Ma'am, could we have your name?"

"Me? Sure. My name is Maggie Morris." Maggie looked from Sam to Karen with curiosity brimming in her eyes.

"Ms. Morris, is this your legal address?"

"Here? I guess so. I only hooked up with Ray about a couple of months ago. Has he done anything wrong?"

"That's what we're here to find out." Karen saw that Sam had seen into the house as far as he could from the front step. "May we come in?"

"Inside? I don't know." Maggie's eyes darted back and forth as if she were trying to make a hard decision. "Sure. I guess so."

"Thank you, ma'am." Sam holstered his weapon, but kept his hand on it.

They walked into the house and stood in the middle of the living room. The room stank from smoke and mold. It smelled like it hadn't been aired out in months. Maggie motioned to them to sit on the couch. Dirty stains marred the faded gold and brown flower pattern. Karen would have bet that if you gave the arm of the couch a hard slap a cloud of dust would fly.

Sam and Karen declined and remained standing. Reading through her notes, Karen looked at Maggie and asked, "So, you've only been living here a couple of months. Where did you live before this?"

Maggie looked down at her feet, then lifted soulful eyes bright with unshed tears. "Before here? I was on the street for a while. Ray, he…he said he liked me. Said I could stay with him until I got back on my feet. He's been real good to me."

"Uh huh. And what about the domestic disturbance call a month ago?"

"A month ago? It was nothing. Nothing at all. We got a little loud and the neighbors called the police. If they'd just minded their own business there wouldn't have been any trouble." Maggie wrung her hands then gripped the front of her shirt near the hem. "We had a little disagreement. Nothing serious. We're fine now. You'll see. When Ray comes home he'll tell you. He'll tell you we're fine now."

Sam and Karen exchanged a glance. Where was the crazy bitch that Raymond's friends described? Somebody definitely had his or her wires crossed. Would she be willing to cooperate? Karen nodded, her head bobbing slightly. She knew what Sam wanted. A look around the house. "Ms. Morris—"

"Ms. Morris? Please, call me Maggie."

"Maggie. Would you mind if we had a look around?"

"Why? Are you looking for something?"

"We're not sure, actually. But we'll know it when we see it." Karen shrugged her shoulders and looked bored. "It's all a matter of paperwork anyway. I could go down to the district attorney's office and get a search warrant and come back here when we've wasted God knows how many hours, or we can just have a look around now." Karen shrugged her shoulders again. "No big deal, really."

"Really? Well, if it's really not a big deal. I don't know what you'll find. Me and Ray, we haven't done anything wrong." Maggie's eyes widened and she smiled.

"Well, then that should make our search easy then, right?"

"Huh? I guess so."

"There's just the matter of your signature. If you'd sign this consent-to-search form, we'll be out of your way in no time."

Maggie stepped only as close as she needed to sign the form. She took the pen Karen offered, signed her name, and stepped back. Karen gave her a searching look before accepting the pen and placing it back in her pocket.

Sam was already heading for the kitchen while Karen made her way around the small living room.

"Detective? The bedroom is that way." Maggie pointed to a closed door.

"Thank you, ma'am." She saw that the woman was going to protest and said, "Maggie, I mean." Karen stood aside. "But we can only search the common areas of the house while Mr. Thomas is away from the premises."

"Mr. Thomas? Oh, you mean Ray." Maggie's lips turned upward into a smile.

"Yes, ma'am."

"What are you looking for? Maybe I can help you out here."

"We're not sure exactly." Karen wondered how much she could say. She looked toward the door where Sam disappeared and made a decision on her own. "We might be looking for a pair of boots or some kind of work shoe."

"Boots? What kind of boots?"

"We're not exactly sure. We'd have to take them in for a comparison to see if we have a match."

Maggie left the room and went into the bedroom. She closed the door behind her. Karen continued to look around the small living room, cringing when she realized that meant she'd even be looking behind the dingy couch. The small house, with so few common rooms, would be relatively easy to search in a short period of time. Karen knew Sam wanted to finish before their suspect arrived home.

Pulling a pair of rubber gloves out of her back pocket, Karen prepared to get to work. The warm, airless room was dark. There was no air conditioning. The only light filtered through the partially covered windows. Karen's hand roamed along the wall inside the doorway looking for a light switch. Finding one, she switched it on. She took in the room as she stood in the entryway, deciding on the best tactic to take.

Karen decided that a logical approach would best suit the situation. She started on her left and figured she'd sweep the room from left to right ending back at the doorway.

Grimy, sweat stained throw pillows were tossed haphazardly about the faded and torn couch. Ashtrays, overflowing with cigarette butts spilled onto the dusty surface of the small tables that bookended the couch. The rest of the dusty, sticky surface held empty and partially empty beer cans. Beer cans and soda cans even littered the floor along the front of the couch and the only chair. Looking up at the ceiling, she could see brown-ringed watermarks where the roof leaked. From the look of the house, it probably hadn't had any repair work done in years.

The room had an unpleasant, sour odor that Karen wrinkled her nose at. The more she stayed in the room, the stronger the odor became.

An avalanche of clothes spilled out of a box in the corner. Karen couldn't tell if they were dirty or clean. Looking for anything that might link Thomas to the crime scene, Karen used a gloved hand to sift through the mess of jeans and t-shirts. Finding nothing, she turned and perused the room. She'd made her way mostly around the room, stopping once to pull the couch from the wall so she could look behind it. As she looked around the room from her new angle, she hoped she'd find something, anything she might have missed.

Her gaze fell on Maggie. She wondered when she returned to the living room and how long she'd been standing in the doorway. Karen looked at what Maggie held in her hands. A pair of brown hiking boots with red laces. They looked to be about the same size as the print they found near the body. Karen crossed the room to get a closer look at them. She itched to snatch them up and examine them closer. Keeping her hands behind her back, she kept her distance in order to preserve the possible evidence.

Karen called out, "Sam, get in here."

Footsteps sounded in the other room. The floor creaked in the kitchen as Sam strode across it and entered the living room.

He stood in the middle of the room, not looking at Maggie. "What'd you find?"

Standing next to Maggie, Karen gingerly held up a boot between her gloved finger and thumb. "How about these?" Sam let out a low whistle.

Karen nodded and smiled. "I think Mr. Thomas has just become a very special person of interest in this case."

"Sykes, how did you find these? Were they in one of the common rooms?"

"I mentioned to Maggie that we might be looking for a pair of boots. She went into the bedroom and returned with the pair you see here."

"Ms. Morris, do you own these boots?"

"Me? No, sir."

"Do these boots belong to Mr. Thomas?"

"Ray? Yeah, I think so."

"Ms. Morris, are you offering these boots to us?"

"These boots? I don't know. I mean, they're not mine, but the detective did say you were looking for boots, and these were the only ones I could find. Do you think I should?" Maggie turned from the doorway and cast questioning eyes toward Karen.

"I can't make that decision for you. You must make it on your own." Karen kept her voice level and tried not to sound too excited. She didn't want to influence Maggie in any way that could lead them to trouble in case they had to go to trial.

"Me? I can't do that. I guess I'd better keep them here and talk to Ray when he gets back." She held the boots close to her chest, hugging them and staring at the floor.

"That's your prerogative, ma'am."

"Sykes?" Sam leaned against the door jam, his eyes narrowing. A crease wrinkled between his eyebrows.

"Yeah, Sam?"

"Let's talk outside."

After explaining to Maggie that they were finished for the moment, Sam and Karen headed out of the stifling little house and into the cooler comfort of their air-conditioned car.

"So, what do you think?" Karen asked while she stripped off the gloves she'd been wearing. Sam had already taken his off as soon as he left the house.

"I think we need those boots."

"But how do we get them if she's not going to give them to us?"

"I don't know." Sam adjusted the vents in the car to blow the somewhat cold air toward his face. "We're walking a fine line here. We can tell her how much they mean to our case, even to Mr. Thomas. If they're not the boots we're looking for they'd help in clearing him. She might be more approachable using that angle."

"If not? Then we hurry downtown and get a search warrant issued as soon as possible," Karen answered, and then asked, "is that even a possibility right now?"

"Absolutely." Sam tilted his chin to let the cold air drift across his face. He sighed. "Okay then. Head back in?"

"Yep, may as well. Let's try one more time."

Sam and Karen walked quickly across the street, through the yard and back up the small rickety steps. Sam knocked rapidly on the door. Once again, it was opened by Maggie. She still held the boots in one arm.

"Ms. Morris, about those boots…"

"These boots? Oh pooh, I decided to let you take them."

"I'm sorry?"

"Huh? You can take them with you. Ray won't mind, I'm sure of it."

"We appreciate your cooperation, Ms. Morris. Maggie." Karen smiled as she watched the shorter woman begin to protest about the use of her formal name.

Sam felt in his pockets then asked Karen, "Do you have another pair of gloves?"

Karen patted her pockets. "No, but I have a pair in the car. I'll grab a paper bag while I'm in there. Be right back."

In a matter of minutes, the boots were secured in a paper bag in the trunk of the car. Karen and Sam drove away from the house in the early dusk. The purple tinge to the night sky made reflections shine extra bright in the car's headlights.

"We got him, Sam." Karen grinned. "I think we should nail this sucker." Karen grinned again and gave a nervous laugh. "I can't believe we're this close. This close." She held up her hand and pinched the air with her thumb and forefinger.

"We've gotta do this right, so we can make the charges stick. You got the woman to sign a consent form so we could search, right?"

"Yep, got it right here in my notebook."

"Good. That's first. You also got her statement about offering the boots to us, right?"

"Yep."

"We need to get these boots to Florida Department of Law Enforcement (FDLE) as soon as possible so they can start testing them to see if they match the print found at the scene."

"How soon do you think we'll know?"

"They're notoriously backed up. Hopefully only a few days." "Good, I want to nail this bastard."

"Well, now we have to figure out why or how Thomas would ever logically be around the Hunts and how he could have left a print on the boy's clothing."

"You think he knew the Hunts?"

"We need to figure that out. And we should run a more intense background check on him. Map out any affiliations he might have that might coincide with the Hunts."

Karen made hurried notes as she kept up with Sam as he talked.

They agreed to get started on the background search first thing in the morning.

CHAPTER TWELVE

Karen stood just inside the door of the restaurant. She'd been to Miguel's before and knew they had good food. She shifted her weight from one foot to the other then shifted back again. Every time the heavy wooden door opened she turned her head to see who came through. Each time she was a little disappointed that it wasn't Mike. However, she also breathed a sigh of relief. She needed another minute to prepare herself.

Susan did tell her that Mike would meet her at seven thirty. And seven thirty it was, on the dot. She had hoped that when she arrived he would be waiting for her, not the other way around. One finger in her mouth, she gnawed absently at a ragged cuticle.

The door opened again. This time the man walking through the door was blonde and handsome. And very sure of himself as he said, "Been waiting very long?"

Quickly removing her finger, Karen hid it behind her as she responded, "No, not long. I actually just got here myself." She threw the hostess a quick look that dared her to contradict her statement.

"Great. This place always smells good. Let's get a table." Karen walked first, behind the hostess as they were led to their table. They ordered drinks and then sat looking at each other. A busboy arrived with a basket of warm tortilla chips and two small bowls of salsa. He placed the items on the table between the two of them and left.

Giving the man across the table a good once over, Karen decided he passed on appearance. He wore a pair of black casual trousers, probably Dockers, and a soft, pastel colored polo shirt. Over the shirt, he filled out and into a black jacket, sports style. Wide at the shoulders and narrow at the hips. Definitely, he passed on appearance.

Unsure of how to start a conversation, Karen spoke first. "So, this is a little awkward."

"Yeah. I guess so."

Each of them looked at anything but each other.

Karen tried again. "How are you?"

"Fine." Mike nodded his head. "Fine."

Karen grappled for something. *Great we're up to two fines already and we haven't even had drinks.* She decided the direct approach might work. "What are you doing here, Mike?" Karen asked as bluntly as possible. She had nothing to lose. She grabbed a chip out of the basket and nervously nibbled on it while she waited for Mike to respond.

rs

Mike blinked. He gave Karen a long look before he answered.
"I—"

The waitress returned with their margaritas. She put a large glass of the frozen concoction in front of each of them. Karen smiled her thanks. Mike remained silent.

After the waitress took their dinner orders, Karen started the conversation again. "You were going to tell me why you're here."

"Yeah." Mike bit his lip then folded his hands together in front of him on the table. "I'm not real crazy about being here, actually, if you want the truth. I'm mostly doing this for Susan. I trust her. She says to give you a second look, so here I am."

"Don't go out of your way or anything." Karen tossed the chip aside.

"I'm serious. Susan usually has good instincts in the field. I figured she had good instincts about this too."

Thanks, I think."

"Relax. I'm not going to bite. Besides, it's just one dinner."

Karen picked up her glass and took a sip. "Right. Just one dinner."

Mike took a deep breath. In an effort to match Karen for bluntness, he went on. "Well, since I'm being so truthful, I guess I better let you know what else." He played absently with the knife and fork in front of him on the table. Looking up, he caught Karen watching him warily. Taking another deep breath, he let it out and said, "I saw something in you. Something that made me think you might be worth a second look."

Karen nearly choked on the chip she'd been nibbling. "You did?"

"Yeah." Mike took a long drink of his frozen margarita. He smiled for the first time that evening. He knew he caught her off guard. "You had a way about you that said, 'look at me, world' and I liked that. You weren't careless at the site and that ranks high in my book."

Karen sipped her drink while Mike talked. He watched her lips purse together from the tang of the lime mixed with the salt on the rim of the glass. Her mouth twitched as if she was biting the inside of her cheek. She said, "I didn't want you to think that I didn't know what I was doing around a crime scene. I have been trained." She sounded almost defensive. Mike watched her search for the right words and try again. "I thought you were kind of a jerk for yelling at me."

"A jerk?" The chip that Mike had dunked into the salsa stopped in mid air.

"Yeah. But I would have probably done the same thing if I were you."

"You think?" Mike placed the salsa-laden chip into his mouth and crunched.

They laughed and a heavy weight fell from Mike's shoulders. She wasn't so bad after all. But he was only doing this for Susan.

"Yeah, that's why I was…" Karen lowered her eyes and studied the table.

Mike wondered if besides the burritos and tacos, more honesty would be on the menu tonight.

"I don't know. I guess I was intrigued by you," she blurted out.

"You were?" He wasn't ready for that much honesty.

"Yeah, but then Susan said you don't date women you work with and I thought that was that."

"Yeah, well, I don't usually. I mean I haven't since…" He looked at Karen's face, studied her eyes and decided she was sincere. "Oh, what the hell. I had a bad break up with someone I used to work with and it got kind of messy. Since then I've kind of had this policy of not dating co-workers. But—"

rs

"But? Then you met me." Karen laughed at Mike. "And you couldn't live without me." She played up the dramatics by placing her hand to her forehead and pretending to swoon. It was her small but inept attempt at trying to flirt.

Mike laughed with her. "Yeah. Something like that."

Raising his glass, Mike said, "To Susan."

Definitely. She raised her glass. "To Susan."

They settled into a comfortable discussion of the day's current events as they drank their margaritas and munched happily on chips and salsa.

It wasn't long until the waitress arrived with their steaming plates of food.

"Listen to that sizzle." Karen wiggled in her chair in anticipation. She caught Mike's bemused expression. "I love fajitas. I don't make them for myself."

"Yeah, I know the feeling. Cooking for one sucks."

Their appetites sated with fajitas, enchiladas, beans, and rice, and comfortable conversation they sat back and sighed.

"Their food is good every time I come here," said Mike as he patted his stomach.

"I don't come here often, but when I do, I always go overboard." Karen sighed again. "I always feel like such a pig." She looked down
at the empty dishes. "I can't believe I ate it all."

"Neither can I. Most women just pick at their food." "God, I'm gonna have to run an extra five miles in the morning just to work this dinner off."

"You run?"

Karen looked at Mike to see what was behind his question. Would he make some smart-ass comment? "Yeah, ten miles every morning. Why?"

"I don't know." He paused. "I run too. I was thinking maybe I'd run with you." Mike rushed on. "If that's all right with you."

Karen thought for a moment. Mike wanted to go running with her. He didn't look like he was making fun of her. Did she miss something? This was more than just pleasing his partner. Then again, it was only a run. Not like a second date or anything. "Yeah, sure. I mean, if you want." She gave him a sideways look. "Do you think you can keep up with me?"

"Well, we'll just have to find out, won't we?"

Karen laughed while she wrote her address down on the back of her business card. She handed it to Mike.

Mike looked down at it and said, "Okay. I know where that is.

It's not too far from me actually. What time shall I meet you?" "Say five thirty?" She wouldn't give in and give him a later time. He started when she did. But he didn't even blanch at the early time.

She had to give him a little credit.

"Sure."

The waitress returned and placed the check in front of Mike. Karen reached out a hand to grab it. She was too late. Mike already held it in his hand.

"Please, let me—"

"No, this one is on—"

"Let's be reasonable, Mike. Can we split it?"

"Why don't I get this one and you get the next one?"

Karen thought for a second or two. She liked the sound of that. "Okay. That works for me. I'll get the next one." Running together tomorrow. A hint of a second date. This was going better than she could have ever expected. Maybe Auntie Susan really did have a magic wand and some fairy dust up her sleeve.

Karen slid sideways in her seat and stretched. She crossed her legs and dangled one sandal off the top of her big toe.

"Great." Mike got out his wallet, laid a credit card on top of the check for the meal, and waited for the waitress to return.

"It was a wonderful meal, and I had a great time, Mike. Thanks."

"Me too."

Karen watched Mike glance around the room at the rest of the tables. He mumbled, "I'm glad I did this." He didn't look Karen in the eye; instead he looked above her head. Probably at the decorations on the wall. "You know. Took Susan's advice." He coughed once then started fiddling with his credit card while they waited for the waitress to pick it up.

"Yeah, me too." Karen wondered where the relaxed Mike went. He sounded like he was trying to force the conversation. What would he be nervous about now? The evening worked out fine.

The waitress arrived, picked up the credit card and the check, then returned with a slip of paper for Mike to sign and the receipt. Karen watched him think for a second, apply the tip, and then add the numbers. He signed his name with a flourish. "There, that's it.

Are we done here?"

"Sure. I'm ready to go."

"Great, let's go find our cars."

Karen frowned. What was the matter with Mike? Here he was, practically pushing her out the door. "I parked near the back. The parking lot was kind of full when I got here."

"Yeah, me too. And I got here later than you."

They walked through the front parking lot and around the building to the back. Karen spotted her car first and headed for it. Mike walked along side her.

She only fumbled once, looking for her keys and then in hand she pushed the unlock button on her key fob. "So, this is me."

"Nice car."

Karen looked over her dark SUV as it shined in the street light overhead. It was a nice car and she was proud of it. It rode like a luxury car but had enough room for all the extra things she felt necessary to carry with her like running gear, plastic gloves, paper bags, and other items she might need on an impromptu case. "Thanks. I like it. It meets my needs."

"Yeah. We have similar tastes in cars." Mike pointed his key fob and pushed a button. A few cars down and over, a dark SUV's lights flickered and the horn sounded.

"Nice."

Mike slapped at a mosquito buzzing around his ear. "Look. I don't know about you, but I don't want to become dinner for these pests. You feel like having a drink somewhere or are you ready to go home?"

Now this was better. Mike was Mike again. For a second, Karen thought about not inviting him back to her place, but forged ahead and said, "Well, I'm ready to go home, but if you don't mind, we can have a drink there?"

"Sure." Mike smiled.

"Why don't you follow me?"

"Okay."

Mike helped Karen with her door then closed it for her when she was safe inside her car. She waved at him as he crossed the parking lot to his vehicle.

Was she doing the right thing? Was it too soon to be asking him to her house? She argued with herself. It's only for a drink. One drink won't hurt. And, besides, he has to go home. He was coming back in the morning to go running.

As Karen drove toward home all the while keeping an eye on

Out fOr Justice • 61

the headlights behind her, she pondered the choice of drinks and whether making coffee was an option at this late hour.

Chapter Thirteen

"If you don't mind, I'm just gonna get out of these clothes into something a bit more comfortable."

"Don't change on my account." Mike looked her up and down, thinking there wasn't anything he'd change about her at all. In her short, body-hugging dress made from some type of soft cotton tshirt material that he wanted to reach out and touch, it was all Mike could do to keep his eyes on his plate during dinner. He found it hard to concentrate on eating and was sure he'd made a fool of himself while talking to her. When she stretched and crossed her legs, he had to force himself to look anywhere but at her. Her body curved in all the right places and he struggled with himself to stop from following the curve not with his eyes but with his hands. He blinked twice and pulled himself back together when he realized that Karen was talking.

"I'm doing it for me, I don't mind dressing up, but when I'm home, I need to be comfortable. I need to be me…in my own space."

"Makes sense." Mike nodded his head. "I understand. Go for it." He admonished himself for thinking sexy thoughts about Karen's body. He had to push those thoughts away at dinner and he swore he wouldn't think of them again. He could feel attraction for someone. He was a man, after all. But he liked Karen the person too, he found out at dinner.

"Okay, I'll be right back."

Karen motioned Mike toward the living room and told him that the drink cart was set up in a corner. Mike listened as she told him to mix what he wanted and she'd be right in.

Not wanting to be so bold and unsure whether alcohol would be a good choice at this late hour, Mike instead wandered around the tastefully decorated living room of Karen's townhouse. He looked at pictures of her as a child with another girl he assumed was her sister and her parents. Everyone looked happy and carefree. More pictures of Karen as she grew up, along with a set of parents that grew older in each picture. Older and more somber. He noticed there were no more pictures of the other sister. A possible death in the family, he wondered as his crime tech intuition kicked in.

He looked at but didn't touch the collection of hand blown glass fish on the shelves in the corner of the room. Instead, he spent his time waiting for Karen to return by staring out the sliding glass doors to her balcony. Her three-story townhouse stood among a row of others just like it.

He liked her quiet neighborhood and felt that it suited her. If he had the kind of job she did, he'd have chosen a quiet place just like this to settle into.

Nervous, he wondered what Karen might change into to get more comfortable. He wasn't sure what she had in mind for the rest of the evening, but he wasn't planning on taking it any further than they'd already gone. He didn't think adding any more alcohol to the evening would help matters. Hearing a door close behind him, he turned away from the sliding glass doors and toward the living room. He breathed a sigh of relief to see Karen in casual clothes and not in something shorter and sexier. "Did you find everything okay?"

"Yeah. But I waited for you."

"That wasn't necessary, but thanks." Karen smoothed down the front of the t-shirt she'd changed into along with a pair of lightweight sweatpants. In her bare feet, she moved silently along the tiled floor.

"You look great, by the way."

"Thanks. I like to be comfortable when I'm home, I hope you don't mind."

"Not at all."

"Let me get that drink—"

Mike stopped her before she could reach the small bar. "Do you mind if we make it coffee?" He asked. He wanted to keep his wits about him. Especially around this woman who not only intrigued but aroused him. She was beginning to get under his skin and he didn't want to do or say anything wrong. For some reason, he wanted to make a good impression. It was important to him.

"No, I don't mind at all. That's a great idea. I'll join you in a cup." Karen busied herself in the kitchen filling the coffee pot and getting down cups. She turned her head to find Mike standing at the breakfast bar watching her.

"Do you need something?"

"No."

"Why are you standing there watching me?"

"I want to."

"Well, stop it, you're making me nervous."

"I've never seen anyone move with such efficiency before. The layout of your kitchen and they way you move from place to place is like watching live art. Did you design the kitchen yourself?"

"Mostly. I had a lot of input when they built it."

"Well, it suits you. It's like it was made for you."

Karen laughed. "It kinda was." She stopped at the refrigerator. "Do you take milk?"

"No, thanks."

"Sugar?"

"Nope. Just give it to me black. It's how I learned to drink it while working in the lab. We barely had time to pour ourselves a cup let alone bother with extras."

"Well, I like creamer," Karen said as she pulled out a small container from the refrigerator. "It gives the coffee a little more flavor. The hazelnut is good, but I like the French vanilla best."

Mike thought that creamer in her coffee suited her. Tough outside but a little soft around the edges. They moved into the living room where he chose a chair while Karen sat on the sofa.

Mentally shaking his head, Mike contemplated his current situation. Here he was, sitting in a co-worker's home, sipping coffee after a great dinner and not twenty-four hours before he'd been protesting this very action. He looked over at the woman who helped change his mind. She sat with one leg curled under her. Comfortable. It made him glad to see that she was at ease around him.

He watched her over the rim of his cup as she took a sip of coffee. She smiled and breathed deep of the aroma. Mike smiled as well. It pleased him that she took pleasure in such a small thing.

"The coffee's good."

"It is, isn't it?" Karen gently put her cup down onto a coaster. "I get the beans ground fresh from a local store nearby. I can't compete with Starbucks when it comes to a latte, but at least I can serve a good cup of coffee."

"Here, here." Mike raised his cup. "To a good cup of coffee."

"Thanks."

Mike sat quietly for a moment enjoying his coffee, then said, "Have you always been a runner?"

"No, I started running during training and I liked it, so I kept up with it even after I graduated." Karen sat up a little straighter on the sofa and turned so she faced Mike. "But I think running is a great motivator for children, especially girls, and can really help their self-esteem."

"How so?"

"Well, I volunteer for a group called Girls on the Run. We use running-themed activities to help girls focus on their emotional, mental, and character development." Karen sat her cup down on the coffee table. "It's a great way to help girls move through that awkward transition of going from little girl to young woman."

"Sounds awesome. I bet you get an immense sense of satisfaction from spending your time with these girls."

"I do, I really do." Karen's face lit up with a wide smile. Animated and using her hands to express herself, she said, "Being given the opportunity to affect a young person's life. To teach them how to be healthy. To develop their emotional character." Karen sighed. "I can't think of a greater use of my services."

"You really enjoy it." Mike smiled back at Karen. He could tell by the way Karen spoke about this program she felt strongly about it. It was another thing to like about her. The way she spoke about the girls, he wondered if she had any young nieces of nephews. Someone with that much energy and enthusiasm should be able to share it with others. "I was looking at your pictures earlier. You have a nice family. Do they live nearby?"

"My parents live in Venice, just south of here, you know, past the Sunshine Skyway. They've retired down there. I try to visit them as often as I can."

"What about your sister? I noticed there weren't any older pictures of her." As soon as Mike said the words he regretted them.

Karen tensed up and seemed to withdraw into herself.

"My sister died." Karen's voice was soft and low as she whispered almost to herself.

"I'm sorry. I didn't mean to bring up sad memories."

"It's okay. I mean, it was a long time ago." Karen stiffened her shoulders. She hesitated, then looked at Mike as if making a decision.

"She was six years old. I was a couple years older. We were playing in the park. I was supposed to keep an eye on her. You know how annoying younger siblings can be." Mike nodded, not talking.

"I just wanted to play with my friends." Karen pulled both legs up so that she could hug her knees. "I ignored Sarah and eventually she went away. I didn't think about her again until it was time to go home. I looked everywhere but couldn't find her." Mike sat still, not knowing what to say.

"We only lived a few blocks from the park, but that afternoon it felt like a million miles. I ran as fast as I could back home when I couldn't find Sarah anywhere. In my own little eight-year-old heart, I wanted to believe that she went home without me. But, deep inside I knew she wasn't there."

Watching Karen's eyes, Mike knew that she wasn't seeing him anymore but was reliving that long ago scene. He wished he could do something to comfort her. "Karen, you don't have to—"

She looked at him briefly, and then shook her head slowly. "No, I'm okay. For some reason, I want to tell you this." She let her chin rest on the top of her knees. "My mother raced back to the park with me, but we couldn't find Sarah. She called the police immediately, but this was before we had the Amber Alert." Karen sighed. "She was already dead before they even got the word out. Her little body was discovered two days later by some kids walking in the woods." Karen shifted slightly. "It was awful. I'd never seen my dad cry before. Sarah was all they could talk about for years."

"Did they ever catch the person who did it?" Mike asked quietly. "No." Karen lifted her chin, balled her hand into a fist, and tapped it on her knee. "The police didn't even have a suspect. The case went on for years. My parents practically put their life on hold while they waited for the police to find the person who killed Sarah." A single tear slipped unchecked down her cheek. "It was my fault. If I had taken better care of my little sister, she'd be here now. I messed up."

Mike couldn't stand it anymore. He slipped out of his chair and slid next to Karen on the sofa. Gently, he placed one hand on her arm and gave it a soft squeeze. "You were only a child, Karen. You can't blame yourself."

"Why not? My parents did."

"You don't really believe that?"

"Sure." Karen swiped at her face. "It was my fault that Sarah was killed. I didn't watch her like I was told. It was my fault we had to move away from our home." One single sob broke loose. "To move to Florida. To get away from the memories." Then another sob broke free. "To get away from all the people who knew. It was my fault..."

Mike slowly drew Karen into his embrace. He let her head lay on his shoulder. He felt her body shake. Making soft shushing sounds, he soothingly patted her back. "You were only a child."

Inside, Mike's heart ached for the little girl who held onto so much pain and responsibility. He held her close as she wept into his shoulder. The tears she cried were good, cleansing tears. He ran his hand over her short, soft hair and curled a section around her ear, so he could see her face. Her sobs turned to sniffles.

Mike looked around and saw a box of tissues on the table behind the sofa. Stretching out an arm, he touched it with his fingertips. Inching forward, he hooked it with a finger and dragged it closer. Grabbing a few tissues, he lightly pressed them into Karen's hand.

She sniffled a 'thanks' then wiped at her face and nose. "What a way to end a great dinner."

"Don't worry about it. I'm sorry I brought it up."

"No, don't be." Karen shifted her body so that she was sitting upright and next to Mike. She laid a hand on his arm. "It means a lot to me that you were here. You're a great listener. I...I haven't cried in a long time."

"Great. I make you cry on our first date."

Karen smiled. She took another tissue and blew her nose. "You didn't make me cry. I imagine it has a lot to do with this new case I've been working on. It brought back a lot of old memories for me."

"You mean the little boy?"

"Yeah." Karen sat up straighter. Her tone grew stronger. "Those parents deserve to know who did this to their son. And I'm going to make sure that I do everything in my power to help them."

"Do you have any suspects?"

"Actually, we do. Remember, we got a match on the fingerprint found on the little boy's overalls snap. And we think we found a match to the footprint found at the scene."

"Speaking of finding footprints, Susan and I were working a scene today that had a similar boot print. FDLE's lab is backed up right now. We won't know anything for a few days or more. We don't even have an ID on the victim. Right now, he's another John Doe."

"Will you let me know as soon as you find out?"

"Yeah. Sure."

"Thanks."

Mike glanced at his watch. Startled to see how much time had gone by, he said, "If we're planning on running at five thirty, we better get some sleep."

Karen laughed. "We?"

"You know what I mean." Mike laughed back, happy to see the smile return to Karen's face. "I better get home and you better get to bed." He pointed a finger at Karen. "If you think you're gonna sabotage my run by keeping me up all night, you've got another thing coming."

"Sabotage? Ha! I can beat you fair and square. Just show up at five thirty. If you dare."

'Oh, I dare, darlin', I dare. Just don't give me any lame-ass excuse about being too tired in the morning." He lightly poked at Karen's shoulder with the finger he'd used for pointing.

Pushing his hand away, Karen said, "We'll just see who's tired."

Mike used that moment while Karen was off balance to draw her into his arms. He gave her a hug and then said, "Thanks for a great time tonight."

Karen hugged him back. "Thank you." She paused. "For everything."

Mike looked into Karen's eyes and saw the gratitude in them. He leaned in closer as if he wanted to kiss her, but then thought better of it and stopped. Now was not the time to get involved, especially with someone from work. He had to distance himself from this woman whom he found so attractive. He broke free from the hug and headed for the door. "I'll see you in the morning."

"Bright and early."

"You bet." And he was out the door, walking down the steps and out to his SUV. He sat behind the steering wheel for a moment before starting the car. He admired Karen Sykes and her desire to find justice. He liked her. And that scared the hell out of him.

Chapter Fourteen

At five-twenty-five in the morning, Karen locked the door behind her and made her way down the stairs to her driveway. With her car in the garage, there would be plenty of room for her and Mike to stretch before the run. That is, if Mike showed up. Karen didn't really know what Mike's physical background was. For all she knew, he could have made an impetuous attempt at offering to run with her without realizing the real implications of his actions. She wouldn't hold it against him if he didn't show.

She thought about last night. He was a strange combination of mixed signals. He enjoyed dinner, but then got stiff when it came time to go. He acted like he enjoyed her company and even let her cry on his shoulder, but when it came time to go, he hugged her. She even thought he was going to kiss her, but then he was standoffish again. Pushing her away. Karen frowned in the darkness. She was determined to get to know him better to see if she could figure him out. He puzzled her and she enjoyed a good puzzle.

Crouching down in the middle of her driveway, she prepared to stretch. Lights from a vehicle coming down the road lit up her neighbor's yard as it turned onto her street. Standing again, she watched the dark SUV as it pulled off the road and parked in front of her yard, next to her mailbox. With the slam of the car door breaking the stillness of the dark morning, Mike sauntered up the driveway and stood near Karen.

"I made it."

"I see that. I was almost ready to give up on you."

"I said I'd be here."

Karen bent over at the waist and grabbed her ankles. Talking into her kneecaps, she said, "I know, but running ten miles is a lot even if you think you're in good shape. I didn't want you to think I'd actually hold you to your promise, just in case you wanted to back out."

"Honey, I wouldn't miss this for the world."

Straightening up, Karen caught Mike watching her with his head tilted sideways. God, she was an idiot for stretching in front of him like that. He was probably enjoying his own private show. Karen stopped berating herself. Let him look. She knew she was in great shape and her body looked good. She worked hard to keep it that way. But if they were going to get any running done this morning, he was going to have to start his own stretches and stop watching hers.

"Why don't you stand over there and stretch." Karen pointed to a place in the driveway about eight feet away.

"Yeah, sure thing." Mike, still watching Karen, stumbled over to the spot she pointed to and mumbled, "I'll be over here, you know, doing my own stretches."

Karen laughed. Sitting on the cold driveway, she put her legs together and leaned over to touch her toes. Her hamstrings tightened and stretched with each attempt. After two repetitions of twenty, she pulled one leg up so that her foot was touching her hip. She leaned backwards until she could feel the coolness of the driveway against her back. Once her quads were properly stretched, she picked herself up and made her way over to the garage door. Mike went with her. Side by side, they stretched their calves by leaning their hands against the garage door and lifting up onto the toes of first one foot then the other while pushing away from garage door.

"Ready to do this?" Karen asked Mike after they finished their stretches.

"Sure thing."

"Last chance to back out."

"No way. I told you. I can hold my own."

Karen looked Mike over enjoying the way he filled out his brief nylon shorts. He was going to regret wearing that cotton t-shirt, but other than that, she couldn't find anything wrong with the way he stretched or what he wore. He looked like he was ready for a run. "Okay. I believe you. Let's hit it." Taking off on a slow jog, Karen led the way as she weaved through the various side streets until they reached Bayshore Boulevard. From there, she picked up speed and set the pace for the rest of the run.

Mike tried to make conversation for the first couple of miles, 80 • Vicki M. taylOr but Karen finally told him that she'd prefer not to talk while she ran. He took the hint and kept his comments about seeing the various wildlife waking up along the bay to himself.

Karen loved running along the bay. She enjoyed watching the water and listening to the waves crash along the walk. The sounds of the birds as they screeched overhead were the perfect background accompaniment to the songs she listened to on her iPod.

Giving herself over to the run, Karen put her mind and body on autopilot. Her shoes pounded the pavement with each stride. She looked to her left and caught a glimpse of the hard chest of the man running beside her. Mike was doing a good job of keeping pace with her. They'd just rounded the corner and finished the first five miles. Breathing lightly and relaxed, Karen felt good. Her legs had stretched through the usual stiffness she felt in the first couple of miles and now she was running easily. They had five more to go on the return run. She gave him credit. He arrived on time and in proper running gear. At least on the outside he looked like he'd be a serious runner.

Like everything else in her life, she took running seriously. Pink Floyd's Dark Side of the Moon blared in her ears from the iPod she had strapped to her arm. She liked the classic rock music even though most of it was from a time before she was born. It gave her a sense of belonging in a world where she didn't feel like she belonged.

Last night, she'd opened up to Mike and even cried on his shoulder. Where that behavior came from, she hadn't a clue. She couldn't even remember the last time she'd cried on someone's shoulder. Not even her mother's shoulder held any memories for a little girl whose life was filled with guilty pain. It had to be this new case that was bringing all these feelings to the surface. Usually she could calmly speak about her sister's death without tearing up. Usually she was in control of her feelings when she was around other people. Usually.

Giving in to her feelings like that made her realize life was passing her by. Of course, she had her job and it was fulfilling in its way, but what about the rest of her life? Where was she heading on a more personal level? Could Mike fit into her plans? Could any man? Where did she see herself in five years? Even in two years? Would she still be living in the same townhouse, alone? Would she still be running these streets, alone? She caught herself smiling. She wasn't alone today. And that should count for something. Maybe there was hope for her yet. After she got him to quiet down, running with Mike wasn't half bad. It felt good to have a companion. To run together, yet still be alone in her own space.

She listened to Pink Floyd sing about Us and Them as she marked another mile gone. Most people had an "us and them" attitude when it came to the police. Most people wouldn't go out of their way to help the police in their investigation. Unless...why was Raymond Alan Thomas's girlfriend so eager to help them? Why did she purposely locate those boots and bring them out. Could she know something? But what could she know? Maybe this was her way of getting a violent and abusive Thomas out of her life? If she did know something and was too afraid to tell, maybe she would think the police would make the connection with the boots. Karen needed more time to think about Maggie Morris's motives and why she had a part in this case. Maybe they needed to interview her again and ask her about any violent actions from Thomas. If they could somehow convince her that she'd be safe. Safe and away from retaliation. That's what kept most women like Maggie from pressing charges in the first place. Karen thought about the time she spent as a volunteer at The Spring, a shelter for battered women, in Tampa. Those women were so brave. Maybe she could use her connections to help Maggie find her way there if she needed to get away. It all centered on how much she knew about Thomas and how much she was willing to tell the police. They needed to know. Was Thomas a violent man?

She needed to talk to Sam. He'd be able to help her flowchart the case and see where the lines connected.

Catching a glimpse of the man running beside her reminded Karen of the most recent events. Was Mike's John Doe case connected? If so, how? Did Tampa have a serial killer that was randomly selecting targets? It didn't make sense. Serial killers had some pattern in their victims. What did a little boy and an unknown man have in common? How were they ever going to make the connection? And where did the Hunts fit in all of this? She laughed at herself. This was one of the reasons she loved to run so much. She could just let her mind go and it would run along whatever direction it wanted, giving her a chance to see various angles of whatever problem she happened to be working on at the time.

Karen marked off another mile. Lights started to come on in the houses they passed. People getting ready for another day. The sun would be coming up shortly. She looked forward to watching the

sunrise. Karen felt a sense of oneness with nature when she ran. She quickly glanced over at Mike. He was doing well. She smiled at him. He smiled back. No sign of stress. He was in good shape.

Karen wondered why she was attracted to him. Was it his good looks? Not really. He did fill out a pair of running shorts very well and it was a sin to have shoulders that wide, but that wasn't it. She liked the way he did his job. His dedication to his job seemed important to him. And that was important to her. Her job meant a lot to her and it was essential that she find someone who understood that. She thought Mike would. But...Mike had issues. He had to have had a pretty bad break up with someone he worked with to not want to date co-workers again. Susan didn't tell her any details, and she wouldn't expect her to. She wondered if Mike would talk to her about it. He wasn't very forthcoming last night, but maybe after they got to know each other a little better he would open up to her. Was that the direction she wanted them to follow?

Checking her watch, Karen noted they'd been running for nearly an hour. It was time to push the next two miles so they could cool down during the final one. This was where Karen would find out if Mike was really in as good shape as he claimed. She picked up the pace. It was time for her favorite part of the run.

Karen had to give Mike credit. He kept up with her. Even though by the end of the run, he was breathing harder than she and she was certain his heart rate was faster than hers, he didn't let the run get to him.

"Not bad," Karen said, standing next to Mike in her dark blue nylon shorts and plain white tank top. Sweat made the shirt stick to her like a second skin.

"Not bad, yourself," Mike said, breathing hard. "You do this every day?"

"Yep. I gotta do something to work off the way I eat."

Mike walked around Karen's driveway, working out the stiffness in his legs.

"Keep walking, Mike," Karen advised. "Don't let your legs stiffen up. You'll get cramps."

"Yeah. Thanks."

"You need water. Stay here and walk. I'll be right back." Karen ran up the stairs to her front door and let herself in. She grabbed two bottles of water out of the refrigerator and ran back to Mike.

He looked better. He sounded better too. He wasn't breathing so heavily. She handed him a bottle of water, then took a long satisfying swallow of hers.

rs

Mike watched as Karen drank deeply from her bottle of water. Small droplets of moisture clung to her neck and throat as if she'd been sprayed lightly. He knew he shouldn't, but seeing her sweating from her run was a major turn on. Something stirred inside of him that he hadn't felt in a long time. Desire. It washed over him before he had a chance to acknowledge its presence.

To cover up his sudden awareness, he took another long swig from his bottle of water. His heart pounded but it wasn't from the ten mile run. Wiping his mouth with the back of his hand, he tried to compose himself and not act like a jerk. So he felt something for Karen. She was an attractive woman. What man wouldn't feel something? So he was behaving like a typical male, with typical male urges. He wasn't dead. He could appreciate a pleasant view when he saw one. And, yes, he saw one. Her small round derriere molded perfectly beneath her shorts. The way her tank top clung to her body like a second skin, clearly outlining the bra she wore underneath that cupped each breast and held them high was a definite turn on.

"Have you sufficiently recovered?"

"Huh?" Mike dragged his thoughts back to the present as he dragged a hand through his still sweat-dampened hair.

"How do you feel?" Karen asked him while giving him a strange look as if he needed her words sounded out separately.

"Fine. I'm fine." Mike bounced from foot to foot. "See. Never felt better. Great run. Gotta go." He knelt down and pulled his key ring from the zippered pocket in his sock. "Don't want to be late for work, right?" Feeling like an idiot, he babbled on, "Thanks for the run. We should do it again sometime, right? Right." Mike lifted a hand to wave then turned and nearly ran to his SUV and hurriedly unlocked the door to get inside before he said anything else to embarrass himself.

CHAPTER FIFTEEN

After a quick shower, Karen dressed with a little more regard for her attire than she usually did on workday mornings. Instead of choosing the usual t-shirt, jeans, and blazer, she opted for a different look. She chose a soft yellow silk blouse that looked great with a dark chocolate colored pair of slacks. Looking in the mirror, she thought it brought out the flecks of gold in her eyes and made her hair appear shinier. Sliding her holster around her shoulders and tucking her gun inside, she slipped into a matching chocolate colored jacket. Checking the mirror again, she couldn't help but grin. She looked good. Probably too good for the bunch down at the warehouse. Was she being too narcissistic to think that anyone would even notice her? It felt good to dress up. It felt good to have a man look at her with appreciation in his eyes. And she definitely saw a lot of appreciation in Mike's eyes when he was checking her out before their run this morning. And afterwards. What an idiot. But a cute idiot. She didn't let on that she knew what he was doing, but she knew. His shorts had been tight and she saw the bulge growing. He got turned on watching her, exciting her as well.

Checking her watch, she sighed. Maybe she shouldn't be dressing up for work. They'd probably just make fun of her anyway. If she had more time, she'd change into one of her regular low-key outfits. Too late now. If she didn't hurry, she was going to be late for work.

Grabbing her purse, Karen poured coffee from the decanter into her travel mug, turned out the lights, locked her door, and hurried to the garage and into her SUV. The extra time she'd taken on getting dressed ate into her traveling time. The drive to work was a blur. Traffic signals seemed to change the instant she approached the intersection. Cars moved out of her way as if by magic each time she needed to pass. Clear of accidents, Karen traveled the Crosstown expressway in record time. She pulled into her parking space with a good five minutes to spare.

Carrying her cup of coffee into work, Karen smiled hello to those she met in the hall. Falling into the chair at her desk, Karen sighed with relief. She'd made it. She sat her coffee cup on her desk and stowed her purse in a bottom drawer.

Seeing Sam, she called out, "Hi, Sam, good morning."

"What's so good about it?"

"In a bad mood?"

"Why are you in a good mood?" Sam growled then looked at her again. "And what the hell are you wearing? You got a court date today I didn't know about?"

Karen fingered the collar of her blouse. "I thought I needed a change."

"You look great, don't get me wrong. It's just…different." "What's different?" asked another detective as he passed by. "Sykes. She looks different today."

"Hey, Sykes. Nice outfit. Can't play basketball in it, though." "I wasn't planning on playing today, Mercer."

"Leave her alone," said Chapman, another female detective in the station. "You look great, Sykes."

"Thanks, Chapman." Karen stood up and twirled around to give everyone a full view. "I can dress like a girl too."

"All right, everyone clear outta here," Sam said. "We got work to do."

"Sam, I was thinking. What kind of connection does our suspect Thomas have with the Hunts? Can you help me flowchart this out?"

rs

"Sure thing. Here. Let's go in here," Sam said as he walked toward an empty conference room. "Hey, on your way in, grab us a couple bagels from the break room, okay?" he said to Karen as she followed him.

Sam hurried to help Karen as she made her way into the conference room, but she waved him off. Notebook tucked under one arm, and coffee in one hand, Karen placed a plate of bagels on the table. She grabbed one for herself then collapsed into a chair. Sam had to grin at her as she focused all her attention on him while she

86 • Vicki M. taylOr

absently munched on a blueberry bagel.

Grabbing a dry erase marker, Sam stood up at the white board. "Let's start with what we know." He wrote names on the board and drew circles around them. He connected the circle from Logan Hunt to the Kelly Hunt circle and to the Mark Hunt circle. Then he drew a circle for their suspect. His name was too big for the small circle Sam drew, so he settled for putting in his initials. R.A.T. Sam underlined the initials then drew a dotted line to Logan Hunt. Along the line he wrote the word 'fingerprint' to indicate how the connection was made.

"I talked to Mike Connelly last night and he said they have a John Doe case that we might be interested in."

Sam raised his eyebrows at the mention of Mike Connelly but left it at that. If Sykes wanted to tell him about it, she would. Otherwise, it was none of his business. "What about the case?"

"They found a footprint near the body. Similar to the one they found near Logan Hunt's body. They figure there might be a connection."

Sam drew another circle around John Doe and connected it to Raymond Alan Thomas with a dotted line. On the line he wrote the word 'footprint.' "Did they give you any indication when FDLE will have processed the evidence?"

"He said the lab is backed up. They don't even have any ID on the body yet. Might be a few more days."

"Okay. Now, look at the board and let me know what you see." Karen studied the board, her face solemn as she concentrated.

"We're missing a circle."

"Who?"

"Maggie Morris."

"Good catch." Sam smiled. He knew if he gave her enough time she'd figure it out. He wrote Maggie's name then drew a circle around it. He drew a solid line from Maggie's circle to Thomas.

Sam looked over at Karen. "Let's spend today running background checks on our major players and see if we come up with any common connections." He capped the marker and placed it back on the white board ledge. "You want the Hunts or the other two?"

"I'll take the Hunts."

"Good. Take your time. Check all sources from their bank to their mechanic. Let's see if any of these circles intersect." Sam paused for a second then said, "Contact the Crime Analysis Section and get them started on the extensive background check. Give them all the
information they'll need to cover all jurisdictions."

"I will."

"And, Sykes," Sam said, "don't leave any stone unturned. Talk to neighbors, friends, relatives, whoever you have to. I want to know if there's any link, I don't care how small, between the Hunts and
Thomas."

"You got it."

"One more thing." Sam knew he was telling her how to do her job, but he wanted Karen to be thorough. "Check out the pre-school where the boy went. See if they hired or did business with Thomas at any time."

"Sure thing." Karen wrote furiously on her notepad to keep up with Sam's instructions. Then she hesitated. "Uh, anything else?"

"No, why?"

"Just checking." Karen grinned. "You're sure?"

"Get out of here and go do your job." Sam snarled at Karen, but only on the outside. He gave her a lot of credit. She would follow through on all of his suggestions with good attention to detail. For a new partner, she was turning out all right.

CHAPTER SIXTEEN

"They act like I killed my own kid!" Mark Hunt pushed open the door to his house. He thrust it with so much force it slammed into the wall behind the door and caused a dent from the doorknob.

"They don't mean nothin' by it, honey." Kelly tried to soothe her angry husband. "They said they do it all parents of…of murdered children. It's routine."

"Routine my ass."

Mark stormed through the kitchen into the living room and threw himself into a chair. He grabbed the remote control and said, "Gimme a beer."

Kelly shut the door behind her, cast a furtive glance at the dent in the wall, then hurried to the refrigerator. She pulled out a can of beer, hustling to hand it to her husband before he thought she wasn't fast enough.

"And who the hell is this Thomas guy and why do the damn cops think I know him? They're gonna pin this shit on me, I just know they are. They always do, you know." Mark opened the can of beer and took a long hard swallow. His throat contracted several times before he tipped the can back upright. "Asking me all those questions about if I ever hit the boy, making it look like I was the one who did this to him. What kind of questions did they ask you? Huh? Did they ask questions about me? What'd you say, woman?"

"Nothing, Mark. Nothing. I didn't tell them anything," Kelly answered quickly so as not to feed her husband's paranoia. She would never tell him what the officers had asked her about him, nor would she ever tell him what she said. She had to tell the truth, they said so, and they said they'd know if she was lying by that machine they hooked up to her. It was all there in the paper they made her sign. She was honest about Mark too, and told the officers that Mark was a good husband and good father. She told them that Mark wasn't involved with Logan's death. She'd swear it. But they asked about particular incidents and she had to tell the truth. She told the whole truth.

Kelly's eyes roamed the room. She was restless. The trip to the police station had frazzled her nerves and now she had a burst of energy to deal with. First thing she needed to do was call the neighbor's house and have them send the girls back home. She didn't like being away from them. Not since Logan died.

Thinking of Logan, she shifted her gaze to the light blue urn that now graced the top shelf of her small bookcase. They'd had Logan cremated and were able to use the money donated to the fund. She couldn't believe how generous some folks could be. Every afternoon, the mailbox was full of cards and letters, saying how sorry folks were for their loss and how they hoped the killer would be caught soon. Kelly remembered the kind words that were said at the memorial that was held for Logan last night. So many people she didn't know came out to say goodbye to her son.

She liked the church. It had a safe, comfortable feel to it. One lady even offered to pick up the girls for Sunday School if she wanted. Kelly didn't know what to say, so she mumbled something and turned away. It wasn't up to her if the girls could go, it would be up to Mark, and Kelly didn't think Mark would let the girls go to Sunday School. He always said that religion was for weak-minded people who couldn't make up their own minds.

The pastor had talked to her before he spoke to the crowd, and he used a lot of her words to describe her son. That made her glad. Afterward, more people stood in line to shake her hand and give her envelopes filled with checks and money. Kelly couldn't believe her eyes when they'd gotten home last night and counted it all. What she truly couldn't believe was how excited Mark got and all the plans he started making. He wanted to get new shocks for his truck and maybe a lift kit, he said. Kelly had sat their quietly letting him talk about all the dreams he had for the money they'd come into. She didn't dare speak up then about how she thought his ideas weren't right. She needed to wait. She wasn't totally without ways to get Mark to do something she wanted. She just had to wait it out and know the right time to make her move. It'd come.

Rousing herself from her daydreaming, Kelly shook herself

back to the present and picked up the telephone to call the neighbor. She wanted her girls back home with her. Where she could watch them herself.

While she dialed, she could hear Mark in the living room, cussing and slamming his hand against the arm of the chair. He still wasn't over having to take the polygraph test down at the police station and if she guessed right, she wasn't hearing the end of it. Nor was she going to feel the end of it, not by a long shot.

CHAPTER SEVENTEEN

Karen called Mike at the lab. She needed some help in finding out what any of the evidence they collected from the Hunt boy told them. She also wanted to talk to him and see how he was doing. After the way he practically ran away from her place this morning after their run, he might be trying to avoid her. Heck, anything was possible. He had looked awfully uncomfortable. Even if he was checking her out.

"Mike? It's Karen Sykes. I'm looking for any final analysis on the evidence you collected from the Hunt boy."

"Hi, Karen." Mike paused then spoke as if taking his cue from Karen's professional demeanor. "Uh, let me get that file and I'll be right back."

Karen waited on hold while Mike retrieved the file. She listened to the hold music and hummed along drawing little circles and boxes on a scrap of paper on her desk.

"Karen?"

"Hmm? I'm still here." She pushed aside the scrap of paper and grabbed her notes for the case.

"Sorry to keep you waiting. I have the file."

"So what did you find out?"

"He had sand and vegetation on his overalls. That tells us that he was probably on the beach and in the woods. Whether it was with our suspect, we still don't know. However, we didn't find any sand in the cast of the footprint we made, so that might indicate that the boy was not together with the suspect while on the beach. The body was found a good distance away from the family's camp. Evidence points to the boy being strangled at the location he was found. So, somehow, the boy got from point A, his camp, to point B, the location where he was found."

"Hmm, how did he get from point A to point B? Did he walk all that way? Doesn't seem logical. Someone would have seen a four year old wandering the campground by himself. If our killer carried him that would explain the print on the overalls." Karen wrote a few more notes then said, "Okay, what else you got?"

"Nothing but dirt underneath the fingernails. No sign that he fought back."

"Nothing?"

"Nope. Nothing. Oh. The only other thing we found was a puncture wound on the bottom of his right foot. Looks like he stepped on a stick that went through his foot. That wound was pre-mortem. There wasn't a lot of dirt or vegetation in the wound, so it doesn't look like he walked very much on it."

"Well, that substantiates the carry theory then."

"I think so."

"I really appreciate all your help, Mike," Karen said tentatively. "No problem. That's what I'm here for." Mike cleared his throat.

Listening hard, Karen thought she heard someone else in the room with Mike while he spoke to her on the telephone.

"Shh," Mike said.

Confused, Karen said, "Huh? What, I didn't say anything." "No, not you, Karen."

Then Mike whispered fiercely, "Okay, I'll ask her, just stop it."

"Mike, are you all right?" Karen thought she heard muffled laughter.

"I, uh, enjoyed our run and thought that maybe, if you want, we could go out again?"

Karen closed her eyes, paused, and then opened them. His erratic behavior this morning aside, he still wanted to see her. "I'd like that. Did you have a particular time in mind?"

"This Friday?"

"Yeah. Sure. Friday. Sounds great. Shall I meet you somewhere, or…"

"I'd like to pick you up if that's okay with you."

"That's fine with me. Thanks."

"You're welcome. I'll see you Friday about seven o'clock?"

"Seven it is. See you then."

Karen hung up feeling much better than when she started the phone conversation. She shouldn't have worried at all. Mike wanted to go out with her again. However, from the sounds on the line, it was probably at the persuasion of someone else. And if she didn't know any better, it was probably Susan who was prompting Mike to ask her out. She sat and stared at the phone smiling until she heard Sam clearing his throat telling her to get back to the background checks on the Hunts.

Pulling the list of names closer to her, Karen read through them again. She was about to delve into a family's private life, entering their world in search of justice for the murder of their son. That family already felt exposed and violated because of the horrific incident; this was only going to make it worse. Karen felt their pain, but put it aside. She didn't have time to feel sorry for them; she needed to find a killer.

She needed to find the killer before the killer decided to kill again.

Chapter Eighteen

Kelly shut the front door after watching her two daughters climb the steps into the large yellow bus. She bit her lip at the aching emptiness in the pit of her stomach. She hated to be separated from them. Even for the few hours they were in school.

Picking up her coffee cup from the kitchen counter, she reached across the clean surface and poured herself a third cup from the glass decanter of the coffee pot. It was one more cup than usual, but she hadn't been sleeping well the last few nights. The extra caffeine would help get her through the day.

"Do you want another cup of coffee, Mark?"

"Of course I don't want another cup of coffee. You know what that shit does to me in the morning." Mark's words bit into the air.

"I'm sorry." Kelly held her cup to her lips and blew across the hot surface. She took a tentative sip.

Trying to be as quiet and unobtrusive as possible, Kelly slid onto a wooden chair at the kitchen table. She watched as Mark shoveled eggs and bacon into his mouth, barely chewing before adding another forkful.

Like most mornings, Mark flipped through the checkbook, going over their money situation. This morning was not different. Kelly waited for the inevitable outburst.

Mark ran his fingers down the entries in the register, stopped, tapped his finger then slowly looked up. "What in the hell did you spend fifty-eight dollars and thirty-four cents on at Walmart?"

"I—I bought the girls some new clothes."

"What's wrong with their old clothes?" Bits of egg flew from Mark's open mouth.

Kelly looked down at the table and stared into her coffee cup. *Don't make him mad. Don't make him mad.*

"You spent too much."

Kelly heard his words, but instead of letting them wash over her, she felt them dig into her soul. How could he be telling her she spent too much money when he's always buying outrageous things for his truck? He spent hundreds of dollars on tools every month and never anything on her or the kids. She had to scrape every cent she used for extras from leftover change from the groceries. It wasn't fair. *Don't make him mad. Don't make him mad.*

The mantra played in Kelly's head but instead of heeding its advice, she shut it down. She closed her mind and opened her mouth.

"I don't think I spent too much." The words carried barely above a whisper.

Mark's mouth hung open. "What'd you say?"

A little louder, Kelly said, "The girls are growing like weeds. They needed new clothes."

A scraping protest rang out as Mark's chair slid back from the table and toppled over. From a far off distance, Kelly heard the crash as the chair hit the floor. Time slowed and movements were on several seconds delay. As if in slow motion, she watched Mark spring to his feet. She didn't feel any pain at first, until she heard the echoing crack of Mark's hand as it made contact with the side of her face.

Tears welled in her eyes while white-hot pain shot through her cheekbone. Biting her lip, she struggled to keep from crying out.

Through a haze of tears, Kelly watched Mark pick up his overturned chair and calmly sit back down. He picked up his fork and pushed another mouthful inside. Between chews he said, "I told you, you spent too much."

He forked more egg into his mouth and chewed before calmly adding, "I'm gonna take some of that fund money and buy me a boat."

The pit of Kelly's stomach twisted. She gripped her coffee cup so hard she thought she'd break it into pieces. Anger built up inside of her and pushed its way out. A part of her mind insisted that she stay quiet and mind her own business. It would be less painful that way.

But she couldn't keep her anger in. How selfish could this man be? In a hesitant voice, Kelly said, "I—I don't think that's what we're supposed to use that money for." Her words grew stronger and faster. "I didn't say anything when you wouldn't let me spend any money on Logan's funeral. You even told me to…to cremate him because it would be cheaper."

Kelly took a deep breath. Then continued. "I even let you talk me into using some of that money on the truck because in a way it benefited the family. But I can't just sit here while you use those people's hard earned money, money that they donated in the name of your son, and buy a boat."

Pushing herself back from the table, Kelly stood and faced Mark. She knew what was coming and braced herself for it.

Mark stood and swung.

Stars burst before Kelly's eyes and intense, searing pain radiated from her jaw. She blinked quickly, holding back the tears. She refused to let him see how much he hurt her.

It didn't matter. Mark didn't look at her again. He stomped past her and grabbed his cooler with his lunch and slammed his way out of the house yelling that he was going to buy a boat and no one was going to stop him not her, not those damn people down at the bank. With the roar of the truck's engine fading in the distance, Kelly finally made a move from where she'd rooted herself and took a stand.

Automatically, she pulled open a kitchen drawer and pulled out a dishtowel. With practice, she folded it, filled it with ice, and folded it again. All the time she thought of how selfish her husband was. How could he only think of himself?

Lightly, with gentle fingers, Kelly prodded at the side of her face. Pain raced from the lower part of her jaw to right behind her left eye. She opened and closed her mouth carefully. Finding nothing broken, she heaved a sigh of relief.

Wincing, she held the towel with ice to her cheek. The entire left side of her face felt like it was on fire. The intense pain spread from her eye socket to the left side of her mouth. It hurt too much even to have the towel touching her face.

She knew better than to contradict Mark when he was talking this morning, but she went and did it anyway. What was wrong with her? She had an opportunity to keep her mouth shut, but she didn't. It wasn't like her. What had gotten into her?

Kelly looked at the telephone against the wall. Moving her head sent startling pain ripping through her face and was an aching reminder that she needed to keep the ice on her bruised face before it swelled any further. Biting her lip, she fought back the tears and placed the towel once again against her cheek.

She considered calling her mother, and then dismissed the idea before it fully formed. What would she tell her? That she talked back to her husband and he hit her? What would her mother say then? "Darling, how many times do I have to tell you that your husband is the man of the house and what he says goes?" Her mother would tell her Mark didn't mean it and she was making a big deal out of nothing. She would get no sympathy from her mother. She never had.

This was her life. The life she'd chosen when she married Mark Hunt. She had to live with her choice. No matter what happened. Her mother said that God gave all of us a choice in life, and we had to live with the choice we made. Kelly sighed. She wondered how other women were able to handle their choices in life and if they had the same kind of husband as she did.

Often times while she bought food in the grocery store or looked for clothes at Wal-Mart, she watched the other women as they shopped. She'd even follow them through the store, mimicking their mannerisms. While doing so, she'd fantasize that she had a husband waiting at home who was loving and attentive. She'd pretend that her husband wanted her to spend whatever she wanted on clothes for herself. She'd look through the racks of clothing picking out a blouse here, or a skirt there. She'd pile the clothes into her shopping cart and wander the store. But she always put the clothes back before she checked out. She didn't have a husband who wanted her to spend money on herself. Kelly knew the real price she'd pay if she wanted to buy a new blouse.

Sighing again, Kelly picked up her cold coffee cup. With one hand, she rinsed the cup out in the sink and placed it in the top rack of the dishwasher. She held the ice wrapped in a towel gently on her cheek flinching from the fresh burst of pain that shot through the side of her face.

She opened the top cabinet above the sink and pulled out the bottle of aspirin. She swallowed two, thought for a moment, then swallowed another one. It was going to be rough going today, trying to get the laundry washed, dried, and folded with the pounding in her head. Putting the aspirin back, she made her way into the bathroom.
Mark always left it a mess when he was finished in the morning. Kelly bent over to pick up the wet towel on the floor and gasped at the intensity of pain that shot through her head. The pounding doubled in strength. She stood up slowly, holding on to the sink vanity with

Vicki M. taylOr

both hands.

Gritting her teeth, biting back the groan, she avoided looking in the mirror above the sink. It didn't matter anyway. She'd seen it before. Kelly took a deep breath and with more caution, bent down and picked up the rest of the wet towels and dirty clothes that were strewn about on the bathroom floor. The gnawing anger in the pit of her stomach grew.

Chapter Nineteen

Karen dropped her blouse into the dirty clothes hamper in her bathroom and slid into a soft, butter yellow robe. She liked the way she felt today in her dress up clothes and the reactions from her fellow officers went a long way to sending her self-esteem through the roof. Getting the second looks and the dropped jaws was more than enough. Hearing the complimentary comments was just icing on the cake. She knew her earlier decision to wear something more flattering was the right choice and it helped her decide that from now on she'd take more care with her wardrobe. Jeans and t-shirts were fine for some occasions, but they didn't do a whole lot to help her feel feminine. And that's what she wanted right now. To feel more feminine. She looked in the bathroom mirror. She had a nice complexion, probably because her mother drilled it into her enough times to take care of her skin and she did. Even to the point of using a sunscreen on a daily basis to help protect from the intense tropical sun of Florida.

Wide, intense hazel eyes looked back at her from her reflection. She was fortunate to have been born with thick dark lashes that brushed the top of her cheeks when she blinked. She knew her eyes were her best feature. Her nose was short, with a small upturn at the end that her father used to gently poke when she was a child to tease her. That was before her sister died. The poking and gentle teasing went away, the same as her mother's smiles and soft laughs.

Generous, full lips slowly turned into a frown as she continued her personal survey. She didn't want to think about her sister's death tonight. Not after the great day she had today. After Mike asked her out, she spent the rest of the day following up on the background checks on the Hunts along with their volatile polygraphs. After the

Vicki M. taylOr

Hunts, she managed to get in touch with several teachers at the children's school, three out of their four neighbors, and the employers for Mark Hunt. So far, she hadn't turned up anything suspicious, but knew that she needed to check with the Crime Analysis Section tomorrow to see if they came up with any unusual banking activity. If the Hunts did hire someone to kill their son, a large withdrawal might show up in their bank transactions.

In her gut, Karen knew it was a long shot, but part of her job was eliminating possibilities along with searching for the answer. Whatever she felt inside, she had to find proof to substantiate her theory. Evidence was the only thing that mattered, and evidence to prove that the parents weren't the perpetrators was as important to the case as fingerprints and footprints of other possible suspects.

Releasing a sigh, Karen turned away from the mirror and headed back into her bedroom. Turning out the bathroom light, she paused for a moment to clear her mind from the day's activities. She'd worked hard today and wanted to unwind. Not ready for bed but still needing some relaxing, she turned the light back on and headed for the tub. Turning on the faucet, she sprinkled a handful of coconut-scented bath salts into the steady stream of water and watched them swirl away. A relaxing warm bath with her favorite scent and a glass of wine would be just the thing to help her recuperate from such an intense day.

While her bath filled, she padded in bare feet to the kitchen to pour herself a glass of wine and grab the latest issue of the *Cosmo* magazine from the counter where she'd thrown today's mail. Glancing at the cover, she noticed an interesting article: *How to Let Him Know You Want Him—Five Easy Steps.*

"Hmm, maybe I'll learn something I can use on Mike," Karen muttered to herself on her way back to her bathroom, magazine in one hand and her wine glass in the other.

Settled in her bath, Karen held the magazine up high away from the water and bubbles. Skipping most of the magazine, she quickly turned to the page with the interesting article and started to read. The article was typical *Cosmo,* listing various ways to let the guy know you like him and quoting experts who say women should be more assertive in this day and age.

Smiling to herself, Karen said, "Mom always used to say if you don't ask, you don't get." Reading further, Karen found out that this

particular author thought men were a lot dumber than women and basically needed to be hit over the head before they'd make a move. Shaking her head and laughing, Karen hoped she wouldn't have to hit Mike over the head, maybe just give him a persuasive nudge or two. Looking over the five steps to let a guy know you want them, Karen giggled. She could handle number one by not coming on too strong, but she drew the line at number two telling her to be a flirt. She didn't know how to flirt and didn't think she'd be any good at it if she tried. The closest she got to flirt with Mike was at dinner last night and she was sure she wasn't any good at it. If anything, looking back at it, she thought she made a fool of herself and wouldn't be trying any flirting in the near future.

She liked number three. She could definitely keep it casual. She wasn't a fancy restaurant kind of girl. Give her pizza and beer and she'd be happy. Jeans and t-shirts were more her thing than dresses, but…it sure felt good to wear that dress to dinner with Mike. He appreciated it. She saw it in his eyes.

Wondering whether asking Mike out fell into the flirting category, Karen thought that she might try it if she could work up the nerve. Her eyes widened as she read number four. How could she let Mike know what she wanted if she was just figuring it out for herself? The article said to be clear about where she wanted things to go. Right. As soon as they cleared up for her first. How in the heck was she supposed to tell a man everything she wanted in life when she was still working on it for herself? Yeah. This article was a lot of help.

Karen sighed. These ways were supposed to be in order of use. How could they jump from being casual to letting him know what you want? And number five? Actually tell him how you feel?

Karen sat up. Shivers ran up her back. Goosebumps popped up on her arms. Was she afraid of telling a man how she felt? She carried a gun, for cripe's sake. She could do it.

If she successfully made it through the four previous points, she could definitely tell one man how she felt about him. However, that was a big 'if'. Like 'if' she could do any of those steps without making a big idiot out of herself. Like 'if' Mike got over his no dating co-workers rule, then she might have a chance. Like 'if' she ever figured out what she wanted in life so she could tell Mike what she wanted in a man. Man, that was a lot of 'ifs'. Maybe she'd just start with if she would ever see him again. A lot could happen between now and Friday.

Like, he could change his mind.

CHAPTER TWENTY

After a satisfying lunch of turkey sandwiches and potato chips at Pickles Sandwich Shop, Karen and Sam headed back towards the house of Raymond Alan Thomas to see if he was in yet. They'd checked once already today to see if he was home, and he wasn't. Sam and Karen didn't get anywhere at Thomas' most recent job. The guy didn't have a steady work record and was apparently between jobs at the moment. They even cruised by the corner store to see if he was hanging out with his buddies. So far, they'd racked up a zero on all tries.

Thomas' girlfriend, Maggie Morris, said that he'd been to the house and left again, and was aware that the police were trying to talk to him. Maggie swore that she gave her boyfriend their messages and promised to call them as soon as he arrived.

"When was the last time you talked to the lab about the shoe print? Did they find a match yet?" Sam asked while he navigated the side streets of Tampa in an attempt to avoid traffic in the higher prone areas.

"This morning before we left to check on Thomas," Karen said, reaching for her notebook to verify. "FDLE said that they're probably still a day or so from getting to it."

"Well, shit. This is getting frustrating. Damn it, I know it's him."

"Can't we do something? Anything?" Agitated, Karen brushed back her hair and blew out a heavy breath that ruffled the hairs across her forehead.

"The problem is we can't find the guy. Why don't we go back to the office and check on some routes out of here and see if he took any of them. We'll check the bus terminal, airport, even the train station. If he tried to sneak out of town, we'll know it."

"Good. Sounds like a plan."

"You're right. We gotta do something." Sam smacked the steering wheel. "I'm tired of waiting for him to just show up. We gotta do some offensive work. See if we can turn anything up we might be able to take to the D.A. for a warrant."

"You mean, like if he left town, we could get him on a probation violation?"

"Yeah, something like that." Making a left turn, Sam headed the car toward the on ramp for the Crosstown. In seconds, they left the city of Tampa behind them as they made their way back to the offices of the warehouse.

"Do you think he'd skip town on his girlfriend?"

"I wouldn't put it past him. Probably leave her holding the bag for the rent on that house too."

"Maybe she's better off without him."

"Maybe."

After negotiating their way through the tollbooth, Sam spoke up. "So, you've been out with Connelly. You two getting serious?"

"What? Me and Mike? We've been on one date and we've gone running together. Hardly serious."

"Going out with Connelly is serious. The guy doesn't date—"

Karen interrupted him with a sigh and said, "Yeah, I know, he doesn't date anyone from work. I'm beginning to think that's a big deal."

"It is a big deal." Sam turned to look at Karen. "He used to go out with a patrol officer." He turned his attention back to the traffic. "She's since moved on to another county, but he swore never again."

"So he's changed his mind."

"Maybe. And maybe he sees something special."

Her face grew warm. "What do you mean?" Karen tried to hide the blush she felt sweep up her neck and over her cheeks by looking out the window.

"Come on, Sykes. You're a beautiful woman. A great person. Someone was bound to see it." "Geez, Sam. Thanks."

"Just don't tell the other guys, okay?" Sam gave a short chuckle. "I'm supposed to be a hard nose, remember?"

"I won't give you away, you old softy."

"Hey, watch the 'old' crack." Sam let go of the steering wheel with one hand and flexed his arm to show off his muscle. "I can still

hold my own."

"Yeah, yeah. We need to finish our game."

"That's right. You were gonna try and sink a basket and beat me, weren't you?"

"And I will too, just let me get back out on the court."

"Well, we'll see if we have time after we do some work this afternoon."

It took Sam and Karen the rest of the day and most of the evening to run down all the possible public exits out of town. If Raymond Alan Thomas left Tampa, he didn't do it on a bus, plane, or train.

"Uh huh?" Karen said into the telephone while she raised her eyebrows at Sam and motioned for him to come over to her desk.

"Great, thanks. We'll be in touch." Hanging up the phone, Karen threw her pencil down on her desk then leaned back and stretched.

"So who was that?" Sam asked as he took a seat on the corner of Karen's desk.

"Raymond's probation officer."

"Oh?"

"He finally returned my calls. Seems our Mr. Thomas has been negligent in his contact with his probation officer and has become a wanted man for reasons other than what we want him for."

"Are they swearing out a bench warrant?" Sam stood and started pacing. He worked better when he was moving.

"The probation officer said he could or we could. It didn't matter which. He'd provide any corroborating evidence if we wanted to make the move."

"All right. Have him meet you down at the courthouse tomorrow morning and you get the warrant signed. Bring it to me as soon as you get it. I'll be staked out at Thomas's house just in case he decides to show up. His girlfriend didn't call by chance to let us know if he returned, did she?"

"No, I haven't heard from her, but she could be covering for him too."

Sam stopped pacing and stood in front of Karen with his hands on his hips. "She could be. That's why I'm going to stake out the house myself." He rubbed a hand over his short hair then said, "I'm tired of playing this game on his terms. It's time to get serious."

CHAPTER TWENTY-ONE

"We just got our fax." Karen waved a paper in the air as she made her way to where Sam was standing. She weaved her way in and out of the short hallways in between cubicles.

"Is that the probation officer's report?"

"Yep."

"Good. Now, I want you to take that and high tail your ass down to the D.A.'s office and get an arrest warrant for this son of a bitch. Tell whoever will listen about the boots and the footprint and our hunch. Then I want you to get over to the Thomas house as quick as you can. We'll sit there all night if we have to, but we're gonna serve that warrant today."

"You got it. Anyone I should talk to in particular?" "Try Martin. He'll listen to you and knows how to expedite." "Martin. Got it." Karen turned as if to go. "Karen."

"Yeah?" She turned back.

"You did good, kid." Sam patted her on the shoulder rather gruffly.

"Thanks, Sam. That means a lot coming from you."

"Now get out of here so you can be done in time for your date tonight." Sam smiled and winked.

Karen took off for the parking lot and her car. She left Sam standing in the hall watching her as she walked away. She thought about him being at the house on his own, waiting for her to return.

A shiver ran through her. She brushed it off as excitement.

Karen strode through the double doors of the District Attorney's office twenty minutes later, excited and nervous. She impatiently tapped her toe as she stood in line to speak to the young woman at

the front desk.

Finally it was her turn.

"Mr. Martin, please."

"And you are?" the young woman asked, as she answered the telephone with, "Please hold."

"Detective Sykes. Tell him Sykes for Detective Sam Anderson." Karen's voice lifted as she finished. She took a deep breath. She needed to calm down. She pressed her hands to the sides of her face, then waved a hand to cool off a hot cheek. She looked around at the others in the room. Weren't they hot too? Wasn't there any air conditioning in this building?

"Detective Sykes. I hear you need to see me." A man rounded the corner from inside an office and smiled as if television cameras were watching him.

"If you're Mr. Martin, then I do." Karen blurted out.

"That's me. David Martin." He smiled more genuinely at Karen then ushered her to his office down the hall. "You said you're here for Sam. Where is he?"

"I'm Detective Sykes, Sam's partner. Sam and I are working on a case, the Hunt boy? Do you know the one I'm talking about? Well, we're pretty sure we've found our suspect. He's violated his probation and here's the probation officer's report." Karen handed Mr. Martin the faxed copy as he rounded his desk and sat down in an overstuff leather chair. She hurried on to say, "We got a fingerprint match and we searched his house and found boots that match the print we found at the scene, well, we think they match, we're still waiting on the report, and—"

"Wait, you searched his house?"

"Yeah, but we got his girlfriend to sign a consent form so we could." Karen's face grew warm. She knew her cheeks had flared to an unflattering beet red. She bounced from one foot to the other impatient to continue her story. "Sam said—"

"Okay. I think I've got the picture. And you're here for an arrest warrant?"

"Yes." Blowing out the rest of her breath she'd been holding, Karen sighed. "Thank you for understanding my blathering mess."

"Not a problem. You're Sam's new partner?" David Martin pulled some papers toward him as he punched up a screen on his computer monitor. "You'll learn a lot from him. He's a good cop."

"I know."

"Okay, hand me the rest of your paperwork, so I can put this warrant together. When I'm finished here, you need to take the warrant down to the third floor and go to courtroom 4B. You'll find Judge Hoffman there. He'll sign your warrant for you."

"I really appreciate all this, Mr. Martin."

"We all want to see this boy's murder solved, Detective Sykes."

Karen watched Mr. Martin click a few more keys on the computer's keyboard then press the Print button. The printer started up with a whir and a clack.

"There. The warrant is printing."

"Thank you."

Martin pulled the paper off the printer and handed it to Karen. "Remember, courtroom 4B. Judge Hoffman will take care of you." In a hurry, Karen grasped David Martin's hand and shook it. She turned to go, but remembered to toss another 'thank you' over her shoulder.

Out in the hall, she pushed the elevator button then bounced from one foot to the other as she waited for the elevator to arrive. "Come on, come on," she mumbled under her breath.

With the ding of a bell, the doors opened and Karen rushed inside and pushed the button for the third floor. She pushed it again and again until the doors closed. A sense of urgency had overcome her. She felt like she needed to be back at the house, waiting with Sam. She had the sense that something big was about to happen and she needed to be there.

CHAPTER TWENTY-TWO

Sam parked his unmarked police car in front of a house two doors down from the Thomas house. It was the best he could do, considering he was trying to be discreet.

The same car as before was parked in the Thomas driveway. It didn't look like it had moved. Sam wondered if it even ran. He sat behind the steering wheel of his car watching the house. From his viewpoint he could see the front door and driveway. He leaned back and got comfortable. Something told him that this was only the beginning.

A couple hours had passed with no activity outside the house. Getting stiff, Sam stepped out of the car to stretch. He pulled his arms above his head and twisted his waist. Several cracks could be heard coming from his spine. He lowered his arms slowly, all the while watching the silent house.

Not knowing if anyone was at the Thomas home at the moment, Sam decided to walk over to the house and knock on the front door. He could come up with a quick excuse if he needed. Especially if Maggie became suspicious about why he was there.

Walking the short distance from the car to the house, Sam patted his right front pants pocket to make sure he had his cell phone. He wanted to ensure he was accessible in case Karen called with information about the arrest warrant.

Looking at the front yard, Sam had the insane feeling that the little concrete garden gnomes were watching him as he walked up the front sidewalk. He shook off the sensation as nonsense and gave a short laugh out loud. His voice sounded strange in the stillness of the day. The neighborhood was quiet; no children played in the yards or raced their bikes along the sidewalks. No neighbors chatted in their yards as they watered dry patches of grass and weeds. It was a strange sensation to feel so alone as he made his way to the front door. Sam knocked briskly and firmly on the warmed and water stained front door then waited for a response. Within a few seconds the door was opened and Maggie stood before him, her short blonde hair in spiky points around her head and her chest heaving rapidly.

Sam wondered what could have put her in such a disheveled mood. "Detective Anderson, what are you doing here?"

"Hello, Ms. Morris. I came by to see if Raymond was at home or if you'd seen him recently." Sam stood waiting on the steps.

"Raymond? Uh, you just missed him. He was here this morning, but took off again. He said if I called the police he'd come after me or have one of his friends take care of me." Maggie looked down as if to hide tears in her eyes.

"We'd protect you, Ms. Morris, he wouldn't be able to hurt you."

"Protect me? No offense, detective, but I doubt you could protect me from Ray or his friends."

Feeling the sweat gathering between his shoulder blades, Sam shrugged his shoulders inside his jacket. He needed to gain Maggie's trust. Her contact with Thomas was their only link right now. "Ms. Morris?"

"Yes?"

"May I come in and talk to you? I'm sure we could work out some sort of agreement that could be mutually beneficial to both of us."

"Come in? Where are my manners? Yeah, come in." Maggie moved aside from the front door so that Sam was able to walk through into the living room. It hadn't changed much since the last time he was there. The air was still stale and dry. The dust layers seemed to have grown thicker, and the pile of empty beer bottles and soda cans was still on the floor.

Sam stepped carefully into the room, watching where he placed his feet. "I appreciate you giving me a chance to talk to you about this."

"Won't you sit down?" Maggie motioned to the couch against the wall.

Sam considered his options and came to the conclusion that if he wanted to gain her trust, he should get her relaxed, and sitting was more comfortable. "Thank you."

Sam eyed the stained couch with distrust. He figured his pants could be cleaned and the stains did look old.

Maggie took the chair opposite the couch after she threw the pile of clothes that were on it to the floor.

Sam took out his notebook and noted the date and time. "So you said Raymond was already here this morning. Did he say why he was avoiding the police?"

"Ray?" Maggie's eyes darted off to her left then came back to look at Sam. She lifted a hand and attempted to smooth down the curls on her head. "He said he's not stupid. He's seen the news. He knows you want to ask him questions about that little boy's murder. He says you're not pinning it on him."

"If he came in to the station to talk to us, we could sort it all out. If he's innocent, it'll all work out to his benefit."

"If? What does that mean? Do you think Ray did it?"

"We're not sure yet, Ms. Morris." Sam shifted slightly in his seat on the couch cushion. It felt like the springs would pop through at the slightest pressure.

"Ms. Morris? Call me Maggie."

"Maggie. We have evidence that puts Raymond at the scene. We need to talk to him about why he was there."

"You just want to talk to him? I don't know, detective. Ray, he probably won't go for something like that. He'll think it's a trap."

Sam watched Maggie's leg bounce up and down as she tapped her foot. Was she nervous because she was supposed to meet Ray somewhere and he was keeping her? Or was she nervous because Ray was coming back to the house. Whatever it was, Sam was going to figure it out. "Does Ray have another place he stays at when he's not here?"

"Another place? I dunno, he doesn't tell me where he's going when he leaves here." Maggie twisted the hem of her t-shirt into a wad around her finger.

Sam leaned forward and put his elbows on his knees. "Maggie, is there something you're not telling me?"

"Me? No, not really. I mean, no. I don't have anything to tell." The twisted cloth around her finger got tighter.

In a softer voice, Sam said, "Come on now. You can tell me. If you think Ray's going to hurt you, we have places where you can go. Where he can't find you." Sam leaned forward a bit more. "We can protect you. But you have to talk to me. Tell me what you know." Maggie looked around the room. Her eyes grew wide. She stopped twisting the t-shirt around her finger. "I don't know, detective. Ray said he'd kill me if I told you about...about...what he did." The last few words came out in a whisper.

"What do you mean, 'what he did'?" Sam tried not to act too eager and kept his hands loose. "What aren't you telling me, Maggie?"

"Me? I'm not sure. I don't remember a whole lot, you see." Maggie stopped and looked around as if she were afraid Raymond would appear around the corner. "I don't think I should be telling you this. What if Ray comes back and sees me talking to you? What do I do then?"

Sam sat up a little straighter, grimacing when the couch springs moved in rusty protest. "Is Ray coming back?"

"Ray? He might."

"Did he say he was coming back? Did he give you a time?"

"A time? Right. Yeah, Ray is always saying he'll be back by such and such a time, but he never shows up. He just comes and goes whenever he wants." Maggie tossed her head and the bright blonde curls bounced.

"Would you feel more comfortable if we went down to the station and you told me what you know there?" Sam wanted to make sure he covered all his options.

"To the police station? No, I don't think so. No, definitely not. I ain't going down to no police station." Curls flew as Maggie vehemently shook her head.

"Stay calm, stay calm." Sam held out his hands in a gesture of peace. "We don't have to go down to the police station. It was just a suggestion because you seemed uncomfortable talking here. We'll talk wherever you want, okay?"

"Are you sure?" Maggie cast a doubtful glance toward Sam. "I can talk here, I guess." She started twisting the hem of her t-shirt around her finger again.

"Let's start with this, shall we?" Sam held up his notebook and said, "You tell what you know about Raymond and what connection he might have with the Hunt boy murder."

"You want me to tell you what I know? I don't know much, that's for sure." Maggie let the hem of her t-shirt unwind then twisted it around a finger on her other hand. "Ray, he came home one night, all high and shit, I mean stuff. All high and stuff. He's talking real fast and I can hardly understand what he's saying. I tell him, 'Ray, slow down, slow down' but he just keeps on talking."

Sam kept quiet and let Maggie continue on with her story. He made notes in his notebook as she spoke.

"I never seen him like this before, you know? I mean, he's all wild and crazy talking. He says he ain't never done anything like that before, but he did a kid. That's what he kept saying over and over, 'I did a kid', real fast like." Maggie used her hands to hold down her knee. It bounced uncontrollably next to the leg of the chair. She pushed a few curls out of her face and went on, "I didn't know what he was talking about, and he was scaring me, you know? He passed out on me and then the next morning, he's all, 'my head, my head' like he's got this massive hangover. He tells me that if I ever tell anyone what he told me last night he'll kill me too. Just like he did the kid."

"He said that? He said, 'just like I did the kid'?"

"Huh? Yeah, he did. And he made choking motions toward my neck when he said it." Maggie held a hand to her throat and swallowed hard.

"Did he say if anyone was with him? Do you know if he went out that night with other people? Maybe some friends of his?"

"Anyone else? No, I don't really remember. He did say when he left that he was going out. That could mean he went out with those assholes he hangs out with on the corner or who knows."

"You don't get along with Ray's friends?"

"Me? They're nobodies. They don't have any ambition. They just want to hang out all day and do nothing but drink beer and smoke pot. They didn't have any sense to see that I was trying to help Ray make something of himself and this place." Maggie grew animated and swung her hands about as she talked. "I tried to fix up this place, you know, I thought the statues made a nice touch in the front yard, but those assholes, all they did was laugh and make fun of them. Ray, he laughed too." Maggie's hands curled into small fists. "They didn't laugh for long. No, they didn't." She took a deep breath, then

refocused. "I thought Ray was different." Sam's pen lifted

from the paper. He paused.

He finished writing then asked if he could use his cell phone to contact his partner. He was eager to find out if Sykes was having any problems with getting the warrant and when she'd be able to drive out to the house.

"Cell phone? Sure thing. I'll give you some privacy. I, uh, have some things to do in the other room. You just stay here and make your call." Maggie quickly stood up and walked out of the room. She didn't look back.

Sam carefully stood up as well, and sighed in relief when the couch cushion springs managed to stay on their own side of the stained and dirty upholstery. He pulled out his cell phone and dialed Karen's cell phone number.

"Sykes."

"Sykes? Sam here. Do you have the warrant?"

"Yeah, Sam. Got it. I'm making my way out of the courthouse now. I can be there in twenty minutes, thirty tops, depending on traffic."

"Great. Maggie Morris admitted that Thomas killed the little boy."

"That's great, right? Now we got him. Does she know where he is?"

"No, or else she's not saying. I have my doubts about her and her story. Something just doesn't sit right with me. We should run a background check on her too. Remind me about it when we get back to the office."

"Sure thing. You getting some bad vibes about this?"

"Yeah. Maybe I'm just getting old and don't trust anyone anymore."

"Maybe. And maybe your instincts are kicking in. I'll be there soon."

"See you when you get here."

"Bye."

Sam ended his cell phone call with Karen then dialed his office to see if there were any messages. He had his back to the room. A sudden sound made him turn around and when he did a foot caught him in the face and sent him hard against the wall. His cell phone went flying. Bright clusters of sharp light broke out all around him. His nose gushed blood as his eyes filled with tears and brimmed over. He knew his nose was broken, but he tried not to focus on the pain. He had to locate his attacker.

Sam's eyes darted left and right as he looked quickly around the room, trying to focus through the blood and tears. Not seeing anything to his left, he held his hands out and turned to his right. From out of nowhere another foot caught him unaware in the throat. He tried to cry out. His breath left his body. He sucked in, but no air would return. It was as if a large vise was tightening around his throat. The last thing Sam heard before his mind went blissfully blank was a loud snap coming from his neck as that foot connected once again.

Chapter Twenty-Three

Kelly stood in the doorway of her home watching the road. The big yellow school bus slowed to a stop in front of their driveway, lights blinking. The red stop sign swung out from the side of the bus, the brakes screeched, and with a loud swish the door opened. Traffic stopped behind the bus.

Amber jumped down the steps of the bus first, followed by her sister Ashley. Kelly watched them as they saw her waiting for them and waved. Kelly could hear Ashley yelling at the top of her lungs even over the bus' noisy engine.

The girls ran from the end of the driveway to the door, each competing with the other until they reached their mother.

"I win!"

"No, I beat you. Momma, didn't I beat her?" Ashley pleaded.

"You both won," Kelly said to soothe her daughters. She let them inside and watched as they dropped book bags and headed for the kitchen. She sighed. Looking down at their bags, she knew she'd have to pick them up before Mark got home. It wouldn't do for him to see the girls' stuff on the floor.

"I want a juice," Amber said as she opened the refrigerator door. "No, I want a juice first." Ashley struck out at her sister and kicked her in the knee.

Amber cried out from the pain then turned and slapped her sister. The sound reverberated in the suddenly quiet room.

"Ashley!" Kelly cried out. "What are you doing hitting your sister?" She placed a hand on Amber's head and smoothed down her hair. "Come here and let me see."

Brushing back the hair from Amber's face, she checked her for any sign of bruising. The only sign was a reddening high on her cheek. "Mommy, it hurts."

"I know, darling. Let me get you some ice." Kelly opened the freezer and took out a small handful of ice cubes and placed them in a few paper towels. She held the ice pack to her daughter's face. Turning to Ashley, she said, "Come here and apologize to your sister. We don't hit each other in this house."

"Daddy hits you," Ashley said matter-of-factly as she stood watching her mother attend to her sister.

"Oh my God."

The color drained from Kelly's face. She gripped the countertop until the knuckles in her fingers turned white. She dropped the ice pack and held her hand to her bruised face. What had she done to her children? Was she turning them into smaller images of their father where they solved all problems with the smack of a hand? She felt like screaming and running from the house as far and as fast as she could. This couldn't be happening. Her chest heaved with emotion.

"Mommy, what's wrong?" Amber said as she picked up the fallen ice pack.

Kelly looked down at the innocent face of her child. Catching her breath, she closed her eyes for a moment, then opened them. She was over reacting. This wasn't that serious. Her daughter was a child and reacted in a childish way the way that kids usually did. She fought with her sister when she was younger. Didn't all kids do it? Replacing the ice pack on Amber's cheek, she smiled and said, "There's nothing wrong, pumpkin. Mommy just forgot something."

"What did you forget?"

"Never you mind. Let's get you some juice, okay?" Taking a deep breath, Kelly helped the girls get the juice out of the refrigerator and pour it into two cups. Her children were normal, she told herself. With shaking fingers, she opened the cookie jar and let the girls help themselves. Pouring herself a cup of coffee, she sat at the table with the chattering girls and listened to them describe their day and what they did in class.

It was only when she heard the familiar sound of Mark's truck pulling into the driveway that she remembered to hurry and pick up the girls' book bags before Mark walked in the door. Kelly tossed the bags onto the girls' beds then rushed back into the kitchen to welcome her husband home from work.

Checking to make sure there was enough beer in the refrigerator, she pulled out a can and handed it to Mark while she said, "You're home early."

"Damn rain started."

"It's not raining yet here," Kelly murmured quietly, motioning to the girls to go to their rooms.

Mark stomped through the living room and threw himself into his chair. "Of course it's not raining here yet. What are you, stupid? It always rains over on the other side of town first. We'll probably get it after supper." He pulled the tie that kept his hair back away from his sweat-stained face, and let his hair fall onto his shoulders. Smoothing out the strands, he yelled, "Tell them girls to shut up or I'll come in there and shut them up."

"I'll take care of them, here's the remote for the TV." Kelly handed her husband the television remote control then hurried out of the room to tell the girls to be quiet.

Kelly heard Mark call out from the living room, "Get me something to eat."

Reminding the girls to play quietly, she rushed out of their room and into the kitchen to find her husband something to eat. She handed him a bag of pretzel twists and said softly, "Supper'll be ready in a couple of hours."

"I don't give a damn if it'll be ready in a couple of minutes. Give me the fuckin' pretzels and leave me alone."

"All right, Mark."

Kelly kept her gaze averted and didn't make eye contact with her husband. He didn't even mention anything about this morning. To him, it's probably all forgotten by now. But it wasn't forgotten by her.

Not this time.

CHAPTER TWENTY-FOUR

Karen made her way out of the courthouse and stepped out into the blazing sunshine. The heat hit her with an intense force after the coolness of the building. She put on her sunglasses and hurried down the sidewalk to find her SUV and get the arrest warrant to Sam.

She let her car idle until most of the hot air blew out the open windows. Putting the SUV into gear, she maneuvered out of the parking lot and into the busy downtown streets. Manipulating her way through the high buildings and narrow streets, she followed the familiar route to I-275. Karen was happy to get back out on the interstate. She rolled up her windows, pressed down on the gas, and her SUV sped up.

The traffic was manageable, so she let her mind wander to the phone call she had last night with Mike. It started out a bit strained, but before she knew it she was laughing and telling Mike stories about the antics of her and her sister from a forgotten time. Mike had been easy to talk to and he opened up as much as she did. She learned that he had two sisters, no brothers, and he was the youngest. His sisters had been merciless about his education into the female mind and tortured him constantly with threats of ruffled dresses and ribbons in his hair. He'd survived with a father who had stuck up for him in a household of women. They managed to get away on fishing trips and camping excursions that only brought them closer together.

Mike asked her why she called, and with a few tips from *Cosmo*, she was able to sound coy and flirting. Couldn't she have just told him she wanted to hear his voice? That she couldn't wait until their date? Karen scoffed at herself. That was too sappy for her even with her latent romantic urges. She had been a bit flustered after confessing but recovered well. She remembered the tactics she'd learned from reading another *Cosmo* article and borrowed a tried and true ploy—get the man talking about himself. It worked. Mike kept the conversation light. He would tell a couple of stories, then insist that she tell one as well. He never tried to monopolize the conversation. It wasn't until Mike said that he'd better go or else he'd get no sleep for work that she realized they'd been talking for over three hours.

Karen smiled then shook herself back to the present. She took the exit for Nebraska Avenue and managed the double lanes of traffic to the now familiar side street and Raymond Thomas's house.

Noting that Sam's car was two houses down the street and empty, she parked in front of the house and locked the car doors. She pocketed the arrest warrant, and walked up the sidewalk and to the front door. Raising her hand to knock, Karen noticed it was slightly ajar. Alarmed and cautious, she pulled out her gun, looked from side to side, and then carefully opened the door. Inside, the room was dark after the bright sunshine. She pulled off her sunglasses, placed them in her jacket pocket and looked around.

Hearing a soft moan, she followed the noise and found Maggie Morris sprawled on the floor of the living room. Sam was next to her, his head at an odd angle. Checking Maggie to verify she was breathing, she then checked Sam. She gasped when she saw the blood covering his face and pooled beneath his head. His pulse was weak, but he was breathing on his own. Leaving the two where they were, Karen searched the small house for any signs of an intruder. The house was empty, so she pulled out her cell phone and dialed 911. Confirming that she was a homicide detective and that there was an officer down, she hurried back to the living room to see if she could help.

Worried and not getting any response from Sam, Karen turned to Maggie. She took in the woman's battered and beaten face and body. Her clothes were torn. It looked like she'd been through hell.

She called out her name. "Maggie." A feeble moan.

"Maggie, can you hear me?"

Another moan. Maggie lifted an arm as if fending off an attacker.

"Don't move, Maggie. Don't move. Help is on the way." "Wh-what happened?" Maggie whispered from swollen lips.

"Maggie, who did this to you?" Karen asked.

"Wh-where?" She slowly shook her head swallowed hard then spoke again. "Ra-Ray."

"Raymond Thomas? Maggie, did Raymond Thomas do this to you?"

"Yes." Maggie forced the word out in one breath.

Hearing sirens, Karen patted Maggie on the shoulder and told her to take it easy, that help was on the way. She left Maggie to go to the front door and wait for the police and EMTs to arrive.

She waved down the paramedics and directed them into the house. More officers followed in various official and unofficial cars. Anyone within hearing distance of the 'officer down' call seemed to be making his or her way to the premises. Karen pointed to the officer in charge and told him that she would be with him shortly. Pushing her way through the room, she managed to make a path to where the EMTs were working on Sam.

"Is he all right?"

"We don't know yet. He's not conscious. He looks like he took a hard blow to the face."

"Where are you taking him?"

"University. We're leaving in two minutes."

"I'll be right behind you," Karen said, then swiveled her head looking for the officer in charge. She needed to talk to him before she left. Spotting him just inside the front door, she left Sam in the capable hands of the paramedics and went to do her job.

"Sergeant Brooks? I called the 911 in. I was on my way back with an arrest warrant and discovered the assault."

"How's Sam?"

"They don't know. He's still not conscious."

"I won't keep you long. I know you want to get to the hospital and check on Sam." Sergeant Brooks patted Karen's arm then motioned for her to tell him what happened.

"Maggie Morris was able to tell me that Raymond Thomas was their attacker."

"The one who the arrest warrant is for?"

"Yes. Sam had been here waiting for Thomas while I went downtown to get the warrant. It was—"

"Was that such a good idea, Detective?" Sergeant Brooks frowned at Karen.

"We thought so at the time." Karen's back stiffened. She held her head high.

"It doesn't seem so now, though, does it?"

"It'll all be in my report." Karen kept her face blank. She didn't want to get into an argument right now. Her first concern was for Sam. She needed to call Sam's wife and have her meet them at the hospital. "If you have no more questions, Sergeant, I'll take off for the hospital now. I want to be there when Sam's wife gets there."

Brooks shook his head. "No, not right now. We'll handle it from here." He stopped Karen from leaving by placing a hand on her arm.
"Sam will make it. Don't worry."

"Thanks." Karen turned toward the door and pulled out her cell phone. She dialed Sam's home number then swallowed hard. The news she had to break to Sam's wife wasn't going to be easy.

"Hello?"

"Mrs. Anderson?" Karen pushed her way through the throng of people who were being kept away from the house by patrol officers. The neighbors stood on the sidewalk and gawked while talking amongst themselves—most in Spanish.

"Yes."

"Mrs. Anderson, this is Karen Sykes. Your husband's partner." "Yes, Karen. How are you, dear?"

"I'm fine, but...but Sam isn't. He's being taken to University Community Hospital. There was an incident. He was assaulted. We don't know all the details yet, but as soon as Sam regains consciousness, we'll know more." Karen found her SUV and motioned to one of the patrol officers that she wanted to move it.

"Oh my God. I'm on my way."

"Mrs. Anderson? I'm so sorry." Karen maneuvered her SUV through the myriad of other patrol cars, fire trucks, and more. It wasn't easy, and she had to honk her horn several times to get vehicles to move out of her way, but she made it to Nebraska Avenue. It was a short distance to the hospital and she could be there in less than ten minutes.

"Thank you. Are you at the hospital now?"

"No, I'm on my way as well. I'll meet you in the Emergency Room."

"Fine. I'll see you there."

Karen pressed the disconnect button to end the call and tossed her cell phone to the passenger seat next to her.

Concerned about Sam, Karen drove with one part of her mind on the road while she pondered the current situation. Sam was hurt. Seriously. Was there something she could have done had she been there? Damn it, their plan sounded so good this morning, where did it go wrong?

Sam had been confident when they'd discussed their idea. He was going to keep surveillance on the house and monitor it for activity. Did he see Thomas go in the house? Did he try to handle Thomas on his own? Without a warrant? There were too many unanswered questions. And all the answers lay with Sam.

Wait, what about Maggie? Karen felt a surge of renewed energy. Maggie Morris had been there as well. She'd be able to explain what happened inside the house and tell her how Thomas had overcome the both of them. Karen's mind raced. She needed to get to Maggie as soon as possible. She had to let the doctors know that Maggie was an important witness who probably needed protection as well.

Turning into the emergency entrance to the hospital, Karen pulled into the first parking spot she saw and hurried inside.

Pulling out her badge, she flashed it at the security guard patrolling the emergency area and asked to see the doctor on duty.

"What does this pertain to?" the guard asked, hitching up his trousers and scratching his stomach.

Karen took a deep breath and managed to speak in an even tone. "I'm Detective Sykes. My partner Sam Anderson and another victim, Maggie Morris, were just brought in here by ambulance. I need to find out how they're doing and talk to them if I can."

"Why don't you go on over there to that room and tell the triage nurse who you are and why you're here? They'll get you back to see your partner as soon as they're able, I'm sure."

The "Thank you" Karen tossed over her shoulder filtered behind her as she hurried into the room the security guard had pointed to. Inside, a nurse stood up from behind a desk and said, "We'll call you in the order of your emergency. Please go—"

"I'm not a patient." Karen showed the nurse her badge. "I'm Detective Sykes and my partner Sam Anderson was just brought here by ambulance. I need to see him."

The nurse took a look at Karen's badge, and then looked at her face. She must have seen the seriousness and no-nonsense behavior Karen portrayed and said, "Please wait right here. I'll go back and see what I can find out for you."

Karen thanked the nurse. She paced the small space in the triage room while she waited for the nurse to return. The longer it took, the more nervous Karen got for Sam and his injuries.

It must have been only a few minutes, but to Karen it seemed like hours when she heard her name from out in the lobby.

"I'm looking for Detective Sykes, she's supposed to meet me here. My husband was brought in by ambulance. I want to see him. Now."

Karen spied Sam's wife talking to the security guard. "Mrs. Anderson, I'm Karen Sykes. I'm sorry we had to meet under these circumstances." Karen helped steer Mrs. Anderson away from the security guard and over to the triage room.

"How's Sam. Have you heard?" Mrs. Anderson kept clenching and unclenching her hands. She would wrap her arms around herself one minute and then smooth out her blouse the second. She acted as if she would normally be in charge, but felt at a loss for her current situation.

"There's a nurse checking right now. She's only been gone a few minutes." Karen lifted a hand to pat Mrs. Anderson on the arm, then dropped it. It was a weak attempt at sympathy and she didn't like it when others did it to her.

"My poor Sam. What happened? Who did this? Do you have the assailant in custody?"

"We've got good police officers working on that right now. The suspect's name is Raymond Alan Thomas and we've got reason to believe he's involved in a murder we've been investigating." Karen lowered her voice. "Apparently, Sam was caught unawares at the suspect's home and was beaten along with the suspect's girlfriend. By the time I arrived, the suspect had fled. I called 911 and here we are." Karen held out her arms to encompass where they stood in the corner of the hospital emergency room lobby.

"Where's that nurse?" Mrs. Anderson spun around searching for anyone who could help answer her questions.

"Wait, there she is." Karen stopped Sam's wife from leaving and walked up to the nurse who was heading her way. "How is Sam? What did you find out? Can we see him?"

The nurse held up her hands as if to ward off the barrage of questions. She cast a questioning look at Mrs. Anderson.

Karen understood. "This is Mrs. Anderson. Sam's wife. I asked her to meet me here at the hospital."

The nurse nodded. "Let's go into triage and I'll explain what's happened so far." She ushered the two women into the small room and shut the door. Instead of sitting behind her desk, she stood as well and said, "Our trauma team is working on both Mr. Anderson and Ms. Morris. They've both suffered serious injuries to the head and face. They've been taken down for CT scans so that the doctors can access the extent of their injuries." "Is Sam awake?" Karen asked.

"No, Mr. Anderson hasn't regained consciousness yet. However, Ms. Morris is conscious and able to talk, albeit very carefully. Her mouth has been injured as well."

The nurse grabbed for Mrs. Anderson's hand. She held it tight. "Honey, your husband is being intubated."

Scared, Sam's wife looked from the nurse to Karen then back again. "What does that mean, intubated?"

"It means that we have a machine breathing for him. He can't breathe on his own right now. The doctors say that this is common in these types of injuries to the neck."

"Ca—Can I see him?"

The woman with the take-charge attitude seemed to crumble before Karen's eyes. She felt so sorry for Sam's wife. She also couldn't help her right now, except to help catch the man who did this to him. She turned to the nurse, "Can I see Maggie Morris? There are a few questions I need to ask her."

"The doctor said you can see her when she comes back from having a CT scan. They'll send someone out to get you."

"Can I see my husband?" Mrs. Anderson's voice was barely above a whisper. Karen looked down at her and was shocked to see that she appeared to have aged ten years. Karen swallowed hard around a large lump in her throat. She didn't know what to say.

The nurse answered, "We'll get you into to see him as soon we can." She patted Mrs. Anderson's arm. "Let me take you back so you can talk to the doctor in charge, okay?"

"Thank you. I'd appreciate that very much."

Karen watched as Sam's wife clung to the nurse's arm as if needing the physical support.

The nurse turned to Karen. "Detective? If you wait out in the waiting room, we'll send someone out to get you just as soon as Ms.
Morris is ready."

"Thank you." Karen turned, left the small room, and stepped into the waiting room. Other people were already there. Several of them were coughing into tissues. One man held a bloody towel around his hand. A young woman rocked a sick baby while another child played on the floor next to her chair. A television blared from one corner of the room with an afternoon talk show. Karen felt drained. She expected to look at her watch and see that it was nearing midnight. But from the sun shining through the windows, it was only afternoon. From her vantage point, she could see the dark clouds gathering for an afternoon shower. Low thunder rumbled from somewhere in the distance.

Karen chose a chair away from those that appeared sick and coughing, and sat carefully. She tried to block out the noises around her, concentrating on the events of the day. Sam had to be okay. He just had to be. Even though she hadn't been Sam's partner long, she still felt close to him. Concern for Sam's wife also surfaced. The poor woman had looked lost and all alone as she walked back to the trauma room.

Drawing on her feelings of grief, she could only imagine the added anguish of losing a husband or wife. Without a significant other in her life, she felt that loss as well. Her thoughts turned to Mike and their date tonight. She wondered if he would mind if she canceled. She didn't think she'd be very good company considering the circumstances. As she thought of calling Mike, her cell phone rang. Hoping for some privacy, she stood and walked outdoors to a small concrete table. It looked like a smoking area for emergency room patients and visitors. She answered her phone on the fourth ring.

"Hello?"

"Karen? It's Mike. I heard about Sam."

"Mike. I'm really glad you called." The door opened and a man came out, lighting a cigarette. "I was thinking about our date tonight and…" Karen frowned at the interruption the cigarette smoker caused.

"I was thinking about it too. I'm guessing you don't want to do anything too public and you'd like to keep the evening quiet?"

"Yes, actually I was thinking—"

"I agree. That's why I changed our plans and you're coming over to my place where I can take care of you."

"You want to take care of me?" Karen wasn't sure she heard Mike right.

"Karen, this is a traumatic time in your life. You shouldn't be alone. Please let me take care of you tonight. I promise a good meal,
nice wine, and some quiet conversation."

Karen's heart melted. "It does sound nice."

"Of course it does. Why don't you come by my place say, seven o'clock? I'll have the coals on the grill and the steaks marinating by the time you get there."

"I'll need directions to your place."

"No problem, you got something to write on?"

Karen pulled out her notebook and pen and took down the directions as Mike told them to her. He was right. She wasn't that far from him. She'd be able to find his house easily. His directions were perfectly clear.

"Thanks, Mike. I really appreciate this." Karen pocketed her notebook and pen.

"No problem. I want to do this."

"I'll see you tonight."

"I'm looking forward to it. Goodbye."

"Goodbye." Karen pressed the end button to disconnect the call. She tapped her chin with her cell phone as she thought about Mike. He kept surprising her. And that was a good thing. As she replaced her cell phone to the holster on her belt, she noticed a nurse entering the waiting room. She hurried back inside to see if the nurse was looking for her.

Seeing the man with the bloody towel stand up and walk over to the nurse, Karen made her way back to her seat and sat down, dejected. What was taking them so long? She had questions and Maggie Morris had the answers. Not able to sit still, Karen stood and paced the waiting room. On her fifth round, she heard her name called.

"Detective Sykes?"

"Yes. Yes. That's me." Karen hurried over to the nurse. "Can I talk to Maggie Morris now?"

"I'm supposed to take you back there. She knows you're waiting to talk to her."

"How is she?" Karen asked as they walked through the doors labeled 'Emergency Room Personnel Only'.

"She's in a lot of pain. She has a concussion. We've given her some pain medication. It's difficult for her, but she insisted on talking to you." The nurse moved on ahead of Karen leading the way. "We're almost there."

"She did?" Karen kept her eye on the nurse's back as they weaved their way around various emergency room personnel and equipment. They passed an elderly man laying on a gurney, covered with a blanket. His eyes were shut and he appeared to be sleeping. As Karen passed, he slowly opened his eyes and stared into space. She could see the pain and confusion behind his watery eyes. She gave him a tentative smiled and continued following the nurse.

The nurse led Karen to an examining room labeled 'Trauma Room 1' and opened the door. She stood to one side and Karen walked into the room.

Chapter Twenty-Five

Maggie Morris lay in a hospital bed with an IV connected to her hand. Her torn clothes were gone and she was wearing a hospital gown. Her face swollen and bruised; her lips puffy and split. There was a new row of tiny stitches above the left eyebrow and a couple in her chin. Her blonde curly hair was pushed back from her face and matted in some places where the blood had dried.

Karen walked to the side of the bed and said, "Maggie? I'm Detective Sykes. Do you remember me?"

Maggie nodded slowly, wincing from the obvious pain.

Karen winced along with her.

"I'm really sorry about this, but I'm going to ask you some questions. I'll try to keep them brief." Karen took out her notebook and pen. "Did Raymond Alan Thomas assault you and Detective Anderson?"

Maggie's eyes widened. She nodded again, fear showing on her face.

"Do you know where he is?" Karen asked her questions softly but clearly.

Closing her eyes, Maggie sighed. She slowly shook her head from side to side.

Karen tried again. "Did he say anything to you?"

Maggie's eyes opened. She looked at Karen and nodded. Working her mouth to try to form the words, Maggie swallowed hard. Her swollen lips moved, but no sound came from them. Making another attempt, Maggie croaked, "Die…bitch." "He told you to 'die bitch'?" Maggie nodded.

Great, Karen thought. Still nothing to go on to catch this guy. "Maggie, would you know where he hangs out, who he hangs out with, or where we can start looking for him?" Karen knew she was grasping at straws now, but she had to keep asking.

Maggie stared up at Karen. Using the hand without the IV, she lifted a glass of water to her mouth and gently put the straw between her lips. She took a long swallow and then another. She sighed and put the glass back onto the bedside tray table. "Ra-Ray…hangs out… corner…store." Exhausted from the effort, Maggie closed her eyes.

Not wanting to show her frustration, Karen bit her upper lip. She needed new information. How was she supposed to bring justice to the poor parents of a murdered boy if she kept running around in circles? Damn it, this guy couldn't just up and disappear. She looked down at the woman who bore the violent marks of the man they were looking for and wondered where he hid himself when he wasn't staying at home. Maybe he had another woman in another house somewhere. Someone was protecting him and Karen was going to figure it out. If she had to spend all her waking moments working on this case, she would. Nothing was going to stop her from solving the murder and bringing justice to the Hunt family.

Karen turned her head when the door to the trauma room opened and a nurse walked in. "We're going to be moving her to a room upstairs, so if you're finished …?" She let her voice trail off.

"Yes, thank you. I'm finished for now." Karen turned to the blonde woman in the bed. "I think she fell asleep."

"It's the medication we gave her. It'll make her sleepy."

"I'll be going." Karen pulled a business card from her pocket and placed it on the bedside table. "Could you make sure this goes with her when she moves to her room? If she remembers anything, please have her call me." The nurse nodded.

Karen turned and left the room. Curious, she looked about to see if she could find where they were treating Sam. The room next to Maggie's was labeled 'Trauma Room 2'. Inside she could see Mrs. Anderson standing beside an empty hospital bed. Her shoulders slumped. Looking from side to side, Karen didn't see anyone who was interested in what she was doing, so she knocked softly on the door.

Mrs. Anderson turned and seeing Karen, opened the door. "Hello, Detective."

"Mrs. Anderson. What is the word on Sam? Has he regained consciousness yet?"

"No, not yet. He's having an MRI test right now. They want to see how much damage has been done to his spine."

"You don't think… They don't think… Is he…?" Karen stammered not able to put into words the horror that she was thinking.

Mrs. Anderson lifted sad eyes to look at Karen. "They don't know yet." She took a deep breath and lifted her shoulders a bit. "They found some swelling around the spinal cord and aren't sure yet how much damage was done. The doctors said they'd know more after this test."

"I'm so sorry, Mrs. Anderson. Please, if there's anything I can do for you…" Karen's voice trailed off in her attempt to think of anything she could do for her partner's wife.

"Thank you, Detective. I appreciate your concern. I'm sure Sam does as well." Sam's wife held out one of her hands and Karen grasped it between both of hers. "Sam's going to wake up soon and he'll be able to tell you what occurred. Just keep praying for that to happen."

"I will, I will." Taking a business card from her pocket, Karen handed it to the woman standing in front of her. "Please take this and call me, anytime, for anything."

"Detective?" Mrs. Anderson looked Karen in the eyes. Her mouth formed a thin line as she pressed her lips together. "Find the man who did this. Please."

"I'm going to, Mrs. Anderson." Karen hoped her eyes and the seriousness on her face expressed all that she wanted to convey to Sam's wife. She would find the man who did this. And when she did, she'd make him pay. Tampa wasn't so big that he could hide forever. A nurse entered the trauma room. "Mrs. Anderson?"

"Yes?"

"We're moving your husband to a room upstairs. Would you follow me?"

"Yes. Thank you." Sam's wife turned to Karen. "Detective Sykes, I'll call you as soon as there's a change."

Karen nodded. "Thank you." She watched Mrs. Anderson leave with the nurse. Her stomach growled in hunger. It reminded her that she missed lunch. She checked her watch. She had just enough time to file her report, get home, and change for dinner. She suddenly had an urgent need to see Mike.

CHAPTER TWENTY-SIX

Karen found Mike's house by the directions he gave. She pulled her SUV into the driveway and got out. Taking a moment to smooth down the hem of her dress, she paused and locked her door. In deference to the heat and high humidity, she'd worn something sleeveless and short. Without stockings, her legs felt free. In flat sandals, she turned and made her way to the front door and rang the doorbell.

Mike answered after a minute or two and by the awed expression on his face, Karen knew she'd chosen the right dress. His appreciation shined in his eyes.

"Hi," Mike said as he stood in the doorway.

"Hi, yourself." Karen pulled her hands out from behind her back and showed Mike what she was carrying. "I brought a bottle of red wine. I hope you don't mind?"

"Not at all." Mike stood to one side and said, "Come in. Please."

Karen walked through the doorway and into a small foyer into Mike's living room. The room was decorated with a casual flair and dark earth tones. There were plump pillows on the sofa and overstuffed chairs. A large, big screen TV took up most of the space at one end of the room while an elaborate sound system and stereo filled in the rest.

"I like this room," Karen said. "It's definitely you."

"Really?" Mike cocked his head to one side as he watched Karen look around the room.

"Yeah. Casual and neat."

"Well, that's me, all right." Mike laughed and put a hand at Karen's back to help lead her toward the kitchen. "I've got the coals hot and the wine chilled. How about I put this bottle away for dinner and we start out with something a bit cooler?"

"That sounds great."

Mike busied himself with pulling wine glasses out of the cupboard and a bottle of wine out of the refrigerator. With a deft flair, he opened the bottle, poured the first glass and handed it to Karen. She smiled her thanks and drank. A bit fruity and not dry. Just the way she liked it. "It's good," she said.

"Thanks. I thought you might like it. It's from Australia."

Karen lifted the glass to her lips and took another drink. "I like it."

After pouring himself a glass, Mike corked the bottle and put it back in the refrigerator. He motioned for Karen to take a seat on the stool behind her at the breakfast bar. He leaned against the counter and his face grew serious. "How's Sam?"

Karen lost her smile. "Not good. The doctors don't know anything definite yet, but they're trying to determine if Sam's paralyzed." "No." Mike's concern showed.

"Yeah. They found some swelling at the base of his neck around his spinal cord. He hasn't regained consciousness yet, so we can only surmise what happened. It looks like he took some violent blows to the head and at least one crushing blow to the throat."

"Any leads?"

"One good one. I've got one eyewitness saying our suspect from the Hunt murder did it."

"Hunt? The little boy found in the campground?"

"That's the one. Our main suspect doesn't want to get caught apparently." Karen took another sip from her wineglass.

Mike straightened up and said, "I need to put those steaks on if we're going to eat anytime tonight. You can come with me or you can sit here and enjoy your wine."

"Why don't I come out and supervise?" Karen smiled to let Mike know she was kidding. "Seriously, though, I like my steaks medium well."

"Good to know." Mike took the steaks from the refrigerator and carried them to the patio off the living room. A large built in grill stood off to one side, away from the house, next to the pool. Karen stepped out onto the patio and looked around. The last rays of sun shot across the sky and melted into the horizon in a blend of deep purple, pink, and orange. The screened lanai kept the pesky mosquitoes at bay. Soft jazz played on the outside speakers.

"You have a nice back yard."

"Thanks. It needs some plants, but I'm not really a gardener, so I'd probably kill them quicker than not."

"Plants just need a little bit of attention, some water, and a little fertilizer now and then."

"You applying for the job?" Mike laughed as he put the steaks on the grill. The meat sizzled and popped as it touched the hot grill.

"Not exactly." Karen laughed with him.

"Darn, I thought I was gonna get me a sexy gardener."

Karen dipped her head. "Sexy?"

Mike walked up to her and placed his hands on her shoulders. He looked deep into Karen's eyes. "Yeah. Sexy."

"Oh." Karen felt the blush of heat rush through her body. Mike's hands felt warm on her bare shoulders. She lifted her wineglass to her lips and tilted the glass slowly. Over the rim of her glass, Karen looked at Mike as he watched the liquid pour into her mouth. Karen saw a spark ignite in his eyes. She never felt so much power over someone before. Knowing that Mike thought of her as sexy was a new experience for her. It made her want to run her fingers through his short blonde hair. It made her want to turn that spark in his eyes into a flame. Flame.

Fire. Fire!

"The steaks!" Karen stepped back away from Mike and motioned toward the grill. "Mike, the steaks, they're on fire."

"Shit!" Mike rushed to the grill. "All right. Don't worry. I can handle this." He picked up the tongs and moved the steaks to another spot of the grill, one that wasn't so hot. "There. No harm done, right?"

"I did say I wanted mine well, didn't I?" Karen chuckled as she watched Mike fuss over the steaks. "Is there anything I can help you with?"

"No. Nothing at all. I'm supposed to be taking care of you tonight, remember?" Mike looked up from the grill and used the tongs to make his point. "You just find yourself a place to sit and relax and I'll take care of everything."

"You do make it easy." Karen eased her body into a patio chair. "It really has been a rough day. I appreciate all of this."

Mike checked the steaks and then walked into the house. Karen shifted in her seat as if to follow, but Mike motioned to her to stay where she was. He reappeared with the wine bottle and topped off her glass. She smiled her thanks.

Karen leaned back against the striped cushions in the chair and gazed up at the darkening sky. One star shined brightly. She wasn't the superstitious type, but the child's nursery rhyme sprang to mind. *Star light, star bright. The first star I see tonight…* What would be her wish? Smiling, Karen wondered if wishing tonight would be the start of something special was too romantic of a wish. With a shrug, she closed her eyes and wished anyway.

Mike walked by and tapped her on the shoulder. "Sleepy?"

"No. Not really." Karen watched as Mike placed skewered vegetables on the grill. "Just relaxing." This was not the time to tell him about her wish. She didn't want to frighten the poor man to death.
"Those look good."

"I have a salad ready and I thought some roasted veggies would be a good addition. The steaks are nearly done, so if you'd like, we can eat out here or in the house. Your choice."

"It doesn't look like it's going to rain yet, why don't we eat outside?"

"Sounds good. I'll get the plates, you just sit back and go back to sleep." He smiled as if to say he was only joking.

Karen grinned. She liked Mike's sense of humor. He was easy to be with and she enjoyed talking to him. She watched as he made several trips to and from the house to bring out plates, silverware, napkins, and more wine. He placed the salad on the table along with a sizzling steak on each plate. Following up with the vegetable skewers, he sat down across the table from Karen and made a face.

"You've outdone yourself here, Mike." Karen complimented him. "Everything looks great."

"I hope you like it." Mike lifted his glass of wine in toast. "To new beginnings."

"To new beginnings," Karen repeated.

rs

Mike watched Karen cut into her steak and place a small piece into her mouth. She chewed with a diminutive smile on her face as if she truly enjoyed her meal. He grinned. He couldn't help himself. His fears about starting a relationship with someone from work were falling to the side, a little at a time. He wasn't totally convinced. Not by a long shot, but he was going to at least make a concerted effort. Karen was sexy, charming, and irresistible. He couldn't get the image of her in her running gear out of his head.

Picking up his fork and knife, Mike tackled his own steak with gusto. They were cooked perfectly, even with the small fire he had to put out. If that was the only hiccup in tonight's activities, he'd call it a successful night. But then, that was his opinion the minute he opened the door and saw Karen in her unbelievably short dress and bare arms and legs.

After taking a sip of his wine, Mike asked, "What about your case, now that Sam's in the hospital?"

Karen put her knife down and looked up at Mike. "It's still my case. I'm going to keep working it. Finding this guy is doubly important. He isn't going to get away with murder or assault on a police officer." Karen speared a slice of roasted red pepper with the fork and popped it into her mouth.

"Well, you know that our department is available to help in any way we can." Mike forked a slice of onion with a piece of steak and put the combination into his mouth. He groaned in appreciation. "I realize that, Mike. Right now, we're focused on finding this Ray Thomas before he strikes again. I know he can't just appear and disappear like magic. He's out there somewhere and I'm going to find him."

"I know you will. You're determined."

"Thanks." Karen cocked her head as she looked at Mike. "So, what are you working on right now? Did you ever get an ID on that
John Doe you found out on the causeway?"

"Not yet. FDLE Lab is way backed up. They said we should have an answer by next week."

"Well, I guess he's not going anywhere, right? No matching missing person's report? Nothing like that?" Karen pushed her plate away and reached for her glass of wine.

"Nope. Nothing to match him with in the system. Guess we'll have to wait for the lab to catch up. It's like this during the summer. They always get backed up." Mike snatched the leftover slice of yellow pepper from Karen's plate and munched happily. "Like you said, he's not going anywhere."

"Please, let me help you clean up. You cooked a fabulous meal. I must do my share of the work." Karen waved her hand with the wineglass.

"Absolutely not. You are to do nothing tonight except relax and enjoy yourself." Mike started collecting plates and silverware. He stood and carried them to the kitchen. In a few minutes he had the table cleared of dishes and returned to the patio. He placed a chilled bowl of seedless red and green grapes on the table and sat back down.

Karen popped one into her mouth. "I love grapes."

"I wasn't sure if you were into heavy desserts, so I thought some fresh fruit might work."

"You made a great choice. Especially after that dinner." Karen sighed. "Much better than a frozen meal any day."

Mike watched Karen pick another grape from the bowl and place it into her mouth, her cheek bulging a bit as she bit into the grape. He wanted to touch that cheek. He almost reached out his hand to do so, but instead covered it up by plucking a grape from the bowl and popping it into his mouth. "I do the frozen dinner thing every once in a while, but it's great to have someone to cook for." He nodded at Karen.

"Well, the next time, I'll cook for you. I make a yummy stuffed manicotti with homemade sauce. You'll love it."

"I'm sure I will." Mike stood up and held out his hand.

Karen looked at him with a question in her eye but placed her hand in his and stood as well.

Giving her a smile, Mike said, "I thought a little after dinner dancing would be nice. What do you think?" He led her away from the table and chairs and over to a cleared part of the patio next to the pool.

"That sounds nice." Karen looked down into the still water. "Just don't drop me in the pool, okay?"

"All right. But you don't have to spoil all the fun." Mike chuckled as he placed a hand at the small of Karen's back and held her close. He swayed gently in time with the music playing through the speakers.

Mike rested his chin on the top of Karen's head and breathed in the soft coconut scent that seemed to emanate from her body. He could feel Karen's hand as it rested on his shoulder. He held her other hand loosely in his. Her hand was warm. And soft. It nestled inside his hand as if it belonged there. Thunder rumbled from far away. He drew her closer, as if he could protect her from the intruding noise. Karen sighed softly and laid her head on his shoulder. Mike tucked her hand beneath her cheek and wrapped his other arm around her small body. It felt good to hold her completely. It was easy to pretend that they were the only two people in the world and nothing else existed beyond his backyard. But, the practical side of him knew that wasn't true and insisted on reminding him that she was a detective for Hillsborough County. Life did exist beyond his backyard—a complicated life. One that would get even more complicated if he gave in to his feelings and took this evening into the direction it was going.

Mike sighed. Karen snuggled in closer to his body. The song ended. They continued shifting their feet, as if the music never stopped. Mike moved one hand up Karen's back and let it rest there, massaging gently back and forth. She didn't tell him to stop. Another song began. The mournful tunes of the wailing saxophone drifted around them, enveloping them in a hypnotic slow beat.

"That feels good," Karen murmured.

Mike rolled his eyes skyward. She wasn't making it easy for him to find a stopping point. "Does it?" he asked.

"Mmm hmmm."

Mike moved his hand lower. "What if I do this?"

"That's nice too," Karen said as she cuddled into the front of his body as if she were an affectionately burrowing bunny. He couldn't get the image out of his mind and almost chuckled out loud. He cleared his throat instead.

Karen lifted her head to lean back and look at Mike. He glanced down and caught her staring at him with warm hazel eyes.

"What?" he asked with a smile.

"I like this."

"Yeah. Me too." Mike watched Karen's eyes focus on his mouth. He knew she wanted him to kiss her. He ran his hands up her back and over her bare shoulders. He cupped each side of her face and tilted her head up further. He stopped moving his feet in time to the music and stood with her body close to his.

She licked her lips in anticipation. Mike swallowed hard past the lump in his throat and brought his head down, capturing her lips beneath his. Her lips were soft. Inviting. They molded to his, matching his seeking, searching kiss. He pressed a little harder and touched her lips with the tip of his tongue. Karen opened her mouth to let his searching tongue enter. He deepened the kiss, using his thumbs to rub her jaw line as he held her face in his hands. Mike felt and heard Karen sigh into his mouth. He moaned in return, equaling her kiss for kiss as their tongues danced a sweet dance of their own.

Karen moved her arms and wrapped them around his neck. She sought out his hair and ran her fingers through it. Mike marveled at her gentle touch; the way it drew goose bumps down his spine. He shivered in delight. He wanted her to feel as much as he was. He moved his hands from her neck and smoothed them down over her shoulders. Drawing her closer, he placed his hands lower onto her back and seductively traced lazy circles along her lower spine. Mike knew he hit the right spot when he felt her tremble in his arms.

Lips touching lips, Mike pulled back a little to breathe Karen's name. She nodded wordlessly and pressed her lips more firmly to his, holding him closer.

Mike slid his hands further down and rested them on the firmness of Karen's behind. She pushed herself into his hands, until his hands were filled with her roundness. Mike kneaded her flesh beneath her dress. He grew more urgent to touch her skin. He worked his way back up to her shoulders and felt for a zipper. He found one at the base of her neck. He grasped the zipper and tugged it slowly down her back. Inch by inch, her body opened up to him. He touched her eagerly, needing the contact. She didn't resist. Karen's hands wandered as well, to the top of his pants where his shirt was tucked. She tugged at it, almost with the same urgency Mike showed, and sighed in appreciation when her hands touched his bare skin. Mike felt the palm of her hand rub his lower torso, her fingers skimming his taut belly. He needed her touch. With shaking fingers, he helped guide her hand to the buttons on his shirt. She got the message and opened his shirt in a matter of seconds. She smoothed back the fabric and ran her hands over his chest. Mike's lips pressed into the side of Karen's face. He kissed her along her neck, reveling in the shivers he induced in her body.

Karen kissed him back as well. She traced a path from his mouth to his chest with her warm, soft lips. Mike's body ached for her touch. His skin tingled with each kiss. He held tight on his control. He could stop any minute if Karen didn't want to go any further. But he was losing the battle over his control on his rule. He searched his mind for a good reason to keep it, but nothing came to mind. With Karen, the rules didn't matter.

rs

Karen let her tongue dart out and lick at one of Mike's hard nipples. It tightened to a taut point in response. She smoothed one hand over the firm hardness of Mike's upper body. She let her fingers play among the blonde hairs of his chest and followed their path down his stomach until his pants blocked her progress. She moaned in frustration then in pleasure as Mike's hands found her bare back and touched her intimately along her ribcage before he let one hand cup her bare breast. Her nipple puckered and pushed at the fabric of her dress. Karen arched her back to give Mike's hand more room inside her dress. His touch gentle but firm. He captured Karen's nipple between his thumb and forefinger, rolling it between them, urging her to respond. Karen opened her mouth wider to Mike's kiss. She wanted to taste him, all of him. She gingerly bit at his lower lip and sucked it between her teeth. He groaned her name. Her restless hands covered his body, seeking, touching. She could feel his hardness pressing into her belly. Her hands sought out his hardness, touching him through his pants. Karen felt him jump and quiver in response.

"Karen, you're a very sexy woman and you're driving me crazy with desire." Mike moaned into her hair, his hands on the front of her dress, cupping her breasts through the light fabric.

"Mike." Karen kissed his chest. "Mike." She kissed him again. "Please make love to me." Karen lifted her chin to meet Mike's mouth with her own. She urged him to respond with her hands and lips.

With no way to speak, Mike nodded as he started walking toward the patio door. He lifted Karen into his arms and held her close. Karen wrapped her arms around Mike's neck and cuddled close, feeling safe and protected in his arms. She placed tiny kisses along his jaw line, marveling at how smooth his cheek felt.

Through the patio door, Karen helped him close and lock it before Mike shifted her back into the circle of his arms and carried her down the hall to his bedroom. The door was open. The room in darkness. Mike dropped his head to give her a kiss as he leaned down and placed her gently on his bed. Karen lay back with her arms tossed above her head. While kicking off his shoes, Mike removed his open shirt.

"Don't move," Mike said.

Karen shook her head from side to side, and stretched like a languid cat. Her dress rode up on her thighs until it barely covered her at all. She knew Mike was looking at her and it made her feel as sexy as he said she was. No one had called her sexy and looked at her they way he did. Her past sexual adventures were nothing but a hazy memory. Nothing compared to the way Mike looked at her, or touched her.

She watched him as he unbuckled his belt and removed his pants. Karen's eyes widened when she saw his penis stretching out to her as if trying to reach her. She lifted one hand to run a finger delicately along its side to the tip. It jumped at her touch. She smiled knowing that she made Mike respond in such a way.

Karen leaned into Mike's body as he lay down beside her, his weight shifting the support of the bed. She touched the side of his face and placed her hand against his cheek. He moved his head slightly to the right to place a kiss inside her palm. She closed her hand around his kiss to hold it tight.

Mike tugged gently on the shoulders of her dress to work the material down her arms. First one arm, then the other was removed from the confines of her dress. As each breast came into view, Mike covered it with kisses. He licked and sucked at her nipples, causing her to shiver as they hardened beneath his lips and tongue. With a few more tugs, Mike managed to work Karen's dress down to her hips and then down her legs. As each leg was disentangled from the dress, he kissed her knees and stroked her thighs. His hands were warm; his fingers long and firm.

With only her panties left, Karen held her arms out so that Mike could move into them. She wrapped her arms about his shoulders and neck, raining light kisses along his neckline until her lips reached his mouth. Her lips captured his and she drank deep of his kiss. She wrapped her legs around his until they were entwined. She wanted to touch as much of his body as she could. She pushed her breasts into Mike's chest; she could feel the velvet hardness of his penis pressing into her leg.

Karen wasn't sure how much longer she could take it. *Cosmo* lessons be damn. She always was a quick learner. "Mike, please. I want you to make love to me."

Mike lifted his head and searched her face. She stared back at him, pleading with her eyes.

"I will, Karen. I will."

Mike lifted himself off her body and knelt over her. He trailed one hand along the side of her face and down her neck until her reached one of her breasts. He kneaded the flesh carefully, rolling her nipple between his fingers. His touch drove Karen wild. She could feel her breast swell within his hands.

"I like it when you touch me like that," Karen breathed.

"Like this?" Mike touched her other breast and gave it the same treatment.

"Mmmm, like that."

Mike let his hands slide down her body and rest on her hips. "What else do you like?"

Karen squeezed her thighs together as she felt the tension build between her legs. "I'll show you." She placed her hands on top of Mike's and guided them between her legs.

"Why don't I get rid of these," Mike said as he pulled down her panties and let them drift to the floor. Mike positioned himself between Karen's legs and looked up at her with a sparkle in his eye.

Karen lifted her head to grin at Mike. She laid her head back against the bed and waited for his next touch. She felt his lips along the inside of her thigh as his hands moved upward to spread her legs tenderly open. She quivered in anticipation as his lips moved higher and higher up her thigh until she could feel his breath stirring the hairs on her mound. Warm and soft, his breath parted the way for his tongue. She felt it tentatively reach out and touch her, then return with more fervor. Karen grinned with pleasure in the dark. She didn't have to show Mike where to place his tongue as he was hitting all the right spots. She tried desperately to hang onto her sanity. She sought for anything to keep her from coming just yet. It wasn't time. She needed more time to enjoy what Mike was doing to her. Karen spread her legs farther apart to give Mike better access. She moaned in appreciation. "God, Mike, you do that so good." A tightness started to build deep within Karen's center. She tensed in response; her thighs squeezing together. Focusing on the swirl and swipe of Mike's tongue, Karen teetered on the edge. She dragged herself back as Mike lifted his head. Panting, she looked down at his smiling face and gasped, "Don't stop, God, don't stop!"

Grabbing fistfuls of the bedding in each hand, Karen tilted her hips up and arched her back. Mike placed a hand on each hip and held her in place. Beads of sweat streaked down Karen's face, wetting the tips of her hair that crossed her forehead. She brushed the hair away from her face in an irritated gesture. Pressure built up until she felt like she was going to explode.

Mike continued his relentless torture with his lips and tongue. Karen could no longer hold back. She strained against Mike as she pressed upward. The bedding pulled away from the corner of the bed as she held on. Mike's tongue drew smaller and tighter circles, focusing on Karen's pleasure points. It was more than she could take. She crossed the threshold and gave in to her bliss. With fingernails dragging across the bedding, she melted into a puddle. Her heart pounded. Her breath escaped her lips in gasps and pants. She floated on a cloud of satisfaction as spasm after spasm shook her body. A smile plastered itself on her mouth. Her eyes closed.

Mike pulled himself up the bed and pushed back the strands of her hair from her forehead. He kissed the tip of her nose, then planted another one on her smiling lips.

"God, you're good," Karen whispered in a hoarse voice.

"I aim to please."

"You pleased. Man, did you please." Karen lifted a weary hand and flexed her fingers. They tingled as blood began to flow back to the tips. She placed her hand on Mike's chest and tangled her fingers in his curling chest hair. "What do you do for an encore?"

"You just wait." Mike pressed his lips against hers and kissed her passionately. She opened her mouth and let his tongue enter. The intimacy of her taste on his tongue overwhelmed Karen. She wanted Mike like she'd never wanted a man to fill her before. She needed to feel Mike inside of her, deep inside of her. It had been way too long since she'd been made love to and she couldn't wait much longer.

Karen pulled at Mike's shoulders. "I want you inside of me, Mike." She opened her eyes and stared into his. He searched her face carefully. "Now," she said.

Mike shifted his body so that he was on top of Karen's. She ran her hands up and down his back as his muscles contracted beneath her fingers. Letting her legs lay open, she could feel the hardness of Mike's penis as it searched for her opening.

Pausing, Mike looked down at Karen with an unspoken question in his eyes. As if reading his mind, Karen answered, "I'm on the pill."

Mike pushed forward with his hips. His penis pressed into her wetness. Mike shifted his hips and thrust effortlessly until he filled Karen completely. She lifted a hand and placed it alongside Mike's face. She stroked his cheek. Mike moved gently at first, back and forth as he plunged into Karen's body. He sought out her breasts and carefully kneaded their soft flesh.

Lifting her hips, Karen met each of Mike's thrusts. She drew up her legs and wrapped them around his waist. As he plunged, she pressed with her legs so that he would go deeper. She kissed a wet trail along his shoulder blade and up his neck. He tasted salty. Unable to keep her hands still, she stroked his back and found his buttocks. She squeezed their firm flesh and felt Mike stiffen. She could tell by his response that he enjoyed her touch.

With each thrust, Karen felt a familiar tightness growing from deep within. The ache of her yearning forced her to lose focus and concentration. She could no longer think properly. All that mattered was Mike's body above hers; moving in and out of hers and the mounting desire that built up and threatened to spill over. Karen continued to match Mike thrust for thrust as their breath mingled. She kissed his lips and clung to his shoulders. Their bodies moved faster; Mike's thrusts grew harder. Karen cried out as a new trembling spasm shook her body. With another thrust, Mike's body went rigid. He shuddered. She smoothed her hands over the tautness of his muscles and held him tight. Mike buried his face into Karen's neck.

They held each other tight until the spasms no longer shook their bodies.

Mike moved first. "I must be crushing you." He made an attempt to roll away, but Karen wrapped her legs around his and held him close.

Karen shook her head. "I like having you here in my arms."

"I couldn't pick a better place to be at the moment." Mike propped his head up on one hand and leaned over to kiss Karen on the nose.

"That was pretty spectacular."

"Yeah, it was, wasn't it?" Mike puffed out his chest.

"Yes, that means you."

"You weren't so bad yourself. I think I lost consciousness at one point."

"Okay. Now you can move. My leg's falling asleep." Karen shifted her hips to alleviate the pressure.

"Sorry about that." Mike rolled off Karen and lay next to her.
He dropped a hand to her head and gently played with her hair.

"Don't be. If I had my way, we'd be joined at the hips from now on."

"That would make it kind of hard to work, don't you think?"

Karen giggled. "Yeah, I guess it would." She thought for a minute then said, "Okay. You are excused for work."

Mike chuckled along with her. "You're so kind."

"Seriously, though. You had this thing about work. Was this just a one-time deal or are we…" Karen stopped talking when she saw the look in Mike's eyes.

Mike stroked the side of Karen's face with his fingers. "I hope we're starting something special here."

"Me too."

"We'll deal with work, however we have to. I know you'll have erratic hours and the same with me. We'll see each other when we can. We'll be with each other as much as possible. We won't let work get in the way of what we have here, okay?"

"Okay." Karen threw her arms around Mike's neck and hugged him. "I knew I saw something special in you."

"Yeah, I couldn't get you out of my mind either."

"No?"

"Nope. Especially after we went running that morning." Mike trailed his finger down Karen's face to her neck and then over her breast. "You fill out a pair of running shorts quite nicely."

CHAPTER TWENTY-SEVEN

Even though it was Saturday, Karen checked in at the office and got caught up giving out status reports to everyone she met about Sam. She broke away from all the talk and went in search of her lieutenant.

Karen stood outside his office door. "Lt. Santiago, I'd like to talk to you."

"Get in here, Sykes. I need to talk to you too."

"Yes, sir." Karen walked into the lieutenant's office and sat in one of the chairs across from where he sat behind his desk.

"You want to stay on the Hunt case, right?"

"Absolutely. I've invested a lot of hours on this case and I know I can find Thomas. He can't just disappear. I'll get someone to tell me where he's at." Karen's knee bounced up and down with pent up energy. "Just don't take me off the case."

"Don't worry. You're still on it. But I'm going to assign you another senior detective."

Karen's face went white. She stared at her boss. "But Sam... He's not... I mean, I don't... You know..." She tossed up her hands in frustration.

"Take it easy, Sykes. Sam's in the hospital. He could be there for a long time. We don't know the extent of the damage yet. You'll need a senior officer to assist you with procedures. Sam trained Hendricks. I've already talked to him. He'll make himself available for you. I want you to catch this son of a bitch as much as you do. We're all on the lookout for him."

"Thank you, sir."

"Now go find Hendricks and let him know I talked to you." Karen stood up and turned to leave. "And, Sykes?"

"Yeah?"

"Be careful out there."

"No problem. I'm serious, sir. I'm going to find him." Karen walked out of her lieutenant's office and made her way to Hendricks' desk. He was waiting for her.

Karen held out her hand. "I'm Karen Sykes. I guess I'll be working with you."

Hendricks shook Karen's hand and motioned for her to take a seat. "Call me John. I've seen you around with Sam. I'm sorry about that."

Karen nodded her head.

"Tell me about the case you're working on. Lieutenant said something about it, but not much."

Karen leaned forward in her chair. "A four year old boy was found murdered in the Hamilton Davis Park Campground. Not a lot of clues, but we did get lucky with a fingerprint. We got a match to one Raymond Alan Thomas. Long term criminal out on probation. We find out his current address, but can't seem to catch him at home. He has a woman living there; she's in the hospital right now as well. Apparently he beat her up pretty badly when he assaulted Sam."

"You know it was him?"

"According to the woman. She named him. Now it's my turn to find him and bring him in."

"Any leads?"

"I know where he hangs out, and with whom. I just gotta lean on them a little harder."

"Any chance you can get more information out of this woman?" Hendricks shifted in his seat. "Do you think she's covering for this guy?"

"That's always a possibility, but if you saw her face, you wouldn't think so. Not after what he did to her. But I'll run by the hospital and talk to her again. She might have remembered something after all." Karen made a move to stand up.

Hendricks motioned her to stay seated. "I don't want to get in your way, Sykes. I know how important this case is to you. But I don't want you running out there half cocked. I'm here for you, okay? You get a good lead on where this character might be hiding, don't try and take him alone. I'll go with you along with some back up patrol, okay?"

"Okay. I hear you." Karen stood up and made her way to the doorway. She turned back and said, "I'm going to go back to the hospital and see if I can get more information out of Maggie Morris. Then I'll check on Sam and see how he's doing."

"Good idea." Hendricks picked up a report off his desk and scanned it quickly. "Remember, I'm here for you."

"Thanks." Karen turned and left Hendricks' office. She stopped at her desk to check for messages then went out into the blazing sun to get into her car and drive to University Hospital.

At the hospital information desk she asked for Maggie Morris' room and was given directions. In a matter of minutes, she was on and off the elevator and walking into Maggie's room. A nurse was taking Maggie's blood pressure as Karen walked in. "Can I help you?"

"I'm here to see Maggie Morris," Karen said as she nodded to the blonde woman in the bed. It looked as if Maggie was sleeping. Her eyes were closed.

"Are you a friend or family?" The nurse finished with the blood pressure monitor and released the Velcro strap. She wrapped it up and tucked it under her arm.

Karen showed the nurse her badge. "I'm here to ask Maggie some questions about her attack."

"Maggie? There's a police officer here to see you." The nurse talked directly to the woman in the hospital bed as if she were a small child.

Maggie opened her eyes slowly. She lifted a hand to carefully touch her swollen mouth. "Who?"

"It's Detective Sykes, Maggie," Karen said. She stepped forward so that Maggie could get a better look at her. "Who?" Maggie asked, blinking first at Karen then at the nurse.

"I don't understand," Karen said to the nurse. "What's wrong with her? She knew who I was yesterday."

"Let's step outside, shall we?" The nurse motioned for Karen to leave the room. Once outside in the hallway, she turned to Karen and said, "We think it is Post Traumatic Stress Disorder. She's been through a very traumatic event. Sometimes people aren't able to recall those events for a while, or sometimes never."

"She's a very important witness. She's gotta remember."

"I understand, Detective. Maggie will be working with the staff psychologist to help her recall as much of the event as possible. She'll need time."

"Time is what we don't have a lot of right now." Karen balled up her fists and shoved them in the pockets of her blazer. Frustrated, she thanked the nurse for her time and turned and left. Angrily, she punched at the elevator down button.

Not bothering to see what surrounded her, Karen followed the directions to the Intensive Care Unit with her mind in a funk. She wondered what else could go wrong today. After giving her name to the nurse at the nurse's station, Karen waited in the small waiting room for Mrs. Anderson.

"Detective Sykes?" Mrs. Anderson walked into the waiting room.

Karen studied her carefully. It looked as if Mrs. Anderson had gained a second wind. She looked stronger today, more sure of herself. "How's Sam?"

"About the same." She patted Karen's arm and then said, "Thank you for coming." She motioned for Karen to sit in one of the chairs flanking a small table, and then sat in the other. "The doctors still aren't positive that Sam's paralysis is permanent. They say they'll know
for sure when the swelling goes down."

"I'm sorry."

"I know, dear. I'm sure if Sam were awake he'd tell you not to worry about him." With restless hands, Mrs. Anderson picked at the front of her light blue sweater.

"Any chance he'll wake up soon?"

"The doctors say that the swelling in his brain will go down. It's just going to take time. They say that in cases like this, the patient usually wakes up once they reduce the swelling. There's just no set time for it to happen. We'll just pray that it works for Sam."

"It will." Karen slapped her fist against her knee. "It has to."

"Yes, it will, I have faith. We just have to be patient and wait for the healing to begin."

"I'll come back again, if I may?" Karen asked.

"You're welcome anytime." Mrs. Anderson stood. "I want to get back in there. I don't like to leave him alone for long."

Karen stood, gave Sam's wife a hug, and left before she broke down in tears. It was too sad for her to bear.

It wasn't easy for Karen to leave the hospital without any new information. She was frustrated and it showed in the way she aggressively drove back to the office. On the way, she stopped to pick

up lunch and breaking one of her own rules for her car, she ate her cheeseburger and fries while driving.

Upset, she stormed into the warehouse and dared anyone within a hundred yards to get in her way. Other officers and detectives obviously saw the dark cloud hovering over Karen's head and stepped quickly to get out of her path.

Only Hendricks ignored her turbulent presence and followed her to her desk. "So, what happened?"

"You don't want to know." Karen tossed her purse into a desk drawer and slammed it shut.

"I wouldn't ask if I didn't want to know. Cut the temper tantrum and tell me what's going on."

Rebuked, Karen lifted her chin and stared at her temporary partner. "Fine." Crossing her arms across her chest, she sat back in her chair. "Nothing's changed with Sam. He's the same. But plenty has changed with Maggie Morris. Seems she's suffering from some post traumatic stress thing and can't remember what happened to her. There goes my one witness who I was relying on to move this case forward. With Sam in a coma there wasn't anyone else there who could tell me what happened."

"Stress? That can be a temporary thing, right?"

"Yeah. Maybe." Karen uncrossed her arms and threw them up in frustration. "I don't know. I talked to a nurse. She said that Maggie's working with a psychologist to sort it all out."

"So this is just a temporary setback. Don't let it get you down." Karen pulled out the Hunt file she'd been working on and sifted through the papers. Hesitating, she let her hand hover over the drawing of the flowchart she'd copied down the day she worked with Sam. She handed it to Hendricks and said, "Look at this. Tell me what I'm missing here."

Hendricks took the paper and studied it carefully. He glanced over at Karen as she waited for him to speak up. "Looks like you need to find out where Thomas is and bring him in for questioning. Next, you need to get an ID on this John Doe."

"I'm waiting on word from the Crime Techs. They say that FDLE is backed up right now and will get to it as soon as they can." Karen sighed. "Looks like it's back down to Nebraska Avenue and checking with Thomas' buddies to see if they've seen him lately."

"Sounds good. Just let me get my things and I'll meet you out front."

"You driving?"

"Of course, why do you even ask?"

Karen laughed. "You guys are all alike."

CHAPTER TWENTY-EIGHT

Mike Connelly took off the latex gloves he'd been wearing and tossed them into the nearest trashcan. After making the shot, he threw his fist into the air and shouted, "Score!"

"Damn it, Mike, you're gonna scare me to death one of these days, you know that?" Susan jumped and held her gloved hand to her heart. She had been leaning over a table of evidence.

"Sorry about that," Mike said.

"Wait a minute." Susan held out her hand. "You're sorry?" She put her hand on her hip. "Just like that, you're sorry? Boy, what's gotten in to you today?" Susan held up her hand and waved it at Mike. "Don't tell me, let me guess. She's about five foot five, short brown hair. You made it with the detective, didn't you?"

Mike shifted his gaze and tried not to smile. He stared at a spot on the wall above Susan's head. "Well, we had another date last night."

"Uh huh. Tell Auntie Sue all about it. What'd you do, where'd you go?" Susan motioned for Mike to talk.

"I cooked her dinner at my place."

"Your place. Hmmmmm. Women really go for that kind of treatment. Did you do it right? Used real dishes? Made more than one course?"

"Yes, yes, and yes." Mike laughed. Then his face grew serious. "It'd been a hard day for her. You know about Sam, right?"

Susan's face grew serious as well. Her hands dropped to her sides. "Yeah. I heard. He's a fighter, Sam is. He's gonna be okay. I'm praying for him to get through this."

"We all are."

Susan smiled. "That's all we can do." She folded her arms across her body and looked at Mike. "So, is it serious?"

"Huh? Oh, you mean me and Karen." Mike shuffled his feet. "I don't know. We're gonna give it a try and see how it goes."

"I knew working together would be a non-issue for you. That was just an excuse to not date after Melissa."

"Yeah. Maybe. I dunno." Mike shifted from one foot to the other. "I still think work can get in the way, but if we try not to let it, we just might have something here."

"Good for you, Mike. I'm glad for you."

"Thanks."

"Oh, hey. Some mail came in while you were down in the lab. Looks like mostly test results and stuff."

"Thanks. I'll take it back to the office where we can sort through it." Mike gathered up the stack of papers, envelopes, and interoffice memos and headed for the door. "Hey, boss," he said to the grayhaired woman standing in the doorway. She was dressed casually with a white lab coat over her clothes.

"I was looking for you two. You're on call today. Got a body in a vacant lot. I need you to get out there now. Who knows how long the body's been in this heat. You'll find all the information on this call sheet." She handed the call sheet to Mike and walked away, her rubber-soled shoes squeaking on the tiled floor.

"You heard the lady, let's go." Susan snapped her gloves off her hands and tossed them in the trashcan.

Mike tossed the stack of papers back on the table where he picked them up. The pile slid onto its side and papers scattered about. "I'll get to these when I get back," he said to no one in particular and raced for the door. "I'll get the SUV started and meet you at the back door." He tossed the message in the general direction of Susan.

"I'm right behind you," said Susan as she grabbed her Crime Tech windbreaker, thrust her arms into it, and zipped it up.

Mike started the big black SUV and backed it out of its parking spot. He stopped it at the back door and waited for Susan to climb in. Handing her the call sheet, he said, "Let's find this place on the map so we don't get lost looking for it." He turned the steering wheel and pulled out onto Lois Avenue. "We're looking for the Los Dos Amigos store on Sligh. You ever heard of it?"

"No, but then that ain't my neighborhood, you know?" "Well, we'll find out what kind of neighborhood it is soon enough."

Mike pulled up at the stoplight and leaned over to look at the spot Susan was pointing to on the map. He nodded that he understood, then turned back to watch the light.

"So, have you talked to Karen yet today?"

"No, but I didn't really expect to. We said we'd get together tonight when she left this morning and hurried back home to get ready for work."

"Oh really?" Susan turned and gave Mike an appraising look.

"What?"

"Nothing. I think it's great. I knew the two of you would get along. I should go into the matchmaking business." Susan looked as if she was very proud of herself.

"One success and you think you're a genius." Mike laughed. "Hey, one success is all it takes."

CHAPTER TWENTY-NINE

Kelly blinked her eyes and stared at the television. She didn't normally have it on during the day, but at the first sound of thunder she turned it on to get the weather forecast. Rain meant Mark could come home early and she always liked to be prepared.

She played the commercial again in her mind. *When love turns to violence.* The image of the young woman with a bruised and battered face dialing a number and talking to a counselor. Another image of her learning to leave safely and getting away. Starting her new life without fear of violence. Could it really be true? Kelly committed the telephone to memory. 555-SAFE. For the first time in her life she felt a spark of hope deep inside.

But what if Mark found out? He'd make her pay. He'd beat her senseless. What if he started in on the girls? He'd never hit them before, but this might push him over the edge. It was too dangerous. She'd never be able to pull it off. Mark was too smart.

What was the harm in calling? Kelly could do that. But when? It had to be before the girls came home from playing with their friends and before Mark got home from work. There would be no other way.

Did she dare call now? What would she say? Would they want to help? Kelly checked the clock on the wall. She had time. Maybe she could get some information from them in case it happened again. For next time.

Kelly's heart raced. She stood and paced between the kitchen and the living room. She squeezed her hands together to keep them from shaking. Stopping in front of the telephone, she reached a hand out to pick up the receiver. Her hand shook. Could she do this? She'd never told a single person about the things Mark did to her except when she had to take that polygraph. Could she tell someone now?
Without being held to the truth?

Pulling her hand back, Kelly doubted her ability to talk with a complete stranger. Would they judge her? She spun her wedding ring around and around on her finger. *You can always hang up,* she told herself. Feeling a little bit stronger, she once again stretched out her hand to pick up the telephone receiver. She touched the telephone. She willed her fingers to curl around the receiver. She picked it up and looked at the numbers. Slowly, pressing each number carefully, she dialed. 555-SAFE. If only that word could mean what it was meant to mean. Safe. When was the last time she felt safe?

The ringing lasted only a few seconds. A woman's voice sounded in her ear. "The Spring, this is Nancy, how can I help you?" Kelly hesitated.

"Hello? Is anyone there?" "I—I saw your ad on
TV."

"Are you safe?"

"Now? Yes. For now. I can't talk when my daughters get home."

Kelly felt a great fear rise up inside of her. "How...how does it work?"

"Let me tell you a little about our organization. The Spring of Tampa Bay is the largest emergency shelter for victims of domestic violence and their families. We have five locations. We not only offer a full spectrum of services to victim families, but we provide intervention services for offenders to help them accept responsibility for their actions."

"Their actions?" Kelly couldn't imagine Mark sitting down to discuss what he did to her.

"It's an option we give to the offender." Nancy's voice was calming.

"How do I leave?" Kelly asked the question, not sure if she wanted to hear the answer.

"Are you ready to be safe?"

Kelly didn't answer. She listened to her own breathing. Was she ready? What would she do when she left? How would she support herself and her children? "How can I ever be safe? What about my daughters?"

"We can help all of you. We have several options for you to help you leave your abusive situation."

"What are they?"

"You can call the police and report the abuse and the police will

bring you to our shelter."

Call the police on Mark? Oh my God, she could never do that. He'd be furious. "No, I don't think I can do that."

"All right. You can drive here on your own. We can give you the address and directions."

Kelly thought about taking Mark's truck. It was his pride and joy. He'd kill her if she did. She knew it just as she knew she had to take another breath to breathe. "No. I don't have a car of my own."

Nancy said that she didn't have to worry. "We also have volunteers that can come to you. We can make arrangements for a pick up time and all you have to do is leave."

Kelly nodded her head. "That sounds like the best option. Do I call you when I'm ready to leave?"

"We can make plans ahead of time. We can set a prearranged time for a volunteer to meet you a few blocks from your house."

"I don't know. This is all so confusing. I know Mark would kill me if he knew I was talking to you. What if he finds out?" Kelly leaned her head into her hand.

"Our location is kept a secret for those particular reasons."

"I have my two little girls to think about as well."

"We have room for both your daughters and you. There's an onsite school and after school activities. The Spring also provides counseling for you as well as your children."

"You make it sound so easy. But—" "I know how difficult it is to leave your husband and his abuse. I went through the same thing ten years ago. It was the best decision I ever made. We're here to help you and protect you. You haven't told me your name yet. Would you like to?"

"Kelly. My name is Kelly. And…and my husband, he hurts me."

"Kelly, would you like a safe place to go with your daughters?" Nancy asked.

Kelly lowered her voice to barely above a whisper. "Yes. Please."

"Let me explain what you'll need to pack. Use a garbage bag if you have to, but put in things like a few changes of clothes, identification for all of you, any medical records you may have, any medications, and anything that was in your name."

"I don't have nothing in my name. Mark, he said I didn't need to own nothing with him."

"The Spring provides you anything else you need like toothbrushes, toothpaste, soap, and other toiletries."

"When can you be here?"

"Any time you'd like. If you want to leave in the middle of the night, we'll meet you."

"No. No, I can't do that. Mark's not a sound sleeper. He'd know if I wasn't in bed. He works during the day when it's not raining. How about Monday after my girls get home from school? Mark, my husband, will still be at work. I hope."

"Kelly whatever works best for you so that you can be safe. Just give me your address and a specific time and we'll make sure a volunteer is waiting for you."

Kelly sighed. It just didn't seem real yet. She gave Nancy her address and told her that the volunteer could meet her at three o'clock Monday afternoon. The girls would be home from school by then. She raised a shaking hand to her face. She had to leave. She couldn't let her girls believe that it was okay for their daddy to hit their mommy— for any man to hit a woman. Not anymore. It wasn't right. She pressed a hand to her stomach. It twisted into a knot. She swallowed quickly before she threw up.

CHAPTER THIRTY

"Look, man. I told you already. We ain't seen Ray." The tall, thin, disheveled man poked a finger at Karen's face to punctuate his words.

"Don't," Karen said with an even but firm tone. "Don't point your finger at me." Karen wrinkled her nose at the sweaty stench emanating from the man. "Get back away from me. You stink."

"He told you we ain't seen him. What more do you want?" A shorter man with a small black moustache whined and squinted up into the sun. "Man, it's hot out here. How long you gonna keep us here?"

Karen exchanged looks with John Hendricks. She shrugged her shoulders then addressed the taller man. "Okay, Jose. Let's say you haven't seen Ray. When was the last time you saw him?"

"I dunno."

"You don't know?"

The thin man shuffled his feet in the dirt and kicked up a cloud of dust. "I don't see him all the time, you know? Sometimes he goes weeks without talking to me. I ain't his keeper, you know?" "Are you believing this shit?" Karen asked Hendricks.

"No. I don't believe one word of it. I think he's lying."

"I'm not lying!"

"Shut up," Karen addressed Jose. "Listen. We're not here to play games. If you don't talk to us, we'll take you down to the station and put your ass in jail. Maybe someone will get around to talking to you then. We'll charge you with accessory and get a warrant to search your place. What do you think your wife will say if we show up at your door?"

Jose's defiant look crumbled a bit under Karen's hard stare. He tried to sound brave, but his hand shook a bit as he wiped sweat from his forehead. "She ain't there."

"Well, that'll make things easy then, won't it? She won't have to know that you've violated probation again and this time the judge might not be so easy on you."

The shorter man spoke up. "Maria'll kick your ass if you get sent to jail. She told you that."

"Shut up, Manny. They ain't gonna take me nowhere and they know it," Jose said.

"Manny's right, Jose," Hendricks said. "You better listen to your friend. He sounds like he's looking out for you. Do you want to have to tell your wife about violating probation?" "What probation? You don't have nothing on me." "Turn out your pockets, Jose," Karen said.

"What?"

"You heard me, turn out your pockets."

"Shit." Jose stuffed his hands into the front pockets of his pants and then pulled them out. He kept his hands closed.

"Now, open your hands."

Jose hung his head. Dejected, he slowly opened one hand and then the other.

"Hmm, what do we have here? You see this?" Karen picked up a small, slender rolled cigarette from among the lint and change. She sniffed it. "I don't think this is part of your probation, Jose." She handed it to Hendricks. "Looks like we got enough to charge him with a probation violation. Imagine that."

Hendricks looked at Manny. "Okay, my friend. Your turn." "Oh, man. Come on." Manny started to back away.

"Stop right there. Don't move. I said, empty your pockets." Hendricks voice carried in the hot air.

Manny muttered under his breath in Spanish then plunged a hand into his pocket. He pulled it out and shoved it in Hendricks' face. "There, you satisfied?"

Hendricks plucked another carefully rolled cigarette from Manny's hand and added it to the one he held in his other hand. "Twins." Karen smiled. "Why don't we add a possession charge as well?" "Might as well." Hendricks smiled back.

"Oh, look, man. You gotta believe us, we ain't seen Ray," Jose begged.

"When was the last time you saw Ray?" Karen asked again. "And

I can tell when you're lying so don't bullshit me."

"No bullshit, man. This is the truth. The last time I saw Ray was about three or four days ago."

"Where did you see him?" Karen pulled out her notebook and started writing.

"My place. He stopped by real late. Said he was laying low and needed a place to crash."

"Did you let him stay?"

"Are you shittin' me? My wife said no, that means no." Jose swiped at his face. "Ray knows that. He must have been desperate to come by my place."

"Did he say where he was going?"

"No, man. He said something about hanging out at the park, to wait for Manny." Jose turned to his short friend. "Did he ever catch up with you, man?"

Manny jerked his head up. "Not me. I didn't go to the park. I scored some—I mean I stayed home that night. He didn't come to my house neither."

"What about his place. Did he say why he couldn't stay there?"

"He just said it was getting too hot to hang there." Jose sneered at Karen. "You cops kept coming by, he said."

Ignoring his sneer, Karen asked, "Did he say anything about the woman that was staying with him?"

"Maggie? Nah. Not really. I think he said something like 'the bitch wouldn't turn him in if she knew what was good for her.' Or something like that." He shrugged his shoulders as if to say he didn't pay much attention.

Karen and Hendricks exchanged looks. Karen bet he was thinking the same thing she was, that Ray might have thought Maggie turned him in and beat her for it. Karen tapped her pen against her notebook and thought for a moment. She looked at the two men who stood before her. They were hot and sweaty. So was she. The miserable heat beat down on her head. The humidity pressed in around her, as if suffocating her. Her t-shirt was stuck to her back beneath her blazer. After leaving Mike's place this morning, she didn't have time for much except a short run and a quick shower. She would have been late otherwise. Getting dressed up wasn't high on her priority list. She couldn't give herself any time to think about Mike. She had a job to do. "Look. I'm going to talk to my partner here about what we're going to do with you." Karen eyed both men. "Don't move."

Karen and Hendricks stepped a few feet away from the nervous men and put their heads together. "You want to bust them?" Hendricks asked.

"Not really. I think they told the truth finally. I doubt they have anything left," Karen said to her partner, but kept an eye on the two men.

"Okay then, it's your call. We'll let them off with a warning." Hendricks blew out his breath. "I'm through with them."

Karen and Hendricks walked back over and stood in front of the two men. Hendricks spoke first, "It's your lucky day, boys."

"You're not taking us in?" Manny asked with a slight whimper to his voice.

"Nope."

"What about our…?" Manny eyed Hendricks hand.

"This? Yeah, right." Hendricks laughed. He held his hand open and said, "Say goodbye, fellas." He unrolled each small joint and let the contents spill onto the ground. For good measure, he kicked at the dirt to mix it up. He crumpled the papers and placed them in his pocket.

"I catch you with pot again and I won't be so lenient." Karen stared hard at the two men. "I'll have your ass in jail so fast you won't know what hit you." Karen pointed a finger at Manny. "What do you think your mother would say if she had to bail you out of jail again?" "Oh, man," Manny whined.

"Shut up, man." Jose growled at his friend.

"I suggest you stay away from Ray Thomas too. He's bad news right now and anyone caught with him is gonna be in some deep shit," Hendricks said.

"Do you understand what we're telling you?" Karen asked.

"Yeah, man. We get you." Looking relieved that he wasn't going to jail, Jose brought back some of his swagger. It didn't last long.

"When we catch up to Ray, we might come back looking for your two anyway, no matter if Ray tells us you two were involved or not." Karen eyed Jose with disdain. "Let's see what your wife has to say about that, Jose."

"We ain't done nuthin'."

"We'll see." Karen motioned with her head. "Now go on, get out of here before I change my mind."

Jose and Manny looked at the detectives standing in front of them then looked at each other. They turned and quickly started walking away.

"You could have busted them, you know?" Hendricks said as he walked back to their car and opened the driver side door.

"I know. But I'm hoping they lead us to Ray." Karen opened the car door and slid into the passenger seat.

Hendricks slid behind the wheel and turned on the car. Hot air poured from the air conditioning vents. "It'll cool off in a minute or two. So, how'd you know they had marijuana on them?"

"I didn't. I just guessed. God, it's hot." Karen pulled at her tshirt and blew down the front. She positioned the passenger air vents so that they pointed directly at her. "Why can't these guys hang out in air conditioned buildings? Why do they always hang out on a hot, dirty street corner?"

"That's a rhetorical question, right?" Hendricks laughed. "Nice guess. It shows you have good instincts. Always trust them."

"Yeah." Karen sighed. "Let's follow these guys and see where they go."

"You're the boss." Hendricks put the car in gear and drove slowly in the direction the men had taken.

"If they know what's good for them, they'll head home. Jose lives down the street here. Manny, he lives further, about three streets over." Karen pointed her finger toward the direction of Manny's house.

"Don't these guys work?"

"Sometimes. They pick up day labor jobs around the end of the month when the benefits start running low. Manny, he lives with his mother and she works."

"Shit. Some kind of life, huh?"

"Jose's got a family. He could make something of himself if he'd just quit the drugs and alcohol. I dunno why Maria puts up with him."

"Maybe we didn't do him such a great favor by not busting his ass. Maybe some time in jail might help dry him out."

CHAPTER THIRTY-ONE

On her way home after her shift, Karen dialed Mike's cell phone and waited for him to answer.

"Connelly here."

"Mike, it's me, Karen."

"Hi." His voice was low and inviting.

"How are you feeling?"

"Tired, but good. You?"

"Same. God, it was hot today. All I want to do is go home and take off these clothes and jump in the shower."

Mike groaned. "Don't tease me like that. I still have a couple more hours here at least."

"That works out then. I'll go home and start the sauce—it takes a couple of hours to cook—while you finish up there…" If Karen hadn't been driving and needed her hand she'd have smacked it up against her forehead. "I'm sorry, I didn't even think to ask. Would you like to come over for dinner?"

"I would like to come over for dinner, yes." Mike laughed. "And I'm excited to see you again too."

"I kind of went a little overboard there, didn't I?"

"Just a bit."

Karen cringed while she kept her eyes on the road. "I hope you didn't think I was just assuming that you would come over. That's not how I meant it."

"I didn't think that at all. As a matter of fact, you saved me a phone call because I was going to call you."

"I'm glad I called first." Karen paused. "Mike?"

"Yeah?"

"Bring your running gear."

One her way home, Karen stopped at her local grocery store and picked up fresh tomatoes, onions, garlic, and ground sirloin for her homemade sauce. She found a box of manicotti and added that to her basket. In the dairy section, she found ricotta cheese and some shredded mozzarella and Parmesan. On her way to the checkout stand, she passed a floral display. On impulse, she grabbed a bouquet of multi-colored flowers and added them to her basket as well. She strolled through the bakery looking for something for dessert when she remembered the display of strawberries in the produce section. After hurrying back to pick up the strawberries and some salad fixings, she sailed through the checkout and loaded her groceries into her car. The ride home was short and it wasn't long before she'd unloaded her groceries onto the kitchen counter and was looking through her array of spices for the oregano and thyme.

While Karen waited for a pot of water to boil, she browned the ground sirloin and added onions, garlic, and a few other herbs. She hoped Mike liked garlic because she used a lot. Turning the heat to low under the ground beef mixture, she sorted through her mail then made the salad. A hissing noise from the stove brought her attention back to cooking. The pot of water was boiling. She dipped the tomatoes into the boiling water and waited for the skins to split. Once they did, she pulled the tomatoes back out of the water and skinned them. After slicing the partially boiled tomatoes, she added them to the ground beef mixture, covered the pot with a lid and let the sauce cook.

Now it was Karen's turn. She picked up her blazer and holster from where she'd thrown them before she started cooking and headed for her bedroom. Looking at her bedroom with a critical eye, she wondered if Mike would think it too feminine. Normally she didn't like ruffles and lace, and considered a v-neck t-shirt dressing up, but there was something innately soothing and comforting about her white lace and lemon yellow comforter, along with the matching pillow shams and bed ruffle. She hoped Mike would see the netting draped around her brass headboard and understand that there was a more feminine side to her than the image she presented at work.

Karen stripped off her sweaty clothes and walked naked to her bathroom to turn on the shower. She let it run for a few moments to get to the right temperature before stepping in and closing the glass shower door. She'd never regret adding a sunken tub and separate shower stand to her bathroom, even though it cost extra and caused a few nightmares for the construction engineer and architect.

Karen soaped her body with a coconut scented body wash and thought of last night and the way Mike had touched her body. She shivered with delight as she recalled the intimate ways Mike had kissed her. She let her head fall back under the flow of the shower as the water soaked her hair. It felt good to wash away the sweat and grime of the day.

After rinsing away the soap and shampoo, Karen turned the temperature a bit cooler and stood in the refreshing stream. Her thoughts turned steamy as she imagined what tonight would be like with Mike. Would he touch her in the same ways? Could they seek even more pleasure and satisfaction? She smiled under the torrent of cool water. Wholeheartedly, her answers were 'yes.'

Remembering that she had left her sauce cooking on the stove, she breathed a heavy sigh and turned off the water. Reluctantly, she stepped out of the shower and toweled herself dry. Slipping into her robe, she knotted it quickly as she walked back into the kitchen to check on dinner.

Stirring the sauce, Karen helped it along by mashing the tomato slices until the sauce was thick. Letting it continue to cook, she pulled out the ricotta, mozzarella, and Parmesan cheeses. Mixing them together with an egg, some fresh parsley from the refrigerator, and a dash of salt and pepper, she let the cheese mixture stand for a few moments while she prepared the garlic bread.

Everything was ready; all she had to do was cook the manicotti and stuff the shells. She started another pot of water to boil while she slipped back into the bedroom to get dressed.

She stood in front of her closet and wondered what to wear. She wanted to be comfortable and relaxed so chose a soft pair of pale blue lounging pants with a drawstring tie and a matching tank top.

Back in the kitchen she put the manicotti shells in the boiling water and stirred the cheese mixture. It was the right consistency for stuffing. Removing the lid from the saucepan, she stirred the sauce and took a little taste. It was just how she liked it. She left the lid off so the sauce could cook down to a thick consistency and checked the manicotti. She didn't want the shells to overcook and be too difficult to stuff. There was nothing worse than limp manicotti. Karen laughed at herself and hummed as she busied herself wiping up messes and putting her kitchen to rights. She liked to clean as she cooked so that when she was done, there was nothing left to clean up.

Reaching into a top cupboard, Karen found a vase. She snipped the ends off the flowers she purchased and placed them in the vase with water and placed the vase onto the dining room table. The timer's insistent buzzing brought her back to the kitchen to rinse the manicotti, stuff the shells, cover them with sauce and extra mozzarella, and slip the whole thing into a preheated oven.

After washing the strawberries and putting them into the refrigerator to chill, Karen cleaned up the final dishes and pans she'd used for cooking, dried them, and placed them back into the cupboards. She looked around. Her kitchen was neat and tidy. Just the way she liked it. Catching a glimpse of the flowers in the dining room, Karen decided they needed some rearranging. While doing so, the doorbell chimed. She checked her watch and couldn't believe how much time had passed. Mike was here already.

Checking her peephole, Karen smiled and then opened the door wide.

"Hi, Mike."

"Hi, yourself." Mike stood in Karen's doorway with a matching grin on his face.

Karen leaned forward and pulled him into her foyer and closed the door. Stepping on her tiptoes, she rested her hands on Mike's shoulders and brushed his lips with hers. Mike held her by the waist while he deepened the kiss. Breathless, Karen broke free. "Wow," Karen said as she touched a fingertip to her swollen lips.

"I didn't think I could miss someone that much," Mike said. "I thought about you all day."

"Me too."

Karen led Mike by the hand into the living room then motioned for him to take a seat on the sofa.

"I'll be right back. I just need to check on dinner." Karen moved into the kitchen.

"Take your time. I'll just sit here and relax."

"Make yourself a drink if you want. I think there's wine on the cart as well," Karen called from the kitchen. She reset the timer for fifteen minutes then went back into the living room to join Mike on the sofa.

"Did you get to see Sam today?" Mike asked as he lifted one of Karen's hands and held it in his.

Karen let her smile fade. "No, but I did talk to his wife. He's about the same, but the doctors have hope that once the swelling goes down he'll wake up from his coma. They're also uncertain about the paralysis." Karen balled her other hand into a fist and beat the sofa cushion. "It's just not fair. Sam doesn't deserve this. He's one of the last good guys."

"I know. Don't beat yourself up about it."

"But if only I'd been there Thomas might not have gotten the jump on Sam."

"You can't change the past. You could play the 'if only' game until you're blue in the face, but it won't change anything. So why start?"

"You're right." Karen sighed. "Of course, I hold onto my right to throw a temper tantrum at a moment's notice."

Mike laughed. "I bet you do."

"Speaking of tantrums, I got assigned a new partner today."

"Who?"

"John Hendricks."

"He's a good man. Experienced like Sam. You'll like working with him."

"I already do. He helped me out today and I really appreciated it." Karen lifted her chin. "He said I had good instincts."

"He did? So what do your instincts tell you about me?" Mike stroked the back of Karen's hand.

"Hmmm," Karen pretended to think about Mike's question. "My instincts say you're completely trustworthy and that I'll always be safe with you."

Mike hugged her as he said, "You do have good instincts."

Karen lifted her mouth and met Mike's as he brought his head down. They kissed slowly and languidly, taking their time as they explored each other's lips.

"So, how long until dinner?" Mike asked between kisses.

"Not long enough."

"Damn."

Karen smiled as she kissed Mike. "It'll be worth the wait, don't worry."

"I'm not worried, just …how should I put this? Motivated. Yeah. I'm motivated."

Karen slid her hand up the inside of Mike's jean clad thigh and felt the firmness of his hard on. "I guess you are motivated." She giggled. "Dinner first. Then dessert."

"I was always a naughty little boy. I never did get that whole dinner routine figured out properly." Mike kissed the tip of Karen's nose. "You say dessert comes after dinner?"

"After."

"Damn." Mike slid his hands up under the hem of Karen's top and stroked her flat abdomen. "Always?" His fingers stretched toward her breasts.

Karen sighed with pleasure. The timer's alarm went off, interrupting Mike's touch. "Always," she said and lifted herself off the sofa.

Mike leaned back and said, "I think I'll just sit here for a few moments, if you don't mind." Karen watched him as he wriggled his hips in an attempt to rearrange himself so that his jeans weren't pressing so tightly onto his groin.

Karen smiled. "I'll be right back. I just have to take out the manicotti and put in the garlic bread."

Mike waved a hand at Karen. "Go ahead. Do what you gotta do."

Karen readjusted her top and smoothed it down over her breasts and stomach. She could feel Mike's eyes on her.

"Oh, God." Mike groaned. "Just don't do that."

"I better get that timer." Karen smiled at Mike then turned away and headed toward the kitchen. She had half a mind to let the manicotti sit in the stove and stay warm while she and Mike indulged with dessert first. However, a cooler head prevailed and she was able to bank the flames of desire for the moment. She knew it would be that much better when they waited.

Using potholders, Karen lifted the manicotti out of the oven and placed it on the counter. Removing the salads from the refrigerator, she set the chilled plates onto the dinner plates already on the dining room table. Looking over the table she couldn't find anything else missing so she walked back into the living room to get Mike.

"Dinner's ready," she said. "How are you doing? You ready?" She cocked her head to the side and gave him a wry grin.

Mike stood up and spread out his hands. "Looks like I'm good to go. Lead on, woman."

"I hope you like it; it's a recipe that my mother gave me." "I'm sure I will. It smells delicious."

"Why don't you sit here," Karen motioned to the first chair, "then I'll sit over here." She slid into her chair.

Mike lifted his glass of wine. "To good food, and to good company." He looked deeply into Karen's eyes. "To us." "To us." Karen lifted her glass and drank.

Their talk settled around light topics and current events. After they finished their salads, Karen took their salad plates into the kitchen and returned with the manicotti. She served Mike then herself. She watched as Mike took his first bite. He closed his eyes as if savoring the taste. She couldn't wait. "What do you think?"

Swallowing, Mike said, "This is the best manicotti I've ever tasted. Even beats out Anthony's downtown."

Pleased, Karen smiled. "Thank you." She lifted her fork and started in on her dinner.

"I'm serious. This is good." Mike eagerly lifted another bite to his mouth.

"I'm glad you like it."

"Maybe there's something to this 'eat dinner first' thing after all."

Karen laughed, nearly spewing the contents of her mouth. She hastily applied her napkin to her lips. "Don't say things like that when I'm eating," Karen said as she grinned. "Look what you made me do."

"You started it by telling me dessert was after dinner."

"Well, maybe we won't have dessert at all," Karen said with a sly grin.

"I'll be good." Mike pasted on a serious look. "See, I'm eating my dinner."

"That's better. We're grownups." Karen couldn't keep a straight face. A giggle escaped. "We have grownup dinners."

Mike's serious look was destroyed with a lifting of the corners of his mouth. "That's right," he said in a deep voice and using his finger and thumb to pull down the corners of his mouth. "Grownups." Karen and Mike finished the rest of their dinner in between talking about current events and making each other laugh. As Karen carried the dirty dishes into the kitchen and Mike carried their wine glasses into the living room, she reflected on the evening so far. She'd never felt so close so quickly to someone before. She felt perfectly at ease with Mike as if she'd known him her whole life. His easygoing attitude and humor gave her a warm feeling. Never had she felt so compatible with one person.

After loading the dishwasher, Karen made her way back to the living room. Mike motioned for her to sit next to him on the sofa. She picked up her glass of wine and cuddled up next to him, tucking her feet underneath her.

Taking a sip of wine, Karen sighed and laid a hand on Mike's thigh. "I'm glad you could make it tonight."

With his arm around Karen's shoulder, Mike stroked her bare arm. "Yeah. Me too."

"Hand me that remote on the table, will you?"

Mike leaned over to reach it. "This one?"

"Yeah." Karen took the remote and pushed a few buttons. Soft music filled the room from discreetly placed surround sound speakers. "Nice," Mike said with approval in his voice.

"Thanks. I had the system put in when the townhouse was built." Karen leaned her head back into the crook of Mike's arm. "This place is my sanctuary away from the drama and tragedy that is prevalent with our business."

"I understand. I feel the same way about my place."

"It's important to have a place to go. To get away from work." Karen rubbed her hand along Mike's thigh. "Sometimes it's just as important to have someone to go to when you want to get away from work."

Mike held Karen close. "I think that's true too." He leaned his head over and kissed her on the forehead.

Karen tilted her head up so that she could look at Mike. "I'm glad you think so."

Mike placed a hand under Karen's chin and brought his lips down upon hers. His kiss started out softly and slowly, with gentle touches. Karen turned into Mike's arms and stretched her body across his. She kissed Mike back, searching and seeking unspoken questions with her lips. He answered back, turning the kiss harder and more ardent. His hands roamed her body, touching her, feeling her soft curves. Karen ached to have Mike touch her completely. She sighed with relief when his hands found the edge of her tank top and moved inside to touch her skin. His fingers caressed her smooth skin, stroking back and forth along her waist and up further until they reached her breasts.

Karen's hands ached to touch Mike. She sought out the point where his shirt tucked into his jeans and pulled until the hem of the shirt broke free. Eagerly, she ran her hands across his hard, flat stomach and up towards his solid chest. Her fingernails lightly scraped through the curled hair.

They twisted and turned about on the sofa, each trying to get a better position to touch the other. "Wait, wait." Karen gasped for air as she pushed herself to a sitting position. "Why are we struggling with this out here when I've got a perfectly good bed going to waste?"

"Makes sense to me." Mike stood up and helped her to her feet. He stood behind her and wrapped his arms about her. As she walked, Mike followed closely behind. In seconds, they were in Karen's bedroom.

She untangled herself from Mike's arms and reached for the lace cover on her bed. "Let me pull the covers down."

Mike reached for the button on his jeans. "On or off?" Karen looked back at him. "Definitely off."

Mike grinned. "Then they're coming off." Kicking off his shoes, he hurriedly unbuttoned and unzipped his jeans and jerked them down his legs. Balancing on one foot, he pulled out one leg, and then the other then removed his socks.

Karen crossed her arms in front of herself and grabbed the hem of her tank top. "How about it? On or off?"

"Definitely off. But wait. Let me do it."

Karen stood quietly and watched as Mike unbuttoned his shirt and took it off. He added it to the pile of clothes he compiled on the floor of Karen's bedroom. Finished, he walked naked to Karen and tugged at her top. Carefully he lifted it over her head and tossed it aside.

Next, he untied the string at the top of her lounging pants and lowered them down her legs kneeling in front of her.

Using Mike's shoulders to help her balance, Karen lifted one leg then the other out of her pants.

As he stood, Mike let one of his hands smooth their way up Karen's leg, across her thigh, and settle over her panty-clad mound. "These have to come off too."

Karen hooked a finger in each side of her panties, pulled them down to her hips, and looked at Mike while batting her eyelashes. "These?"

Mike's voice grew rough with desire. "Those."

Planting a quick kiss on Mike's lips, Karen pushed her panties over her hips and kicked them off. She turned and crawled into her bed and beckoned Mike to follow her.

Mike paused for a moment, reaching down for his jeans. "I know we didn't... I mean we kind of rushed into..." He pulled a condom out of his pocket and held it out to Karen. "We didn't use any protection last night, and I don't want to make that same mistake again tonight."

"I don't know if you remember, but I'm on the pill."

"That takes care of pregnancy issues, but what about...?" Mike lowered his eyes and lifted his eyebrows.

"I haven't had sex in three years. I think I'm free of any sexually transmitted diseases, unless you...ummm...might be...?

"Me? No." Mike said hastily. "My last physical, I got a clean bill of health. And I haven't had sex in a while either."

Karen smiled and held out her arms. Dropping the condom, Mike slid into Karen's arms and kissed her full on the mouth.

"Well, I'm glad that's taken care of," Karen said as she stroked Mike's back.

"I had to ask."

"I'm glad you did. Even if you blushed."

"I didn't blush!"

"Whatever you say." Karen chuckled. "Although, you're right. We should have had this conversation last night."

"Conversation is over." Mike grinned with a wicked look in his eye as he looked down at Karen. "Now it's time for other things." He kissed her quick. "Fun things." He kissed her again. "Very fun things."

Karen pushed at Mike's shoulder and rolled him over onto his back. She balanced herself across his body. "Comfy?"

"Yes, why?"

"It's my turn to have some fun, you just lay back there and relax and let me concentrate." Karen trailed kisses from Mike's jaw line, down his neck and across his chest.

"Yes, ma'am." Mike laid his head back on a ruffled pillow and grinned.

Karen ran her hands across Mike's firm chest and tweaked his nipples. She pinched them lightly between her thumb and finger until they grew as hard as little pebbles. She flicked her tongue out and tasted one nipple and then the other, feeling their hardness with her lips.

She slid her body lower over Mike's and continued to trail kisses down his chest, then his stomach, finally reaching his groin. His penis, large and heavy, pushed outward like a pointing arrow. She wrapped one hand around it, smiling as it quivered in her hand, sensitive to her touch.

Flicking out her tongue, she licked from one side to the other, amazed at how hard Mike was beneath the velvety softness of his skin. Karen took her time, licking then lightly blowing each spot with her warm breath.

Mike groaned deeply in response, reaching for Karen with his hands and running his fingers through her hair.

Mike's response spurred Karen on to take Mike's penis into her mouth, sucking at it lightly. His hardness filled her mouth. She breathed deep of his scent, filling her senses.

"Baby, you've got to stop," Mike gasped, sucking in air to fill his lungs.

Karen shook her head.

Insistent, Mike pulled Karen up and lifted her onto his penis. His wetness found hers and he pressed deep inside of her. Filling her completely. Totally.

Karen moved up and down as she rode Mike's body. The sensations built inside of her. She knew she was coming and she didn't want to stop it. Giving herself over to the mounting emotions as she straddled Mike's body, Karen let her head fall back. She closed her eyes and focused on the pleasures she was experiencing. A small voice inside of her wondered if Mike was feeling as much pleasure as she, and knew he was. Karen marveled at her heightened sensory perception. It was as if she and Mike were one being, sharing the same awareness.

She opened her eyes and looked down at Mike. He watched her with a thoughtful expression on his face. Trembling, she smiled. He smiled in return as he lifted his hips and thrust deep inside of her. His moves were slow and deliberate, his stroke sure. Karen matched his strokes, moving her body above his, meeting his thrust.

The tension started to build even more; she knew she was close. She arched her back, her movements quicker. Her hands spread across Mike's chest, seeking, searching for a strong hold. Mike increased the rhythm, letting Karen set the pace. Faster and faster. A low growl built up in the back of her throat, breaking free. She gripped Mike's shoulders, hanging on. In seconds, she was over the top, bursting into a million pinpricks of light as Mike thrust again and again as he exploded along with her. Their bodies covered with glistening, slick sweat, they fell into each other's arms, gasping for air. Mike held Karen close, her chilled skin warmed by his arms and the rest of his body.

It was several long minutes before Karen could stir herself to move. She slid along and over Mike's body until she was lying beside him, her arm thrown across his chest. She waited for her breath to slow before she spoke. "We never did have dessert."

Mike forced a laugh from his exhausted body. "What was dessert?"

"Strawberries. Fresh ones."

"Strawberries? Mmmm, I like strawberries."

"Well, then you just stay where you are and I'll be right back." Karen slid out of bed and reached for her robe. She belted it as she walked into the kitchen. Opening the refrigerator, she pulled out the chilled bowl of strawberries and grabbed a couple of napkins.

Returning to the bedroom, she handed Mike the bowl and napkins so that she could remove her robe and crawl back into bed.

"Hey, this is cold!" Mike exclaimed as he sat up in bed.

"They've been in the refrigerator, silly." Sitting cross-legged next to Mike, Karen picked up a strawberry and held it to his mouth so he could taste.

Mike chewed thoroughly, savoring the sweetness. "They are good." He licked his lips and eyed the bowl with hunger. "How'd you get strawberries now? Isn't picking season over here in Florida?"

Karen watched the expression of longing on Mike's face and grinned. She picked up another strawberry held it out to him, and then popped it into her mouth instead. She laughed as she chewed. "The package said California. Guess they have a later season."

"That was not fair. I'm bigger than you. I should get twice as many berries." Mike pushed out his lower lip to pout.

"You want to come between me and food? I don't think so."

"I should know better by now."

Nodding her head, Karen said, "Yes, you'd better." As a consolation, she picked a big strawberry from the bowl and let Mike eat it from her fingers. When he was finished, she wiped her hand on a napkin.

"You know," Mike said thoughtfully, "I think these strawberries could be put to good use."

Karen lifted her head and looked at him, "What do you mean?"

Mike carefully set the bowl aside. He picked one strawberry from the bowl and bit it in half. As he chewed one half he looked at the other half in his hand, then looked at Karen.

She eyed him with a wary look. "What are you going to do with that?"

Mike cocked his head and with a sly look grinned at Karen, "Want to find out?"

Karen's breath caught in her throat. "I think so."

He brought the strawberry to her breast and wiped strawberry juice gently across her nipple. The juice dripped only a little. Leaning over, he kissed and licked at her nipple until all the juice was washed away.

Karen shivered. "Now that's a recipe you won't find in Betty Crocker's cookbook."

Mike placed the other half of the strawberry into his mouth. "It's my personal favorite." He kissed Karen's lips sharing the juices of the strawberry with her.

"I like how you share," Karen said as she licked her lips.

"I'm really a friendly guy."

"I'm beginning to see that. I like people who share." Karen used her napkin to wipe a spot of juice from the corner of Mike's mouth.

"Does that mean you like me?" "Oh, that definitely means I like you."

"Good, because I like you too." Mike kissed her quickly on the mouth. "I'm never going to hear the end of this from Susan, though."

Karen lifted her head. "Susan?" Biting her lip, she said, "She did push awful hard to get us together, didn't she?"

"Yep. And, she's quite proud of herself, as a matter of fact." Mike chuckled tossing another strawberry into his mouth.

"Remind me to send her a thank you card." Karen selected a berry from the bowl and bit into it. She chewed quickly when she saw Mike's head moving closer to hers.

Mike leaned over and pressed his mouth to Karen's juice stained lips. "Send one for me too." He kissed her deeply and thoroughly.

When Mike lifted his head, Karen gasped for air. This man literally took her breath away. How could one man make her life so perfect and turn it upside down at the same time?

CHAPTER THIRTY-TWO

Sunday passed with Kelly walking on eggshells around Mark and keeping the girls entertained so that they didn't bother him. It was one of the longest days she'd ever experienced. Monday couldn't have come soon enough, although it too dragged by.

She checked her watch for what must have been the hundredth time. She couldn't believe how slow the day was going. And just to make her even more nervous, the day started out cloudy and gray with a threat of rain. She'd already sent up a dozen prayers that Mark wouldn't come home early from work today.

She managed to get the girls off to school and Mark his breakfast with minimal trouble. But she'd failed miserably at trying to stay out of Mark's reach. Touching her swollen cheek, she winced a bit at the sting of pain. His temper had been short as soon as he saw the clouds in the sky.

If she had any doubts about not leaving today, her mind was definitely made up, thanks to the latest damage Mark inflicted. Her face hadn't healed from the last time he'd hit her, so this new bruise was in addition to the others on her face.

Kelly paced the house, looking to make sure everything was in order. She'd already thrown up twice and didn't think her nerves could handle much more stress. Chewing the side of her fingernail, she went over the plan again in her head.

As soon as the girls got home from school, she'd help them pack their backpacks and choose one toy each. She felt bad that they would have to leave their toys behind, but she'd make it up to them somehow. She hoped that sometime in the future they'd understand why she was making them leave their home and their daddy.

Kelly checked her watch again. She groaned in frustration. The minute hand seemed to creep along. She thought about eating, but knew it would only make her upset stomach worse. Instead, she concentrated on her breathing. Slow and steady. Deep breaths in and out. It didn't seem to have any affect on her rapidly beating heart. Anxious, Kelly chewed her thumbnail.

Agonizing about whether she was doing the right thing, Kelly wondered what Mark would do as soon as he found out they'd gone. He'd call her parents, she was sure of it. It hurt her that she couldn't call her parents and tell them what was going on, but she knew that as soon as she was safe at The Spring, she'd be able to call. It was going to be hard enough telling them that Mark hit her and she wasn't going to take it anymore, let alone explain to them that she had taken her children and left Mark for good.

Left Mark for good. The words repeated themselves over and over again in her mind. She needed to throw up again. Hurrying to the bathroom, she lifted the lid on the toilet and bent over. Her stomach contracted. She heaved into the toilet, but nothing came up. Her stomach was completely empty.

Lifting her head, Kelly brushed back her hair from her face. She went to the sink and splashed a handful of cool water on her warm skin. Patting it dry with a towel, she looked around the bathroom. Was there anything she'd forgotten to pack? She checked the medicine cabinet. No. She'd packed everything that was important. Doubting herself, she went back into her bedroom and checked to make sure she hadn't left anything in there that she might need. She hated second-guessing herself, but she knew she only had one chance at this and she wanted to do it right.

Hearing the familiar squeal of the school bus's hydraulic brakes, she hurried to the front door and opened it. Kelly watched her daughters jump from the bus's last step to the ground and race to the house. This was it.

"Girls, listen to me. We're going on an adventure and we have to hurry up and get packed."

"An adventure, Mommy?" Amber asked.

"Where?" asked Ashley.

"It's a surprise," Kelly told her girls. "Let's take your things into your room and get started." Kelly kept her voice light and a smile on her face. She didn't want her daughters to sense that anything was wrong.

Kelly led the way into the girls' bedroom. "The first thing I want you to do is dump out your backpacks on your beds." She helped
Amber unbuckle her backpack. "Right there, dump it out."

"Like this, Momma?"

"Yes, Ashley, just like that. Now. I want you to each get your favorite toy and put it next to your backpack."

"Can I bring Henry?" Amber held up her stuffed teddy bear. "He says he wants to go on an adventure."

"Put Henry next to your backpack. Now, listen to me. I want you to each pick a favorite book to read," Kelly said as she opened the girls' dresser and sorted through their clothes. She pulled out underwear, socks, t-shirts, and shorts for them to pack. She made sure to grab enough for several days. She didn't have room for anymore.

"Did you pick a book? Hurry up, Ashley, pick one book. No. Just one." She dropped clothes next to each backpack. "Now, I want you to put your clothes in your backpack."

"Why?" Amber looked up. "Are we spending the night?"

"We might." Kelly helped her youngest put her clothes in her bag. "It's always good to be prepared, don't you think?"

"Yes."

"Yes," Ashley repeated her sister's response, and nodded.

"Are we packed?" Kelly asked.

The girls nodded.

"Good. Now, put your book in your bag and carry your toy. We're going for a short walk."

"Where?"

"Who's house are we going to?"

"I told you, it's a surprise." Kelly led the girls out of their bedroom, down the hall and into the living room. She picked up her bag from next to the door and looked at her watch. It was finally time. "Are we ready?" Kelly looked down at her brave girls.

"Yes."

"What about Daddy?" Amber asked, looking around the room.

Kelly didn't know what to say. She scrambled for something to tell her daughters.

Ashley spoke up first. "This is a girl adventure, no boys allowed." She looked up at her mom as if seeking reassurance.

"That's right." Kelly sighed with relief. "This is a girl adventure. You guessed it, Ashley."

Opening the front door, Kelly let the girls out then took a deep breath. She shut the door behind her. Biting her lower lip, she tightened her grip on her bag of clothes. She stood straight and squared her shoulders. This was it.

Chapter Thirty-Three

Karen turned the doorknob and entered the darkened house. No windows had been opened and the air smelled dank and dusty.

She gave herself time to orient on her surroundings, recalling the last time she was here when she'd discovered Sam's badly beaten body. After her eyes adjusted, she was able to make out the dirt and grime clinging to the furniture. It looked the same, just messier.

Not knowing where to start, Karen walked deeper into the living room and glanced around. Furniture had been pushed aside from the wave of police and rescue personnel that had crammed into the small house that eventful afternoon. Karen pulled a pair of latex gloves out of her pocket and put them on. She wasn't sure what she was looking for, but didn't want to compromise it once she found it.

Sweat beads sprung up on Karen's forehead. She used the sleeve of her jacket to wipe them away. She couldn't concentrate with the room in the condition it was so she set about righting it. She picked up an overturned end table and placed it back where she thought it went and pushed chairs back to their original positions on the stained floor. That was better. This was how she remembered the room.

She put herself back to the day of the event. She had talked to Sam on his cell phone and everything was fine. For Ray Thomas to get a jump on Sam, he must have attacked Sam first. Then he attacked Maggie. Otherwise, Sam would have heard the attack on Maggie and responded. What made Maggie stay and not run for help while Sam was beaten? Did Thomas have a gun as well? Sam was beaten severely about the head and face. Did Thomas use an object? What could he have used? Karen looked around the room for anything that might have been used as a weapon. She checked under the couch cushions and cringed at the dirt and garbage she found, glad she was wearing gloves.

Not finding any possible weapons in the living room, Karen entered the kitchen to extend her search. She looked in drawers and pulled open cabinets all in vain. Wiping her brow with the sleeve of her jacket, she tossed a used spatula back into the sink with the other dirty dishes and sighed. She wasn't getting anywhere in there. There were only two rooms left—the bathroom and the bedroom. Not looking forward to either one of them, Karen chose the bedroom first. She pushed open the door and entered. At first glance, the room was sparsely furnished. There was a bed that took up most of the room and that was it. The closet door was wedged open with a pile of clothes that Karen didn't dare investigate further to determine if they were clean or dirty. The bed held an assortment of mismatched sheets and a couple of flattened, sweat stained pillows. Karen took a deep breath of the sour, stale, hot air and started her search. She looked under the bed and under the mattress, trying her best not to let any of the dirty bed linen touch her.

She kicked her way through the various piles of clothes on the floor until she got to the pile in the closet. At first kick, she encountered nothing but more clothes, but her second kick hit something hard. Kneeling down, Karen pushed aside the array of clothes until she uncovered the object she'd practically stumbled across.

Blinking twice, Karen stared at the pair of hiking boots buried beneath the pile of clothes. Using her forefinger and a thumb she carefully picked one of the boots up and held it up to her face so that she could see it properly. It was nearly identical to the pair they'd removed from the house earlier. Only smaller. Karen picked up the other boot in the same way with her other hand and stood up. She examined them with growing suspicion. Which pair of boots was the right pair to match the footprint found at the little boy's murder site? Now Karen had a choice for FDLE's lab to consider.

Looking around the room, she figured she looked in all the logical and illogical places where someone could hide a weapon. She had to tell herself that it was possible that Thomas had taken the weapon with him when he fled the house. Giving up on her search, she carried the pair of boots in one arm as she exited the house. Using her keys, she opened the back of her SUV and unfolded a large paper bag. As she was putting one boot into the bag, a spot on the outside of the boot caught her eye. She held it up and turned it

this way and that to get a better look at it. With the sun as her light, she examined the blotches along the toe and side of the boot. The coloring was darker than the boot and looked dried. She scraped at a bit with her gloved finger and noticed tiny flakes caught on the tip of the glove. Holding the boot to her nose, she took a tentative whiff. It didn't have a particular smell. Nothing recognizable, like motor oil or gasoline. She'd have to get the lab to tell her what the substance was and if it related to her case.

Shrugging her shoulders, she placed the boots into the paper bag and folded the top of the bag over. She secured it in the back of her SUV, and then she closed the back door and slipped into the driver's seat. Sighing with relief, she started the car and positioned the air conditioner vents to blow on her full force.

She needed to get back to her office at the warehouse and go through her notes. Something wasn't adding up and she was going to find out what it was.

Karen drove back to the warehouse with only half her attention. She considered the presence of a second pair of hiking boots and how they fit into her investigation. She needed to turn this pair over to FDLE as soon as possible so they could determine if they fit the footprint or not. She needed to talk to Sam. She guessed she'd have to settle for the next best thing: John Hendricks.

Dialing her cell phone, she waited for Hendricks to pick up.

"Hendricks."

"John, it's Karen Sykes. On a hunch, I checked out the Thomas house. I found another pair of hiking boots. Similar to the first pair we were given by Maggie Morris. I—"

"What were you doing in the house?"

"I thought maybe I could find the weapon Ray Thomas used to assault Sam." Her defensive tone rang in her ear.

"That was good thinking, but damn it, Sykes, why'd you go there alone?"

"It was a spur of the moment kind of decision."

"I could have gone with you. What if that bastard showed up and—"

"He didn't, so stop worrying. I'm going to stop at FDLE and turn over these boots and check on the status of our other evidence. Maybe I'll get lucky and they'll be finished with some of it."

"Yeah. Maybe. You just shouldn't have gone alone. You're my responsibility, Sykes." "I need to find this guy, Hendricks. I'm going to find him. He can't hide forever."

"All right. Get in here as soon as you can."

"Will do."

"Oh, hey. We got a call from the hospital. Sam's coming around."

"For real? That's great news. When can I talk to him?"

"I don't know. The report from the hospital said he was coming around. Don't know anymore than that."

"I think I'll stop by there before I go home today."

"Come find me when you get in."

"Yes, sir." Karen pressed the end button on her cell phone and disconnected the call. Sam was coming around. Her heart soared. This could mean that he'd reached a turning point. The swelling could be going down and he could regain consciousness. Karen pounded her steering wheel with her fist. "Yes!" she exclaimed with each whack she made on her steering wheel. "Yes!"

After finding an open parking space near the door, Karen carried the large paper bag with the hiking boots into the FDLE lab. She filled out the proper paperwork to turn over the boots and add them to her case, and then turned on her heel and retraced her steps back to her vehicle. Even that short time in the sun brought the temperature in her SUV to blistering levels. In a matter of minutes, Karen was back on the road and on her way back to the office.

She knew Sam's recovery would take a long time, but she couldn't keep the elation down for this first small step. Karen practically skipped into the warehouse and to her desk. She stored her purse and rang Hendricks' office to let him know she made it in. Her mind still couldn't quite wrap itself around the good news. Sam was coming around.

Chapter Thirty-Four

Kelly couldn't believe how physically tired she was. She'd closed her eyes only for a moment while she rode in the car that picked up her and the girls. The woman that drove said her name was Amanda. She'd had juice boxes for the girls and a cold soda for Kelly.

Now, as the car bumped over the driveway entrance to a large house, Kelly opened her eyes and stretched.

"We're here," Amanda said.

"Already?" Kelly put a hand over her mouth and yawned.

"I didn't want to disturb you, so I let you sleep."

"Thanks. I guess I'm tired."

"We're going to stop in the office first so you can meet your case manager." Amanda helped the girls out of the back seat and grabbed Kelly's bag of clothes. "Maybe I'll see you at dinner, okay?"

"Okay, thanks." Kelly held her daughters' hands and followed Amanda's retreating back into the big house. She looked up at the large trees and heard the birds calling to each other.

"Denise, this is Kelly and her two girls. I just picked them up." Amanda dropped the bag of clothes at Kelly's feet and turned to go. "Hi, Kelly."

"Hi." Kelly looked around the brightly painted foyer and felt shy.

"Let me tell Rosie you're here." She turned and left the room and entered one of the closed doors off to the right.

In a few seconds, she returned with another woman that Kelly assumed was Rosie. She was a small Hispanic woman with a round face and a wide smile.

"Hello, Kelly. I'm Rosie. Who do we have here?" She crouched down so that she could be face to face with Kelly's daughters.

"This is Amber," Kelly laid a hand on her head, "and this one is Ashley."

The girls stared back without saying a word. "They're quiet."

Kelly nodded.

Rosie nodded as well. Then she said softly, "Because they had to be?"

Ashamed, Kelly nodded again. For something to do, she picked up the bag of clothes at her feet.

"Don't worry about it, sweetheart, you're safe now." Rosie put a hand on Kelly's arm and squeezed. "This is a safe place."

Kelly felt tears stinging her eyes. She brushed at them with the back of her hand then gripped the bag of clothes a little tighter.

"Let's go find you a room and then we'll take a little tour."

Confused, Kelly followed Rosie through a maze of halls and rooms until they stood in front of a door. "Here it is," Rosie said. She opened the door and stepped aside so Kelly could enter.

Inside, Kelly saw a room with two beds. Off to the side was a door that led to a bathroom. Kelly stood in the middle of the room and looked at Rosie. "This is ours?"

"For as long as you're here."

"Thank you."

"Why don't you put your bags down and we'll take a tour of your new home."

Kelly lifted the garbage bag and placed it on one of the beds. She helped the girls remove their backpacks and place them on the other bed. She touched the homemade quilt and fought back tears.
This was already beginning to feel like home.

Rosie led the way out of their room and down the hall. Walking into a large room with tables, Rosie said, "This is our cafeteria. We eat all of our meals here. Our meal schedules are included in the paperwork in your room. You'll find a welcome packet on the dresser along with a bag of personal care items for you and your daughters."

"It's big."

"Wait until you see it at dinner tonight." Rosie turned toward another door and said, "Let's go out this way." They left the cafeteria and headed out a door at the back of the house.

Outside, Kelly saw a smaller house surrounded by sidewalks.

Rosie pointed at the smaller house. "This is the Kid's Team House." She opened a door. "Let's step inside. In here, the children

have counseling sessions. Your girls will attend a group session at least once a day."

Kelly looked down at her daughters. They were wide eyed as they held hands, watching the group of children sitting in a circle in the center of the room.

"Counseling sessions are very important part of our children's growth. Did you know that seventy-nine percent of boys who witness domestic violence will become abusers when they are adults?"

Kelly shook her head. "Do you think Mark was abused when he as a kid?"

"There's always that possibility." Rosie patted Kelly's arm and motioned to another door. "Let's step in here."

Kelly ushered her girls in ahead of her. The room was empty of other people, but held a lot of toys. The shelves were filled with all sorts of games, dolls, and balls of all kind. Kelly felt a tug on her leg.

"Mommy, can I play with that doll?"

Not sure what to say, Kelly looked up at Rosie for help.

"We sell these toys to the kids here. They buy them with something we call 'bonus bucks'." Rosie bent down until she was level with the girls. "Bonus bucks are earned every time you go to group, when you help your mom, do extra chores, and for getting good grades in school. Do you think you can do that?" Amber and Ashley both nodded.

Rosie stood up and led them out through a gate. They entered the playground area. Kelly looked at the brightly colored benches, rings, monkey bars, and two playhouses. She touched Ashley on the shoulder. "Do you think you could have fun here?"

"Can I go play now?"

"Not yet. Let's finish with this nice lady before we go running off."

"We always make sure the children have plenty of time to play," Rosie said. "Why don't we go over to the school?"

"You have a school here too?" Kelly was surprised.

"You won't be able to send your girls back to their regular school. Your husband will go there to find them." Rosie led them into another brightly painted room with desks, computers, and books.

Kelly pondered Rosie's statement as they walked into the schoolroom. The teacher came up to them and held out her hand to introduce herself.

"Hello. I'm Miss Sandy. And who do we have here?" She looked down at the two girls standing next to their mother.

Kelly laid a hand on the head of each girl and introduced them. "This is Ashley and this is Amber."

"Hello, Ashley. Hello, Amber," Miss Sandy said. "It's nice to meet you. School's over for the day, but you're welcome to color." She took the girls to a small table and gave them each a drawing of a puppy and some flowers and a box of crayons.

Miss Sandy returned to Kelly and Rosie and said, "The Spring School is a Hillsborough County Alternative School with teachers, aides, and social workers all supplied by the county. We're the first domestic violence shelter to open a school on site."

"The classes are small so the kids can catch up on the work they may have missed while living at home," said Rosie.

Kelly looked confused. "Why would they be behind in their work?"

"Kids living in an abusive home live in fear. They may not be concentrating as well as they should while in school and might be behind on their basics like reading, writing, and math."

"I didn't know that. I thought they were doing fine." "We'll find out and don't you worry. We give our kids lots of personal attention and your girls will catch up in no time."

"But why didn't I know?"

"Honey," Rosie said as she touched the side of Kelly's bruised face. "I think you had other things to be worrying about."

Kelly lowered her head, ashamed of the marks on her face. She held a hand up to try to cover them.

Rosie smiled gently. "We're here for you. Don't hide or be ashamed. We've all been through it." Rosie looked at Miss Sandy who nodded as well. "Why don't we take the girls to the Kid's Team
House, and you and I go talk in my office?"

Kelly lifted her chin a little then nodded. "Thank you."

Kelly followed Rosie back out of the school and down the sidewalk until they came to the Kid's Team House. She told the girls that they'd be able to see her again once they were done. She gave them each a tight hug and a kiss.

"I think your girls will get along fine," Rosie said when she returned from taking the girls inside.

"I hope so. This has all been kind of confusing to them, I think."

"It's confusing for you too, isn't it?"

"Kind of. I keep wondering if I did the right thing." Rosie led the way into her office. She motioned for Kelly to take a seat in the chair across from her desk. She picked up a camera. "Do you mind if I take some pictures?" Rosie took aim and snapped the camera. "You will need these pictures if you decide to press charges against your husband."

Kelly lifted a hand to the side of her face. "I guess so. I ain't never told anyone before that Mark hits me. I've never even told my parents, not the whole truth anyways." Kelly's mouth formed a perfect oval. "I have to call my parents. Mark will call them thinking we went there. He'll worry my mom."

Rosie took a couple more pictures. "We'll let you call your mom, don't worry. You just can't tell them were you are, only that you're safe. I'm sure they'll be happy to hear that once you tell them what happened."

Kelly brushed away at the tears that welled up. "We are safe, right? Mark, he can't find us, can he?"

"You're safe here." Rosie nodded. "What we can do for you is get you a meeting with our on-site attorney. He'll help you get an
Injunction for Protection."

"Injunction for Protection?"

"Well, it'll say that if Mark sees you outside this facility, he needs to be at least five hundred feet away from you at all times." Rosie shuffled some papers on her desk. "These kinds of things will help you if Mark tries to get custody of those adorable little girls."

Kelly's head snapped up. "What? He can do that?"

"Don't worry. Our attorney knows his stuff. He works for Bay Area Legal Services. We can get you an appointment right away. Just tell us when."

"Thank you. I...I..." Kelly hung her head. Tears fell along her bruised cheeks. "I just don't know what to do. I can't ever go back to my husband. I don't have a job. How am I going to raise my girls by myself?"

"Honey, we're here to help you." Rosie offered Kelly a box of tissues. Kelly took the box, smiling her gratitude.

"How can you help me?" Kelly sniffled into a tissue she plucked from the box.

"We can offer you a place to stay while you look for work or go back to school. You'll go to counseling and so will your girls. Once you're ready, you'll apply for Aftercare." Rosie handed a pamphlet to Kelly. "Aftercare is a transitional stage for women and families who need safe, secure housing. You'll need to work hard to be accepted. But I know you can do it." Rosie handed Kelly a small stack of forms. "Why don't we get started?"

Overwhelmed, but confident with each form that she was doing the right thing, Kelly filled out the required paperwork and answered the rest of Rosie's questions. Afterward, she found her way back outside and waited for the girls to finish their group counseling session. They walked out of the Kid's Team House with smiles on their face.

"Momma, can we stay here?"

"Please?"

Kelly knelt down and hugged her girls tight. She kissed each one on the cheek. "I think we'll stay here for a while."

Chapter Thirty-Five

"What am I missing here?" Karen rubbed her fingertips along her temples.

"Let's break it down." John Hendricks pulled out a pen and drew a few circles on a pad of paper. "You got the murder victim. We know we can link him to his parents here." He drew another circle next to the boy's, drew a line to link them, and wrote in the parents' names. "Then we got your suspect here." Hendricks drew another circle and wrote in the name of Raymond Alan Thomas. "Now the suspect is linked by a fingerprint." He drew a line linking the two circles and wrote the word 'fingerprint' along the line.

Karen added, "We have Maggie Morris, linked to Thomas. And now we can add the hiking boots we found at the house to her link. So put a dashed line from her to the victim. And write boots along it." Karen ran a hand through her hair and pushed it away from her face.

Damn, she still needed to make an appointment to get her hair cut. "What about a link between Thomas and the parents?"

"We did background checks and haven't come up with anything." "So all we have is a fingerprint that puts Thomas with the kid, and a footprint found at the scene?"

"Yeah, that's about it."

"Didn't you have a John Doe with a similar footprint?" Hendricks drew another circle and linked it with a dashed line to the little boy's circle. He wrote 'footprint' along the line.

"Yeah. Parker and Connelly found the print next to their John Doe out on the causeway. I haven't heard back from them about it. Let me give them a call and see what's holding them up."

"Get on it." Hendricks threw down his pen. "Hey, did you see the paper this morning?"

Karen shook her head.

"We're getting some good coverage about our missing suspect. The reward just went up. If he's out there, someone will spot him and turn his ass in just for the reward."

"I hope so." She rubbed a hand at the back of her neck. "I'm heading for the hospital. I'm gonna try and talk to Maggie again and see if she remembers anything. I'll check on Sam while I'm there."

"Yeah, sounds like a good idea. See if you can lean on this Maggie a bit. She might remember more than we think and just doesn't want to talk about it." Hendricks grinned. "Keep it light, but watch her."

"Will do." Karen shoved her chair away from her desk and grabbed her purse out of her desk drawer. She checked to make sure her cell phone was attached to her belt.

While she walked to her car, Karen dialed Mike's cell phone number.

"Connelly here."

"Mike, it's Karen."

"Hi."

"Hi, I'm calling about the footprint on the Hunt case. Did we get a match on the boots?"

"I received a batch of reports yesterday, and I'm going through them today. I'm sure the report is in there."

"I hope so. I just found another pair of hiking boots at the Thomas house. A smaller pair, I'm thinking they were Maggie Morris'. I've turned them over to FDLE to identify a substance I found on the boots." Karen found her car, got in, and started it up.

"Good. I hope FDLE is getting to their cases quicker. They've been behind for a while now."

"They didn't give me an exact day when they'd get back to me. But there were a lot of people working in there." Karen drove out of the parking lot and headed toward the Interstate.

"You sound like you're in your car. Are you on your way home?"

"I'm in my car, yes, but I'm not on my way home. I'm heading for the hospital to see if I can get anymore out of Maggie and check on Sam." Looking behind her, Karen signaled to merge into the traffic speeding by on the highway.

"If you get a chance to see Sam, tell him I said 'hello'."

"I will. I hope he's conscious. It'll be good to have him finally out of the woods."

"Um, Karen, I don't want to tell you how to do your job, but what were you doing at the suspect's house? Alone?"

"Mike? What the hell?" Karen bit out the words. "This is my job. My number one priority is to catch the son of a bitch who put Sam in the hospital and who possibly killed that little boy."

"That's right. Your partner is already in the hospital because of this maniac. I don't want to see you end up there too."

Karen swung the steering wheel to the left to avoid a driver changing lanes. "I won't."

"Just follow procedures. Use your partner."

"Don't tell me how to do my job, damn it. We're sleeping together. You're not my boss."

"Shit. I knew this would get complicated."

"It's not complicated at—stay in your own lane, asshole!" Karen leaned on the horn while she verbally assaulted the driver next to her. She rolled her shoulders. She didn't need this right now. What she needed to do was get to the hospital without anymore interruptions.

Traffic or boyfriend-wise. "Mike, just let me do my job."

"Karen, I—"

"Look, Mike, I'm driving. I have to go. I need to concentrate."

"Right. Okay. Fine then."

Karen heard the clip of each word, but she didn't have the time to deal with Mike at the moment.

"Bye, Mike."

Karen ended her call and tossed her cell phone onto the passenger front seat. She followed the now familiar exit for the hospital and after a series of long traffic lights she pulled into the hospital parking lot. Finding a parking space was difficult, but she managed it and parked her SUV.

Determined to get some answers out of Maggie, she focused on finding her room and developing a list of questions she wanted to ask. There must be something she could say that might help trigger Maggie's memory, PTSD or no PTSD. Maybe if she talked about Sam. That might do it.

Karen walked into Maggie's room. The woman lay back on the hospital bed, absently changing channels on the overhead television.

"Maggie?"

"Mmm?" Maggie turned her head to see who was at the door.

"Hi, I'm Detective Sykes. Remember me?"

"You're the police?"

"That's right. I'm here to ask you a few questions, is that okay?" Karen stood next to the bed and looked down at Maggie. The bruises and cuts on her face stood out against the paleness of her skin.

"Questions? Sure, I guess. I don't know how much help I can be. The doctors say I can't remember much because of the shock." Maggie turned off the television and laid the remote control on her bedside table.

"Well, let's start out with a few simple questions and then we'll go from there." Karen took out her notebook and flipped to a blank page. "How far back can you remember? Do you remember with whom you were living with before you were brought to the hospital? Do you know whose home you were in?"

Maggie screwed up her face as if trying to remember. Wrinkles appeared between her eyebrows and in her forehead. "Living with? I'm not sure. I think I was living with a man." Maggie paused. "Yeah.
I think I was living with a man."

"That's good, Maggie. Do you remember who this man was?" Maggie scratched the top of her head. "Who? Maybe. I dunno. Everything's all scrambled up in my head. If I go back in my mind, I think I was living with another guy before this one. But we got in a big fight and I left." Taking a sip of water, Maggie tried to focus on the question. "But this guy, he wasn't like the others. We did stuff." Maggie lifted the hand with the IV inserted and stared at it. She paused for several seconds. "Yeah, I think I remember doing stuff."

"What kind of stuff?" Karen reined in her frustration at the lack of direction in Maggie's answers.

"I dunno. Just stuff."

"Did you have fun with this guy? What kind of fun things did you do?"

"I don't know how much fun we had. I'm trying to remember. It's hard, you know?"

"I know, Maggie. But it's real important that you remember. We want to find the man that did this to you and to my partner, Sam. Do you remember Detective Anderson, Maggie?"

"Detective Anderson? Who's Detective Anderson?" Maggie looked at Karen with round, wide eyes.

"He was with you the day you were attacked. Detective Anderson was there to arrest the man you were living with."

"The man I was living with? Why would he want to do that?"

"We have reason to believe that the man you were living with may have been involved in a homicide." Karen debated with herself about how much to tell Maggie. She hoped that by telling her as much as she could, it might jog her memory.

"A homicide? Do you mean murder? Someone I was living with murdered somebody?" Maggie held a hand to her heart. Her chest heaved as her breathing came fast and shallow.

"Calm down, Maggie. Don't get yourself all worked up. You're safe now, here in the hospital. They won't let anyone hurt you." Karen looked toward the doorway hoping a nurse would wander by. Getting Maggie all worked up wasn't her main objective. She wanted to possibly shock Maggie into remembering something, but she didn't want to give her a heart attack in the process.

"But murder? That's serious stuff." Maggie lifted her glass to take a drink then sat it down again. "What about that detective? The one you said got attacked too. How's he doing?"

"He's in the Intensive Care Unit, here in the same hospital. He's been beat up pretty bad."

"Does he…does he know what happened to him?" Maggie kept her eyes down as she asked her question.

"He's been unconscious since they brought him in. The doctors say he's coming around, so I'm hoping to talk to him after I finish here talking to you. He might be able to tell me who did this to him."

Maggie's head swung up. "He can tell you that?"

"I hope so." Karen watched Maggie's face change expression. Her eyes went blank before her eyelids fluttered closed, and her mouth turned down into a frown.

"Could you go now? I'm real tired, detective. I don't think I can answer anymore questions."

"I'm sorry, Maggie. I didn't mean to tire you out. I'll leave now and let you get some rest." Making a final mark in her notebook, Karen snapped it shut and put it back into her pocket with her pen. "You take care of yourself. And don't worry about a thing. We'll find the person who did this to you."

Maggie lifted her hand slightly in a halfhearted wave. She leaned her head back on the pillow and sighed.

Turning to go, Karen stopped and asked over her shoulder, "By the way, Maggie. Do you like to hike?"

Maggie opened her eyes. "Hike? I don't know what you mean?"

"We found a pair of hiking boots in your house. I was wondering if they were yours." Karen watched Maggie carefully to see what her reaction would be.

Maggie closed her eyes and rested her head back against the pillow. "Boots? I dunno. I don't remember."

"Well, don't worry about it. I'm sure it's nothing." Karen bit the inside of her lip. Was she going to keep running into brick walls when it came to Maggie Morris? Karen walked out of Maggie's room and headed toward the elevators to take her to the

Intensive Care Unit. She hoped that Sam would be awake enough to talk to her. Grateful that the elevator was empty, Karen relaxed against the wall. What was with Maggie today? Could she really have suffered such a shock to her system that she couldn't remember even the simplest details about the last few days? Or was there something more to Maggie's attitude? Did she know something and wasn't telling? Did she still harbor feelings for the man who attacked her? Karen stopped second guessing herself when the elevator sounded its final stop. She exited the elevator and headed for the ICU.

"Detective Sykes, is that you?"

Karen looked for the person calling her name and recognized Sam's wife. "Hello, Mrs. Anderson. I came by to see Sam, if I can?"

"Sam's been awake now for a couple of hours or so. I was just thinking about calling you. I think he wants to see you."

"How is he?"

"He's still on a respirator so he can't talk. He's alert, but seems confused. Why don't you come see for yourself, dear?"

"Thank you," Karen said. "I'd like that."

Mrs. Anderson led Karen through the double doors into the Intensive Care Unit. The large nursing station buzzed with activity. Nurses watched various computer and video monitors with patient data. The noise level was low, but with a heightened sense of urgency. Mrs. Anderson seemed to know her way around the area and led Karen to a small group of nurses congregated around one monitor. She motioned to the nurse closest to her and said, "I'm taking my husband's partner in to see him for a few minutes, Dottie."

The nurse lifted her head and looked at Karen. She paused before saying, "Only for a few minutes, Mrs. Anderson. We don't want that husband of yours to tire out now that he's awake."

"I won't. Just for a few minutes. Sam wants to see Detective Sykes."

Karen watched the nurse named Dottie smile at Mrs. Anderson then go back to watching the monitor with the other people she was standing with. Following Sam's wife, Karen quietly walked into the room a few doors down from the nurse's station. She kept her face neutral as she took in the room and Sam as he lay in his hospital bed. There were so many beeping and blinking machines around the top of the bed. The one that was helping him breath was making soft sucking sounds. Tubes and wires led from the machines to Sam's body. He looked smaller than she remembered, or maybe it was just the large hospital bed. Tears gathered at the corners of her eyes. She tried to brush them away without drawing attention to them. Mrs. Anderson had taken the get-well cards that were sent and taped them up along the walls and windows of the small room. She had put them at eye level for Sam to see. And Sam could see them. Eyes open, he watched as Karen entered the room and looked around.

"Why don't you stand over there, so Sam can see you without having to move too much." Mrs. Anderson pointed to a spot next to Sam's bed.

Karen sidestepped her way over to the place Sam's wife pointed to and said, "Hi, Sam."

Sam blinked and a crooked grin tried to form on his lips around the tube protruding from his mouth.

"We've worked out a blinking system, haven't we, Sam?" Mrs. Anderson said as she gently patted Sam's bruised hand. "One blink means yes and two blinks mean no."

Karen smiled down at Sam. "I think I can figure that out." With worried lines creasing her forehead, she asked, "Do you know why you're here in the hospital?" One blink.

"Good, Sam. Do you know what happened the day you went to Ray Thomas's house to arrest him?" One blink.

"Sam, did Ray Thomas attack you?" One blink. Then another.

"Two blinks? That means no, right?" Thinking that she had made a mistake, Karen looked at Mrs. Anderson for confirmation.

Mrs. Anderson leaned over her husband to look into his eyes. "Sam, did you understand Detective Sykes' question?" One blink.

"He understood me. So he's saying no to my question. What does that mean? Who attacked you, Sam?" Agitated, Karen began to pace along side Sam's bed. "Maggie said that Ray attacked her. Who else could have been there? Did he have an accomplice?" Karen stopped pacing and stared down at Sam. "Was that it, Sam? Did Ray Thomas have an accomplice?"

One blink. Then another slow blink.

"No. He's saying no again. What does that mean, Sam? Who else was there?"

Sam's hands bounced up and down on the sheet covering his bed. Mrs. Anderson covered one of his hands with hers. "He's getting upset, dear. Maybe we should stop."

"I'm sorry, you're right. This must be making him anxious." Karen wrapped her arms around her waist and stood to one side of the room. A buzzing noise startled her, until she realized it was her cell phone vibrating against her waist. She checked the caller ID and recognized Mike's telephone number. "I'm going to take this in the waiting room," she said to Sam's wife.

Mrs. Anderson waved her on while she tried to soothe her fretful husband.

Karen walked through the double doors and out of ICU and into the waiting room. She answered her cell phone, "Hello, Mike?"

"Yeah, it's me. Wait, before you say anything, this is strictly a business call. I got some news for you. Let me start by saying I didn't know the report had come in. It got mixed up with some other stuff when my mail fell and we just now got it all sorted out."

"What report?" The cell phone reception wasn't that great, so Karen moved closer to a window in the waiting room.

"The boots. We got a probable match on the boots you found and the footprint we cast in the campground."

"That's great. We got a match. That puts Thomas in the campground with the kid. We already got his fingerprint on the kid's snap, this just confirms it. We can charge this guy with murder just as soon as we bring him in for questioning."

"That gets me to the next report."

"You got another report? For me?"

"Yes, on the John Doe we found on the Courtney Campbell Causeway?"

"Oh right. How does that relate to me or my case?" Karen stood at the window and watched the thunderclouds rolling in.

"Listen carefully, Karen. We ID'd the body. His name is Raymond Alan Thomas."

CHAPTER THIRTY-SIX

"Who?" Karen held one hand up to her ear to block any noise coming through. "Who did you say the ID was?"

"It's Raymond Alan Thomas, Karen. The guy you've been looking for."

"But, it can't be. He…he can't be dead. That would make him dead for more than seventy-two hours. That would make him dead before—"

"Before Sam got attacked," Mike finished for her.

Karen wiped a hand across her face. She needed time to process this information. Sam blinked no to her questions about Thomas. Thomas didn't attack him. She had to talk to Sam again. Find out what he knew. Hurrying back through the double doors, Karen slipped past the nurse's station and down to Sam's room. She practically ran into Mrs. Anderson who was on her way out of the room.

"Sam. I need to talk to Sam," Karen said.

"I'm sorry, dear. The nurse gave him a sedative to see if it would calm him down. He was way too upset after you left."

"But he knows who attacked him. I have to find out who it was," Karen begged.

"He's sleeping. He won't be talking to anyone for a while. I'm not sure he should talk to you again."

"Oh, please, Mrs. Anderson. Sam wants to tell me who attacked him. If I gave him a pen he could write it down. He doesn't have to try and talk."

Sam's wife cocked her head to one side as she considered Karen's proposal. "I don't know. Maybe. We'll see after he wakes up." "Please call me as soon as he wakes up. I'll be close by." "I will, dear." Mrs. Anderson patted Karen's hand.

"Thank you." Karen turned to walk away. She stopped and turned back. "Sam was moving his hands. Does that mean…?"

"The pressure is slowly subsiding from his spinal cord. The doctor says that with time and rehabilitation, Sam should be able to regain full use of his arms and legs."

Karen reached out and gave Mrs. Anderson a hug. "That's wonderful! I'm so happy for you and for Sam." Karen stepped back. "He's going to get better then?"

"Yes. It'll be slow going, but Sam's a fighter."

"Please call me when Sam wakes up. I promise not to get him upset. This is important to our case."

Sam's wife nodded. "Okay, dear. I'll call you."

"Thank you. You have my cell phone number?"

"Yes, it's on the card you gave me. I have it in my purse."

"Good. I'm going to go back and visit Maggie Morris. I think Sam's information will be helpful." Pushing her way through the double doors, Karen left ICU. She followed the now familiar route to the elevators and up to the floor where Maggie's room was.

Karen entered the dark room. The only light coming from the television. "Maggie?"

Maggie sat up in bed and muted the television. "Detective Sykes? I didn't know you would be coming back today." With hands that shook slightly, she smoothed the sheet that covered her body. "What can I do for you? I've already told you everything I can remember."

"I know you did." Karen watched Maggie carefully. "I've just been to see Detective Anderson. He's awake."

"Really? Well, that's good news then, isn't it?" Wide eyed, Maggie made eye contact with Karen then quickly shifted her glance to the quiet television. She watched it for a moment then glanced back at Karen. "Was there something else?"

On impulse, Karen said, "Sam's told me who attacked him."

Eyes narrowing for a split second before returning to their wideeyed, innocent look, Maggie coughed. She reached for her glass of water and took a long, slow drink.

The silence spoke volumes to Karen. Something in Maggie's mannerisms was too calculated, too perfectly orchestrated. Karen wanted to see what Maggie's reaction would be to her next statement. "We know what happened, Maggie." With Thomas dead before the attacks, that left only Maggie. Karen didn't know if she had an

202 • Vicki M. taylOr

accomplice, but wondered how she could have gotten the drop on Sam. Maybe that's what Sam was trying to tell her. Maggie was the one who attacked him.

Maggie placed her glass of water on the bedside table and pushed it away from her. She kept her head down. Her hands shook as she folded and refolded the top of the sheet. Finally, she lifted her head and looked at Karen. "I...I'm not feeling very well at the moment, detective."

"I'm sorry, would you like me to get the nurse?" Karen took a half step back and made a motion as if to go to the door.

"No," Maggie cried. She lowered her voice and said, "I mean, thank you, but no. I think I need some rest. My therapy session was rather difficult today."

"Difficult? It's too bad you can't remember what happened that day. But that's okay actually. We don't need your memory anymore now that Detective Anderson is awake." Karen watched as Maggie stopped smoothing the sheet and clenched her trembling hands together.

"That's good," Maggie said through tight lips. "If you could just go now?" She let her head fall back against the pillow and turned away from the door.

"Absolutely. You get lots of rest, Maggie. You're going to need it." Karen turned and left Maggie's hospital room. She knew that Maggie was involved in Sam's attack. She just hadn't worked through all the details yet. Maggie's reaction to Sam's condition meant that she wasn't happy to hear the news. That much Karen had figured out. Did Maggie inflict all that damage on herself? Could she have possibly beaten Sam, as big as he was? Karen laughed at herself for thinking up such far-fetched ideas. But she was sworn to follow every lead and this one was worth checking out. She headed for the elevators, noticed there was a crowd waiting to board, and detoured to the stairwell. Taking the stairs would be quicker and she'd be able to use her cell phone in the process.

Karen dialed Hendricks' number as she pushed open the heavy door to the stairs.

Listening to the phone ring for the third time, Karen bounded down the stairs. Suddenly, with a slam to her back, she fell forward and dropped her cell phone. "What the hell?" She pushed herself up to a crouching position and looked backward at what had nearly pushed her down the stairs.

She couldn't believe her eyes. It was Maggie. But a Maggie like she'd never seen before. Eyes sparked with anger. Lips curled backward over her teeth, snarling in a low growl. Her fast, heavy breathing could be heard echoing in the stairwell. She wore only her hospital gown and had bare feet.

"Maggie! What are you doing?" Karen stood up and reached out a hand to the angry woman a few steps up from her.

"Don't touch me, bitch." Maggie made a swipe at Karen's hand with her fingers clenched like talons.

"Settle down, Maggie." Karen brought her hand back and looked out of the corner of her eye to see if she could find her cell phone. It was three steps below her on the edge of the stairs. Her far-fetched idea about Maggie being the assailant wasn't sounding so crazy anymore as she kept an eye on the feral woman getting ready to attack.

In a flash, Maggie sprang forward and launched herself at Karen. Teeth and nails flailed. She punched and tore at Karen's body.

Karen fended off Maggie's assault as best she could. A fist found a way into her sternum and she lost her breath. Pain burned along her cheek as she felt nails rake her face. Her head slammed into the concrete wall of the stairwell as Maggie grabbed her arm and flung her to the side. Bright lights flashed before her eyes. She blinked twice to bring everything back into focus.

Maggie tore at her jacket and pulled it up and over Karen's head. Karen flipped easily out of the sleeves of her jacket and flung it away from her. Another flying fist caught her in the chin; she bit hard on her tongue and tasted blood. Grabbing one of Maggie's arms, Karen tried to subdue the wild woman by pulling Maggie's arm behind her back. With bare feet, Maggie kicked at Karen's legs and connected right below the knee. Karen's leg buckled. She grabbed for the wall to help her maintain her balance. Stumbling, she grabbed for the handrail and held on as Maggie pushed at her to make her fall.

From below, Karen heard one of the heavy doors open. She opened her mouth to scream for help when Maggie's fist connected with her left temple. She slumped over as bright flashes of light blurred her vision and blackness crept in along the edges.

CHAPTER THIRTY-SEVEN

Frustrated, Mike tossed his cell phone across the table. He couldn't get through to Karen. She wasn't answering her cell phone and that wasn't like her. Their other conversation didn't go well, but not so well she'd screen his calls. Or would she?

A gnawing feeling deep in his gut wouldn't go away. Something wasn't right. Karen was in trouble and he needed to find her. Would this be what he had to look forward to in a relationship with a homicide detective? Would he be left on the sidelines, waiting, wondering? Could he endure this kind of nervous suspense on a regular basis? Doubts crept into the back of his mind. Memories of his last failed relationship with a fellow officer flooded forward. He didn't need this. Not again.

Mike paced between the office and the lab. A knot of frustration in the back of his neck ached incessantly and a feeling of helplessness that he couldn't get over nagged at him.

"Hey, Mike. Haven't you left yet? You're gonna wear a path in the hall. What's got you all in a twist?"

"It's Karen. I was on my way out and thought I'd give her a call. I can't get her to answer her phone."

"When was the last time you spoke to her?" Susan's eyebrows lifted.

"A couple of hours ago. I found some reports that got mixed up with the filing and called her to give her the results. Since it related to the case she was working on, I figured she'd want to hear the results right away."

"Yeah. Makes sense." Susan shifted her purse strap higher on her shoulder. "Did she say where she was at the time?"

"Yeah. She was at the hospital. Checking on Sam and talking to Maggie Morris." Mike stopped pacing and leaned against the wall. He rubbed the back of his neck. "Something just doesn't feel right, Susan. I don't know exactly. But, I got this feeling."

"Feelings are good. What exactly is troubling you? Is it that you can't get her on the phone?"

"No, not exactly." Mike forced a laugh. "You're gonna think I'm crazy or something. Maybe it's just nothing."

"Mike, you're talking to me. Auntie Susan. I'm not gonna laugh. Tell me what's bothering you. It's obviously something, or you wouldn't be acting this way."

"All right. But don't laugh."

Susan crossed her heart. "On my honor," she said.

Mike paused, took a deep breath, blew it out then forged ahead. "I have this feeling that Karen's in trouble. Something inside tells me that whatever she's doing, it went wrong." Susan smiled.

"See, I knew you were going to laugh." Mike lifted a fist and hit the wall he'd been leaning on.

"I'm not laughing. Do you hear me laughing?"

"No."

"All right then. Do you have a way of getting in touch with her new partner?"

"No. Wait. Yeah. Maybe, if I can remember his name. What was it?" Mike screwed up his face in concentration trying to remember Karen's new partner. He couldn't focus. The name didn't come to him. "What was it? Hicks? Something like Hicks. But that's not it."

"Why don't you call over to the warehouse and see if anyone can tell you who it is?"

"That's a good idea. Why didn't I think of that?" Mike smiled at Susan.

"Cuz you're not smart like me."

"Right." Mike stood in front of Susan, shuffling from one foot to the other, anxious to get to his cell phone.

"Go on. Call already." Susan moved out of his way to the lab doorway, where he'd thrown his phone earlier.

Mike hurried into the room to retrieve his cell phone.

Susan called after him, "I'm gonna need a full report tomorrow."

Mike turned back and poked his head out of the doorway to look at Susan. "Hey, thanks for all your help. And thanks for listening."

"That's what I'm here for." Susan blew him a kiss and walked down the hallway toward the exit.

Buoyed by his conversation with Susan, Mike picked up his cell phone and dialed the number to the Sheriff's office warehouse location. While he waited for someone to answer, he looked over the report he'd given to Karen earlier. It suddenly dawned on him that if Raymond Alan Thomas had been dead for over seventy-two hours, then a killer was still on the loose. Someone attacked Sam. Someone who may have left him for dead in that house. Could that same person want to hurt Karen as well? Mike's stomach turned over with a sickening thud.

His hand shook as he ran it through his hair and rubbed absently at the top of his head. A voice answered and he hurried to explain his situation.

"This is Mike Connelly, crime scene technician. I'm trying to get in touch with one of your detectives and I'm not sure of his name. He's partnered with Detective Karen Sykes temporarily. Do you know who I'm talking about?"

"Just a moment, sir. I'll check for you."

Mike heard a click then a recording of summer safety information played into his ear. He didn't listen as the recorded voice gave helpful tips to make this summer a safe one.

Another click and the voice came back on the line. "Sir, that would be Detective Hendricks. Would you like me to connect you?"

"Hendricks. That's it." Mike breathed a sigh of relief. "Yes, please. I'd like to talk to him."

"I'll ring his desk. Have a good day." The voice disconnected. Mike heard ringing and waited.

"Hendricks here."

"Detective Hendricks. This is Mike Connelly. Crime Scene Technician and a…friend of Karen Sykes. I don't know how to ask this, so I'll just come right out with it. Have you heard from Karen today?" "Connelly? Yeah, I heard that you and Sykes were an item. What about her?"

"She's not answering her cell phone." Mike paused. "That's not like her, detective."

"Yeah? She's a big girl. She can take care of herself. She's probably at the hospital checking on Sam."

Mike didn't like the way Hendricks was giving him the brush-off. "Maybe. That's where she was when I called. But I gave her some information that affected her case and it has me worried."

"Like what? What did you tell her? And why the hell wasn't I informed?"

"You know the Hunt case she'd been working on?"

"Yeah."

"Well, the main suspect she's been after, Raymond Alan Thomas? He's been dead for more than seventy-two hours. We found his body on the causeway a few days ago. He was our John Doe."

"Damn. That means—"

"Yeah, it means that whoever attacked Sam is still out there and could be going after Karen as well."

"Okay, this is what I want you to do. You stay by your phone in case she calls. I'm going to take a drive over to the hospital and see if I can track her down."

"All right. I'll do that. It's just…"

"I know. But like I said, Karen's tough. She can take care of herself. Sam always had good things to say about her. I just hope she remembers to call for back up instead of trying to bring this guy in by herself."

CHAPTER THIRTY-EIGHT

Sam opened his eyes and winced at the dim light above his hospital bed. Even though it wasn't bright, it still hurt his eyes. He blinked several times to help his eyes adjust. With the beeping, whirring, and faint sucking sounds of the machines surrounding his bed, it took him several minutes to realize that there was someone else in the room with him. Someone he couldn't see, but could hear their heavy breathing.

With a breathing tube down his throat, hooked up to the ventilator, he had no range of motion for his head. He couldn't turn to see who was in his room. Nor could he speak and ask who was there.

Discouraged, it reminded him of his frustration earlier when Karen was here with his wife. He felt helpless and upset that he couldn't make her understand. She asked about the day he was attacked. Of course he remembered it. How could he ever forget?

He'd been on the cell phone with Karen talking to her about the arrest warrant for Raymond Alan Thomas. Karen had secured it and was on her way to the house so that they could serve it when Thomas arrived. He'd just ended the call to check for messages when he heard a faint noise behind him. From that point on, it seemed like everything around him slowed down. He turned and saw a foot coming toward his face. With no time to react, he took the full brunt of the kick while his face exploded with pain and blood. Blackness threatened to creep across his vision as he tried to shake himself alert. While he went into slow motion, the kicking foot pounded his head and face. Through a stream of blood that flowed from a cut that had opened up on his forehead, Sam saw blonde hair and a face full of rage. Maggie Morris screamed as she slammed her foot into his chest and knocked him backward, staggering into the furniture.

A table on his right overturned. He struggled to get back to his feet while he fumbled inside of his suit jacket searching for the handle of his gun. His hands wouldn't work. He felt like they were weighted down with lead weights. He couldn't lift his arms. He couldn't ward off Maggie's attacks. Again, he watched as her foot came toward his face and the heavy blow hit his throat and neck. A loud popping noise echoed in his ear as a warm sensation started in his neck and ran down his back and along his nerves to his fingertips and toes. The blackness that had threatened to overcome his vision crowded inward, obscuring his sight. He knew he slid down, but there was no sensation. Unable to lift his arms to protect his body, his head crashed into the floor as the darkness enveloped him.

The next thing he remembered was waking up in this room with his wife's face looking down at him, concerned and scared. He wanted to tell her he was all right, but couldn't make the words come out of his mouth. He panicked. Inside he was thrashing about, but outside his body remained abnormally still. The doctors said that with time he'll regain the use of his limbs. They said that in time the swelling will go down and the paralysis will leave his body. Time. But he didn't have time. Karen was in danger now and he had to figure out a way to tell someone.

Sam rested his mind and listened. Whoever was in his room was still there. He moved his eyes as far to the right and left that he could, seeking any movement or shadow. A low rumble in the distance told him that a storm was coming.

Tiny alarms were going off in his mind. Having someone in his room like this wasn't right. It wasn't the calm breathing of his wife, nor would she stay out of his line of sight. Concentrating hard, he fumbled with his left hand and managed to move it a mere fraction of an inch on the sheet. If only he knew where the call button was for the nurse. He slowly moved his fingers along the sheet, searching for something solid to hold onto. Anything he could find that might make noise.

The breathing was getting closer. Sam could hear it plainly now even over the noises of the machines surrounding his bed. He could hear the faster beeping of his own heart rate as it raced with fear. His heart thumped in his chest. Even as his chest rose and fell with the steady breathing of the ventilator. Up and down. In and out.
Steady, even breaths.

210 • Vicki M. taylOr

He moved his eyes and looked quickly to the right. Something moved. He was sure he saw something. There, he thought he saw it again. He could feel the sweat breaking out on his forehead. He blinked hard to keep the beads of moisture from running into his eyes. Anxious, Sam listened for any noises coming from the hall. Wasn't it time for a nurse to come into his room? How long had he been awake? A flash of color. Sam blinked. Blonde hair. He blinked again. Maggie's face. His heart jumped in his chest. Her face grinning down at him with a maniacal twist to her lips. She was laughing at him. Fear ripped through Sam as he lay helpless in his bed.

Crooning softly, Maggie's hand reached up and stroked his forehead. He willed his body to move away from her heated touch. He couldn't turn his head away and had to endure her fingers on his skin. Inwardly, he groaned in frustration. With half of his attention on listening for someone to come down the hall, Sam only partially heard Maggie as she spoke in whispers.

"…never find me in here." Her hand moved to Sam's cheek and stroked the few days' worth of stubble. "You'll be gone, just like everyone else. Soon, soon you'll be gone too," she crooned softly.

"What do we have here?" Sam could see that Maggie was no longer watching him but eyeing the machines that blipped and whirred around him. "So many machines for one man. I wonder what this one does?"

Sam could no longer see what Maggie was doing, but he knew in his heart it wasn't good. She shouldn't be touching those machines. His life literally depended on them. He wanted to take a deep breath and shout, but the only noise that could be heard was the faint sucking and whirring of the ventilator as it took its steady, even breaths.

"You should never have come back, you know that, detective?" Maggie moved back into Sam's line of vision.

Sam stared at her with wide, frightened eyes. He sought out her hands. They were no longer touching any machines. Sam blinked while maintaining eye contact with Maggie. "You understand me, don't you?" Sam blinked again, slow and deliberate.

"Yes. That means 'yes,' doesn't it?" Elation brightened Maggie's face as she eagerly watched Sam's eyes. Thunder rumbled in the distance. The storm was drawing closer.

Blink.

"Good, then you'll understand what I'm going to say to you. That makes it all the better. You'll know. But you can't do anything about it." Maggie stopped twisting her hands together along the hem of her hospital gown and touched the side of Sam's face. "Yes, you poor thing. Stuck here in this bed. Not able to move." Her hand touched the hose that was connected to the tube in Sam's mouth. "Not able to breathe."

Alarms went off inside Sam's head. She was going to remove his hose. He couldn't let her. He had to keep her talking, but he didn't know how. He blinked rapidly while surreptitiously moving his right hand along the edge of his bed. There had to be a nurse call button somewhere.

"Are you scared, detective?" Blink.

"You should be scared of me. Everyone should be scared of me, but are they? No. No one is. No one ever suspects little Maggie." Maggie practically spit the words out as she kept her voice down.

Blink.

"Well, that lady detective won't think I'm so nice the next time I see her. I gave her a taste of what I gave you." Sam felt a hand touching his face again.

"Yes, you are badly bruised. But not bad enough. You know, you weren't supposed to make it." Maggie pinched his cheek. "You're such a bad man. You didn't die like the others." She slapped his face, but Sam noticed she was careful not to make a loud sound. "We can fix that, though, can't we?"

Blink. Blink. Sweat slipped down the side of Sam's face. He knew she had plans to interfere with his life support. He urged her to keep talking with his eyes. He had the impression that she didn't need much encouragement. It was as if she wanted to talk to him. Wanted to tell him.

"No, you didn't die like the others. But then it was easier with them. They made it so easy. The idiots. They're so gullible. So easy. So stupid. Such a waste of my time."

Sam watched as Maggie got a faraway look in her eye. He blinked slowly. Lightning flashed. Thunder roared outside the window of his room. The storm was closer, nearly to the hospital.

"Talk about a waste of time. You and that partner of yours wasting taxpayers' time and money running around trying to find

Ray when Ray was dead all along. You never figured it out." Maggie leered at Sam. "What a waste of energy. I could have told you. Any time I could have told you. But I didn't. It was more fun letting you
think Ray was still around. Wasn't it fun?" Blink. Blink.

"I had fun with Ray, but he had to get all righteous on me and start freaking out about killing that kid. He sure was enjoying it while we did it, but afterward he had to go all paranoid and spooked. Do you know what it feels like to hold someone's life in your hands and know that you have the power to take it?" Maggie snapped her fingers. "Just like that?" Blink. Blink.

"I do. It's better than any high you could ever imagine." Maggie cocked her head to the side. "Do you get high, detective?" Blink. Blink.

"You should try it. Too bad we couldn't try a little now before…" Maggie smiled. "Well, before you have to go."

Sam knew what she meant. He knew she meant to kill him.
There was still time for him to find the call button. His fingers crept along the sheet, a fraction of an inch at a time, searching.

Sam heard voices in the hall. He couldn't help himself; his eyes darted in the door's direction.

Maggie heard the noise as well. "Close your eyes," she demanded. "Close them, damn it." She reached for the ventilator's hose. "I'll pull it right now. Close your eyes!" The words spat from her mouth.

Afraid, Sam did as he was told. Before he closed his eyes, he saw Maggie duck out of sight. The voices drew closer. The storm rumbled outside. Was someone stopping at his door? He could only imagine. Would they come in? He willed whoever was out in the hall to come into his room. There were two people just outside of his room. He could hear them talking about the storm.

"I hope the power doesn't go out like last time."

"We have the backup generators. It'll be okay."

"Let me look in on Mr. Anderson."

"Mary?" Another voice from further down the hall.

"Yeah?"

"Is that Matthew with you?"

"Yeah, it's me."

"I need you both to come help me. We have a new patient checking in from surgery. Apparently he's a rather large patient and I'm going to need both your help."

"We'll be right there. Let me just do a quick check on Mr. Anderson."

CHAPTER THIRTY-NINE

Karen shook her head, but winced in pain as fresh stabs of light burst before her eyes. Slowly she stood up holding onto the concrete wall and laid her hot head against the coolness of the cement. Counting to five, she opened her eyes and looked around. Maggie had disappeared.

She wasn't sure how long she'd been knocked out. She checked her watch and realized less than ten minutes had passed. That was ten minutes too many as far as Karen was concerned.

Footsteps sounded on the stairs. Karen vacillated between racing after Maggie and calling for back up. Her head made the choice for her. She needed to get help. She found her cell phone and pushed the send button to redial Hendricks' number and held it to her ear. No sound. She tested the phone by trying to dial again, but still nothing. She placed it back into her belt holster and hurried down to the lobby floor. Beaten and bruised, she flew down the stairs taking them one and two at a time. "Police business," she said to the two people coming up the stairs, mouths gaped open, as they watched her rush by. Her first task in getting help would be to get in touch with hospital security and have them find Maggie. Next, she needed to find a hospital telephone and get back up sent as soon as possible. She had a dangerous situation on her hands. A very angry and lethal Maggie Morris was loose in the hospital.

Karen knew by the look on the security guard's face he'd caught a glimpse of her ravaged features. Before he could say anything, Karen showed him her badge. He sprang to attention immediately. "I'm Detective Sykes from the Hillsborough Sheriff's office. I was attacked by one of the patients here in the hospital. She's about five foot two, one hundred fifteen pounds, and has short blonde hair.
She was wearing a hospital gown and had bare feet."

"Yes, ma'am, we'll do what we can to help you. My name is David and I'll gather a team to search right away. You say a patient did this? We need to notify the hospital administrator. This is serious." He reached for the telephone with his left hand. "Here." He handed Karen a box of tissues. "You might want to get those wounds looked at in the ER."

David spoke quickly into the telephone, his tone urgent. He relayed all the pertinent information, said 'Yes, sir, a Code Gray' several times, then hung up. "We'll cooperate as much as possible to get this situation under control quickly."

Taking a few tissues from the box, Karen held them to her face to stop the blood from dripping. She shook her head. "I'm not going to the ER right now. We need to find this woman." Karen gave the security guard Maggie's room number and suggested that they start their search there. "My cell phone is broken; do you have a radio I can borrow to stay in contact while your team searches the hospital?"

David reached across the desk and under a newspaper. He pulled out a radio. "This one we keep at the desk, but I think you can take it for now."

"Thanks." Karen tossed the bloody tissues into the trash can.

Talking into his radio, David contacted the other security guards in the hospital and gave them Maggie's description. "Did she have any kind of weapon, detective?" The security guard directed his question to Karen.

"No. No weapon. But she packs a mean punch," Karen said as she gently touched the deep scratches on her face.

David nodded and went back to talking into his radio.

"Can I use your telephone to call for back up?" Karen said when she noticed the telephone partially covered by the newspaper on the guard's desk.

"Yeah, sure thing."

Karen dialed 911. She mused that tonight's excitement was probably more than security guard David was expecting when he came to work today. Once she connected with a 911 dispatcher, Karen explained the situation and asked that additional officers be sent to the hospital. Karen told the dispatcher that she would meet the officers at the main entrance of the hospital.

Explaining her plan to David, Karen said, "Stay in radio contact

with me and let me know how the search progresses. I'm going to brief the officers when they arrive and we'll proceed upstairs and join the search."

"Yes, ma'am."

The front lobby of the hospital was crowded. Karen watched the throng of people moving in and out of the open area carefully searching for a familiar head of short blonde hair. She wouldn't expect Maggie to try and waltz right out the front door, but then she didn't expect her to attack the way she did either.

It wasn't long before Karen spotted the familiar uniform of the Tampa police. Two officers walked through the front door. She waved them over to where she was standing against a wall.

"I'm Detective Sykes. We have a dangerous patient running loose in the hospital."

One of the officers pointed at Karen's face. "She do that to you?"

"Yeah. She attacked me from behind on the stairwell." Karen gently touched the side of her bruised face and gave a lopsided grin. "It's gonna leave a mark, isn't it?"

"Yes, ma'am."

Karen read his nametag. "Thanks, Officer Lopez. I appreciate the honesty." She motioned for them to stand closer so she could discreetly tell them who they were searching for. "She's about five foot two, one hundred fifteen pounds. Twenty-eight years of age.
Short blonde hair. Last seen wearing a hospital gown and no shoes." "Well, unless she changes clothes, she should be easy to spot." "Yeah, man," Lopez said to his partner.

"Let's get started. I'm in radio contact with the security guards. They're actively searching the hospital now. Lopez, you come with me." Karen glanced at the second officer's nametag. "Burke, you start in the ER. She might try to sneak out of the hospital where there's a lot of foot traffic."

"Yes, ma'am."

"Stay in radio contact, you two. Lopez can update me with your reports, Burke."

"Yes, ma'am." Burke swung around and headed for the Emergency Room at a good pace, his head swiveling from side to side as he scanned the crowd.

Karen turned to Lopez. "Let's take the stairs in case she decides to try using them to escape."

"So what's she wanted for?" Lopez asked as he held the stairwell door open for Karen.

"She's wanted for questioning in a homicide investigation."

"Homicide, huh?"

CHAPTER FORTY

"Did you check on Mr. Anderson?" Mary's voice carried from the corridor.

"He's asleep," Sam heard Matthew answer. "Why don't we let him sleep through the storm?"

No! Sam screamed in his mind. *I'm not asleep. Walk into the room. Walk into the room, please!* He felt tears form behind his closed eyelids. The voices were moving away. He'd lost his chance. Lightning cracked and thunder answered. No one would hear.

"Very good, detective."

Sam slowly opened his eyes. Maggie stood beside his bed looking down at him. Lightning lit up the room behind her very close body. The thunder rumbled and echoed. Outside, the rain slashed the windows.

"Now where were we before we were so rudely interrupted?"

Sam searched his mind. She was going to kill him and there was nothing he could do to stop her. He moved his hand another fraction of an inch hoping to encounter something he could use that would make enough noise to draw someone's attention.

"You're not very talkative, detective. Cat got your tongue?" Maggie slid her palm along Sam's cheek. She tweaked his nose.

Inwardly, Sam cringed, trying to shrink back away from her touch. He blinked twice, hoping to catch her attention and keep her talking.

"What do you want, detective? Do you want to beg for your life?"

Blink. Sam knew he looked like a coward, but knowing that all that stood between him and death was the flip of a switch he'd gained a new appreciation for life. Damn it, he wanted to live. He wanted to spend more time with his wife. Maybe take a trip or two to see their grandchildren. Spend time with his family. Those were things he promised to do if he only made it safely through this situation.

"The big brave detective is afraid of little bitty ol' me?" Maggie whispered with glee. "Good. You should be. I say who lives or dies. Me. Not God. Me. I have the power." Lightning flashed outside, once again turning the room from dark to light. Maggie slapped her chest with one of her hands, the sound covered up by the echoing crash of thunder. "You will die. Your lady partner will die. Why? Because I say so." Pointing at herself, Maggie raged on with savage whispers, "No one is ever supposed to suspect sweet, innocent, Maggie. Never. I'm the good one. Me. I didn't beat the shit out of myself for nothing. I'll make you pay. I'll make all of you pay!"

With surprising speed, Maggie leapt up onto Sam's bed and sat on his stomach. The brunt of her weight forced air to exhale from his lungs. In shock, Sam watched with wide eyes as her hand moved up to the IV machine next to his bed. He watched with horror as she pushed the off button. Fluid halted in mid-drip.

Blink. Blink. Blink. Sam's mind screamed for help.

"Now, which one should I turn off next?" Maggie pointed to the other various machines that beeped and whirred around his head. "This one?"

Sam's heart raced. "How about this one." Maggie flipped a switch. Then another. And another.

Sam closed his eyes.

CHAPTER FORTY-ONE

Karen spoke into the radio she held close to her mouth. "Any reports?"

"Nothing yet, ma'am," the voice of David, the security guard, crackled from the radio. "I've checked with my men and they haven't found her."

"Keep looking," Karen responded. "Officer Lopez and I will move to the third floor."

Karen pushed through the stairwell door and took the stairs two at a time. Officer Lopez fell into step beside her. "She can't hide in this place. Not in a hospital gown. We'll find her."

"We better. She's wanted for assault on a police officer." "On you?"

"And my partner. I think she tried to kill him." Karen opened the third floor door and strode out into the corridor. "He's here in the hospital right now. ICU." Karen considered she'd probably make Sam proud by calling for back up and working with the other officers instead of ramming head on into the thick of it without anyone's help. She guessed she'd learned something after all. It felt good, organizing a team and keeping them working. Searching for this deranged woman.

Karen worked through her mind where in the hell Maggie could possibly be and then it hit her.

"Sam!" Karen took off running pushing past people in the hall. She didn't look back to see if Officer Lopez was keeping up with her. Instinct told her that Sam was in trouble and that Maggie was the cause.

With a thud, she pushed through the swinging doors into the Intensive Care Unit. Nurses were calling out to one another. When they saw Officer Lopez's uniform, they pointed down the corridor and yelled, "The police are here!"

ICU staff waved Karen and Officer Lopez past the nurses' station and toward Sam's room. Karen knew. She swallowed a large lump that forced its way up her throat.

"Officer. Here, come quick." Karen followed.

"She's sitting on top of him. She says she's going to turn his ventilator off."

"Oh my God."

"Hurry!"

Karen rushed to the door of Sam's room. She pushed others out of her way and told them to stand back away from the door. "Get back, damn it. Let me in, I'm a police officer." She could hear Officer Lopez moving people away from Sam's door behind her.

"Maggie, what on earth do you think you're doing?"

"Back off, detective. I've turned off everything else. I only have one more switch to go." Maggie's hand hovered over the off switch to the ventilator.

Karen held out her hands in a gesture of faith. "Look, Maggie. It doesn't have to be like this. We'll get you some help. What do you say?"

"I say hell no. I know what kind of help you're talking about. You want me to admit I'm crazy. Well, I'm not. No one can make me go back to that damn place." She shifted slightly so that she was sitting more firmly on top of Sam's body. "You can all just go to hell." Lightning flashed and thunder boomed. The storm raged outside. Wind blew and rain battered the windows.

Without taking her eyes off Maggie, Karen motioned to Officer Lopez. She knew she had to follow procedure on this one. Sam's life was at stake. Out of the corner of her mouth, she said, "Call for back up. We need a negotiator."

"Already put in the call. Anything else I can do for you?"

"Yeah, get these people back. Move everyone down past the nurses' station. I need room to work."

"You got it." Lopez turned to the crowd. "All right, everyone. Back up. Go on. Get back. I want everyone on the other side of the nurses' station. Move."

Karen sighed with relief after the crowd of people moved further back. She had never participated as a hostage negotiator, but she remembered the training she received. Ensure public safety and keep the hostage taker talking. Don't antagonize the suspect. She rolled her shoulders to help ease some of the tension and turned her full attention back to the situation at hand. "Maggie. Let's work this out. Why don't you get down from there and let's go someplace and talk." Reminiscent of a rabid dog, Maggie snarled and snapped at Karen's suggestion. "Right. You want to go someplace and talk. You mean to jail. I'm not going to jail." She leaned further toward the ventilator and put one hand on the hose connected to Sam's mouth and kept the other on the power switch.

"Let's talk here then." Karen shifted her weight from one foot to the other. Could she burst in the room and tackle Maggie? Would she be able to reach her before she had time to hit the switch? Karen wasn't sure.

Lightning lit up the room. The thunder crashed.

"What do you want to talk about detective? You need my advice on what to wear? Want me to do your hair? I don't think so." Laughing, Maggie said, "I'm not into that girl talk kind of shit. So just back off."

"Why don't you tell me what happened to Ray? Wasn't he your friend? Didn't you care about him?"

"Ray? You want to talk about Ray? Fine, let's talk about that stupid son-of-a-bitch. He had to get all freaked out on me. I don't know what his problem was. He couldn't handle it. He said he could, but he didn't. Weak-ass bastard. He didn't have what it takes to be God. He couldn't handle the power. The control over other people's lives." Maggie lowered her head. "He became a drag, so I let him down easy." Her voice trailed into a sing-song pattern. "Nice and easy. Just get 'em high, and give 'em a little more and that's all it takes. Nice and easy." Maggie lifted her head. A twisted smile splayed across her mouth. "He never suffered. Too bad for him."

"Do you like to let your victims suffer, Maggie?"

"They need to know who's in control. God doesn't control their lives, I control their lives."

"You're not God, Maggie."

"Don't you say things like that! I have the power! Me!" Maggie yelled at the top of her voice. She screamed in anger. She beat her fist on Sam's chest. "I should have killed you. You should be dead! I could be out of here. Gone. No one would have to know. Damn you!" Maggie slumped over, one hand on the power button. She pushed the switch.

Sam's machine let out one last gasp and all was quiet. Lightning flashed. The thunder answered from a distance.

Karen shot into the room and launched herself at Maggie. She screamed for Lopez to get someone into Sam's room to turn the machines back on. With a solid collision, the force of her impact with Maggie's body brought them both up and off Sam's bed and onto the floor. Karen's head bounced off the wall near the window. She fought through the pain. Maggie wasn't going to get the best of her this time. Forcing Maggie onto her stomach, she planted a knee into her back and grabbed Maggie's arms and pulled them behind her back. "Stay where you are. Don't move!" Karen said through clenched teeth. "You're under arrest." Karen fumbled for her handcuffs and brought one end down onto Maggie's left wrist then twisted and cuffed the other hand. She let out the breath she'd been holding and stood up, keeping one foot planted in the middle of Maggie's back.

Lopez stood at the doorway with his gun drawn. A nurse stood next to Sam's bed, trembling as she hurried to switch on the various machines connected to Sam. The ventilator gasped back to life, forcing air back into Sam's lungs.

More police officers appeared at the door of Sam's room. Back up had arrived. Karen smiled when she saw Detective Hendricks at the front of the pack. She waved.

He waved back. "You all right?"

"Yeah." She looked down at the small, blonde woman lying at her feet. "Boy, have I got something to tell you."

"Your boyfriend called. He was worried about you."

"I can take care of myself."

"So I see."

"I couldn't have done it without help, though."

"Yeah?"

"It's not so bad working with a team."

"Good for you. Now why don't you give that guy of yours a call and let him know you're okay."

"Sure thing. One sec. Lopez? You want to help me with this?" Karen pointed down at Maggie Morris. Lopez helped Karen lift Maggie to her feet. "Read her her damn rights."

"Yes, ma'am." Lopez pulled Maggie out of Sam's hospital room and into the hall.

Thunder rumbled from a distance. The storm had passed.

"Sam?" Karen looked down at the man in the hospital bed.

A nurse spoke. "It looks like everything is okay. I'd like to get a doctor in here to check him out." The nurse fussed over Sam, straightening his sheet and smoothing the wrinkles out of his forehead. Karen looked into Sam's eyes. "Okay, partner?" Blink.

"Good. You can't check out on me yet." Karen reached down and held Sam's hand. Blink. Blink.

"Okay, I'm glad you don't want to either." Blink.

"Did I do okay?" Karen squeezed Sam's hand gently. Blink.

Karen felt movement in her hand. Sam was moving his fingers. She looked down and watched as his fingers closed over and his thumb stood up. Tears welled up in Karen's eyes. She returned his thumbs up gesture. "Thanks, partner."

CHAPTER FORTY-TWO

"You were worried about me?"

Mike drew a heavy breath. He held Karen close as if to never let her go. "Damn right, I was worried."

"I am a police officer." "I know."

"And I work Homicide."

Mike drew another deep breath. His stomach twisted into a knot. "Karen…"

"Hmmm?" Karen gently caressed his arms while he held her tight against his naked body.

"Karen?" Mike shifted his position. He needed to see Karen's face when he talked to her.

Karen shifted herself as well and pushed away so that she sat up on the bed. She pulled a sheet up and tucked it under her arms and over her breasts. She looked at Mike expectantly.

Mike saw the growing affection in Karen's eyes. They'd already moved so far into their relationship. She meant the world to him. And what he went through today made him age ten years.

"Today scared the shit out of me," Mike said in a soft even tone, although he felt like taking her by the arms and shaking her to her senses. "I wasn't even there and it scared me."

"It was dangerous. I won't argue that. But I followed procedure. I called for back up. I handled it." Karen looked at him with her head cocked to one side as if she were asking him if he questioned her abilities.

"I know you're a great detective. You proved that by the way you figured out it was Maggie Morris who was the actual killer. It's just…" Mike paused. "I don't know if I can handle going through that every time you're on a case." He lowered his head. "Mike." Karen touched his shoulder. "Mike, look at me." He lifted his head.

Karen smiled at him. "I won't deny that there are going to be times when my job will put me in dangerous situations. Maybe even life-threatening. But I'm a trained police officer. And thanks to today's events, I even figured out that working as a team is better than going it alone." Karen touched his face gently with her hand, caressing his cheek. "You have to have faith and believe I'm going to be all right.
And you have to trust me to take care of myself."

Mike leaned into Karen's touch. "This is so damn frustrating." He pulled away and shook his head. "I'm usually so sure of myself and in control. But around you…" Mike lifted Karen's chin with his thumb and forefinger. "Around you, I melt into Jell-O. What's the matter with me?"

Karen giggled. She kissed the tip of Mike's finger and then let his thumb slide past her lips. She sucked it lightly. "Maybe…I don't know." She gave him a smile that caused his chest to contract and lose his breath. "Maybe you more than 'like' me?"

Mike didn't laugh. Karen's tongue swirled around his thumb. It sent hot shivers up and down his body. Did he more that like her? Could that be it? "Karen, all I know is that I've tried to figure out what to do both ways. With you and without you. And without you I'm lost. I'm incomplete." He gave Karen a dejected look. "I can't imagine myself as a functioning human being. My life becomes meaningless."

Karen kissed his thumb, held his hand and turned it over so that she could kiss the palm. "And with me?" she whispered.

Mike sucked in a breath. His stomach contracted and he felt a familiar longing that started between his legs and swelled upward. "With you…" He pulled Karen to him. He pushed the sheet aside. "With you…" Touching her soft skin, stroking her exposed breast, watching the nipple contract and harden. Mike tenderly pushed Karen onto her back. He stroked her thigh, lightly running his knuckles up the inside touching her delicate skin. He leaned over her. Pushed a stray strand of hair back behind her ear.

"I meant to get a haircut this week," Karen apologized while pushing her hair away from her face.

"Shhhh." Mike touched her full lips. He kissed her once. Then leaned back in for another longer, more thorough kiss. When he

lifted his head he said, "With you, the world starts spinning again." He shifted his legs so that his hardness stroked her thigh. "With you, my heart starts beating again." Mike kissed her on the tip of her nose. "Yes, Karen. I think I more than like you."

Mike lowered his body, gently pushed Karen's thighs apart with his knee, buried his hands in her hair, and kissed her full on the lips. "Let me show you exactly how much I love you." Then he kissed her again, deeply, with his tongue entwining with hers.

"Mike," Karen gasped after his kiss. "I love you."

"Good, I'm glad we have that straightened out. Now," he nibbled on her lower lip, "it's time for a little show and tell."

EPILOGUE

"To Sam!" Karen lifted her glass and toasted the man sitting in his favorite recliner enjoying all of the attention.

Echoes of "To Sam" were heard from those standing in groups in Sam's living room. After the well wishes quieted down, Sam took a drink from his glass then put it down on the end table next to his chair. "Wait a minute, wait a minute," he said loudly. "When will we be celebrating something for you two?"

Karen leaned back into Mike's arms and whispered into his ear. Mike nodded and smiled. Karen lifted her left hand and showed it to the room. "You're all invited to the wedding," she said with a big grin on her face.

Karen smiled at those who wished her good luck and congratulated her on her engagement. Leaving Mike to talk to all those who crowded to their side, she carefully made her way through the throng of people to the side of Sam's chair and knelt down to talk to him.

"This is your day, Sam. You shouldn't have got them started on us."

"Why not? This isn't just my retirement party. It's about moving on. Moving forward. And that means you." Sam made a motion with his hand. "You, 'Ms. Accommodation for capturing a serial killer wanted in three southern states'."

Karen blushed. "I was just doing my job." She shrugged. "I don't know. It just feels weird moving on without you. You're my partner. I really never thought I needed help, but now I know we're all a team. I'm going to miss you."

"We haven't really worked together in more than nine months. What with me going to physical therapy every week and you working with Hendricks. Hendricks is working out okay, isn't he?"

"Oh, yeah. Hendricks is great. He's like you in a lot of ways. But it's just not the same, Sam."

"He helped you work through your first homicide case, right?"

"Yeah. We got Maggie Morris on murder one for the death of Ray Thomas. We had her DNA in the hiking boots that matched the print found on the causeway, and of course, it was your blood on the boots that nailed it for assault on you. Then we got her for murder two for the Hunt boy. She's pleading insanity and looks like she'll have a good case considering the number of years she lived in Georgia's state psychiatric hospitals before she escaped, so the lawyers and State Attorney's office will have all that to work out. I'll leave it all up to them and just say my piece when they call me into court."

"You're going to do okay, Karen. You have what it takes to make a great detective. I should know. I trained you." Sam laughed.

"Thanks, Sam."

"Did you get in touch with the Hunt family and let them know what happened?"

"I didn't have to actually. I got a call from Mrs. Hunt letting me know her new address and telephone number in case we had any new information. I was able to give her the good news myself." Karen shifted her weight. "Did you know she's left her husband? I knew there wasn't something right between the two of them. She's divorcing him and has started a new life with her girls. I'm glad for her actually. It took a lot of courage and strength for her to leave an abusive relationship. She sounds like a whole new person."

"See, moving on and moving forward."

"I guess so."

"What?"

"I always thought my first homicide case was about finding justice. That I had to do it on my own. But it was more than that. It was about justice and working as a team." Karen held Sam's hand. "I wanted to find justice to prove that I could do it on my own. That my parents would somehow see what I've done and forgive me after all these years."

"But?"

"I talked to them. They said they never blamed me. I guess it was my own guilt that kept me from believing that. We cried a bit, then they said they were proud of me."

"And that was good, right?"

"Yeah. I learned a lot. I think I've become a better detective for it. And I've forgiven myself for what happened to my sister."

"I know you've learned quite a bit. I'm proud of you as well."

"Thanks."

"Now, go back to that man of yours and enjoy the party. Don't be sitting here with the old man all night."

Karen leaned over and kissed Sam on the cheek. She stood up and looked over at Mike. He caught her gaze and smiled. Karen smiled back. Life had a funny way of working out. There she'd been, bemoaning the lack of a personal relationship in her life and now, thanks to one persistent crime scene tech who moonlighted as a fairy godmother, she couldn't be happier.

ACKNOWLEDGEMENTS

Writing a book takes a lot of hard work and research. I wouldn't have been able to accomplish my part in this endeavor if it weren't for the hard work and dedication of those experts who gave of their time to help me.

Thank you to Sarah-Jane Lehoux, my editor at Mundania Press, LLC for helping me with the details of getting this story grammatically correct and consistent. And to all the other production team members, I say a great big THANK YOU!

The wonderfully informative people working at the Hillsborough County Sheriff's Office exchanged countless e-mails with me answering all of my questions. Specifically, I'd like to thank Lt. Rod Reder the HCSO Public Information Officer at the time I was doing my research and Lt. JR Burton. Thank you very much for taking the time to talk to me and helping me develop my crime sense and realistic crime scenes.

I'd like to thank Dr. M.J. Price for helping me with the Crime Scene Technician aspect of my story. The information she provided helped me present realism and practicality.

I'd also like to thank Special Agent John F. McDonald of the Florida Department of Law Enforcement (FDLE) for his insight and knowledge.

As for the sports and running technology, I must thank Bryan Prushinski. Without his invaluable expertise, I wouldn't have understood the running philosophy.

Of course, I'd be nowhere if it weren't for the caring helpful staff of The Spring Women's Domestic Abuse Shelter. They provide a wealth of information for women in need.

All of these experts gave their knowledge and time to help me with my story, however, if anything is out of character or wrong in anyway, I take full responsibility for the error or omission.

ABOUT THE AUTHOR

Award winning author, Vicki M. Taylor writes dramatic stories with strong women as her main characters. A prolific writer of both novel length and short stories, she brings her characters to life in the real world.

When she's not writing, you can find her lurking about the many writing boards dispensing and receiving little pearls of wisdom from her computer in Tampa, Florida where she lives with her husband their dog, Jack and their parrot, Bailey. To find out more about Vicki and her writing, visit her website at http://www.vickimtaylor.com

www.ingramcontent.com/pod-product-compliance
Lightning Source LLC
Chambersburg PA
CBHW061230170626
46809CB00007B/2591